Praise for
ANTHONY DOERR

"It's fair to say that Anthony Doerr is doing things with the short story that have rarely been attempted and seldom achieved. . . . Doerr has set a new standard, I think, for what a story can do."

—Dave Eggers, author of *Zeitoun* and *What Is the What*

"Doerr has a way of saying the ordinary that makes you rethink the way the English language is used."

—*The Denver Post*

"Doerr writes about the big questions, the imponderables, the major metaphysical dreads, and he does it fearlessly. The stories in *Memory Wall* shouldn't work at all, and yet they do, spectacularly."

—*The New York Times Book Review*

"It's rare to encounter a writer who is able to make us see the world around us in new ways. And yet Doerr does so on every page."

—*The Boston Globe*

More praise for
THE SHELL COLLECTOR

"If you have stopped reading short stories because they have turned pretentious, silly, or meaningless, *The Shell Collector* is a good reason to come back. . . . The stories in this collection are polished jewels. They will draw you back . . . first to marvel at what Doerr is telling you, and then to see how he has performed his magic."

—*The Cleveland Plain Dealer*

"Stunning. Eight stunning exercises in steel-tipped feathery fineness that no writer can read without envying. . . . [Doerr's] is the all-knowing, all-seeing eye we find in D. H. Lawrence, Tolstoy, Hemingway, Pynchon, DeLillo, Richard Powers—writers able to pin down every butterfly wing and fleck of matter in the universe, yet willing to float the unanswerables about the 'hot, hard kernel of human experience.'"

—*The Philadelphia Inquirer*

"These complex, resonant, beautifully realized stories sing. . . . A remarkable first collection."

—Andrea Barrett, National Book Award–winning author of *Ship Fever*

"[Doerr] centers his stories on taciturn hunters and fishers with deep reservoirs of emotion—inept conversationalists and husbands whose senses only come alive in the woods. . . . Doerr's wilderness contains a touch of the magical, too: a blind shell collector on the coast of Kenya discovers a miracle cure in a snail's toxic sting. Tourists land a carp so huge it can't be photographed. A woman finds she can divine the dream of animals by feeling them. 'Want to know what he dreams?' she asks her husband after touching a grizzly's fur. 'Blackberries. Trout. Dredging his flanks across river pebbles.' These are tales that capture the wonder and the icy indifference of nature, and Doerr tells them exceedingly well."

—*Outside*

"Anthony Doerr is a wonderful new writer. His stories reach deep and mine the forgotten places, as well as the never-before-discovered. These stories don't just describe beauty, they help create it."

—Rick Bass, author of *Where the Sea Used to Be*

Also by Anthony Doerr

About Grace
Four Seasons in Rome
Memory Wall

THE
SHELL COLLECTOR

Stories

Anthony Doerr

Scribner

NEW YORK   LONDON   TORONTO   SYDNEY

SCRIBNER
A Division of Simon & Schuster, Inc.
1230 Avenue of the Americas
New York, NY 10020

First Scribner trade paperback edition January 2011

SCRIBNER and design are registered trademarks of
The Gale Group, Inc., used under license by
Simon & Schuster, Inc., the publisher of this work.

For information about special discounts for bulk purchases,
please contact Simon & Schuster Special Sales at 1-866-506-1949 or
business@simonandschuster.com.

The Simon & Schuster Speakers Bureau can bring authors
to your live event. For more information or to book an event contact
the Simon & Schuster Speakers Bureau at 1-866-248-3049 or visit
our website at www.simonspeakers.com.

DESIGNED BY KYOKO WATANABE
Set in Spectrum

Manufactured in the United States of America

9 10 8

Library of Congress Control Number: 2001040031

ISBN 978-0-7432-1274-8
ISBN 978-1-4391-9005-0 (pbk)
ISBN 978-0-7432-2362-1 (ebook)

Most of the stories in this collection have appeared elsewhere,
in slightly different form: "The Hunter's Wife" in *The Atlantic Monthly*;
"So Many Chances" in *Sycamore Review* and *Fly Rod & Reel*; "For a Long Time
This Was Griselda's Story" in *North American Review*; "July Fourth" in *Black Warrior
Review*; "The Caretaker" in *The Paris Review*; "A Tangle by the Rapid River"
in *The Sewanee Review;* and "The Shell Collector" in *The Chicago Review*.

for Shauna

CONTENTS

The Shell Collector   *9*

The Hunter's Wife   *40*

So Many Chances   *73*

For a Long Time
This Was Griselda's Story   *96*

July Fourth   *115*

The Caretaker   *130*

A Tangle by the Rapid River   *174*

Mkondo   *184*

THE SHELL COLLECTOR

The shell collector was scrubbing limpets at his sink when he heard the water taxi come scraping over the reef. He cringed to hear it—its hull grinding the calices of finger corals and the tiny tubes of pipe organ corals, tearing the flower and fern shapes of soft corals, and damaging shells too: punching holes in olives and murexes and spiny whelks, in *Hydatina physis* and *Turris babylonia*. It was not the first time people tried to seek him out.

He heard their feet splash ashore and the taxi motor off, back to Lamu, and the light singsong pattern of their knock. Tumaini, his German shepherd, let out a low whine from where she was crouched under his sleeping cot. He dropped a limpet into the sink, wiped his hands and went, reluctantly, to greet them.

They were both named Jim, overweight reporters from a New York tabloid. Their handshakes were slick and hot. He poured them chai. They occupied a surprising amount of space in the kitchen. They said they were there to write about him: they would stay only two nights, pay him well. How did $10,000 American sound? He pulled a shell from his shirt pocket—a cerith—and rolled it in his fingers. They asked about his childhood: did he really shoot caribou as a boy? Didn't he need good eyes for that?

He gave them truthful answers. It all held the air of whim, of unreality. These two big Jims could not actually be at his table, asking him these questions, complaining of the stench of dead shellfish. Finally they asked him about cone shells and the strength of cone venom, about how many visitors had come. They asked nothing about his son.

All night it was hot. Lightning marbled the sky beyond the reef. From his cot he heard siafu feasting on the big men and heard them claw themselves in their sleeping bags. Before dawn he told them to shake out their shoes for scorpions and when they did one tumbled out. It made tiny scraping sounds as it skittered under the refrigerator.

He took his collecting bucket and clipped Tumaini into her harness, and she led them down the path to the reef. The air smelled like lightning. The Jims huffed to keep up. They told him they were impressed he moved so quickly.

"Why?"

"Well," they murmured, "you're blind. This path ain't easy. All these thorns."

Far off, he heard the high, amplified voice of the muezzin in Lamu calling prayer. "It's Ramadan," he told the Jims. "The people don't eat when the sun is above the horizon. They drink only chai until sundown. They will be eating now. Tonight we can go out if you like. They grill meat in the streets."

By noon they had waded a kilometer out, onto the great curved spine of the reef, the lagoon slopping quietly behind them, a low sea breaking in front. The tide was coming up. Unharnessed now, Tumaini stood panting, half out of the water on a mushroom-shaped dais of rock. The shell collector was stooped, his fingers middling, quivering, whisking for shells in a sandy trench. He snatched up a broken spindle shell, ran a fingernail over its incised spirals. "*Fusinus colus,*" he said.

Automatically, as the next wave came, the shell collector raised his collecting bucket so it would not be swamped. As soon as the wave passed he plunged his arms back into sand, his fingers probing an alcove between anemones, pausing to identify a clump of brain coral, running after a snail as it burrowed away.

One of the Jims had a snorkeling mask and was using it to look underwater. "Lookit these blue fish," he gasped. "Lookit that *blue.*"

The shell collector was thinking, just then, of the indifference of nematocysts. Even after death the tiny cells will discharge their poison—a single dried tentacle on the shore, severed eight days, stung a village boy last year and swelled his legs. A weeverfish bite bloated a man's entire right side, blacked his eyes, turned him dark purple. A stone fish sting corroded the skin off the sole of the shell collector's own heel, years ago, left the skin smooth and printless. How many urchin spikes, broken but still spurting venom, had he squeezed from Tumaini's paw? What would happen to these Jims if a banded sea snake came slipping up between their fat legs? If a lion fish was dropped down their collars?

"Here is what you came to see," he announced, and pulled the snail—a cone—from its collapsing tunnel. He spun it and balanced its flat end on two fingers. Even now its poisoned proboscis was nosing forward, searching him out. The Jims waded noisily over.

"This is a geography cone," he said. "It eats fish."

"*That* eats fish?" one of the Jims asked. "But my pinkie's bigger."

"This animal," said the shell collector, dropping it into his bucket, "has twelve kinds of venom in its teeth. It could paralyze you and drown you right here."

‿

This all started when a malarial Seattle-born Buddhist named Nancy was stung by a cone shell in the shell collector's kitchen. It crawled in from the ocean, slogging a hundred meters under coconut palms, through acacia scrub, bit her and made for the door.

Or maybe it started before Nancy, maybe it grew outward from the shell collector himself, the way a shell grows, spiraling upward from the inside, whorling around its inhabitant, all the while being worn down by the weathers of the sea.

The Jims were right: the shell collector did hunt caribou. Nine years old in Whitehorse, Canada, and his father would send the boy leaning out the bubble canopy of his helicopter in cutting sleet to cull sick caribou with a scoped carbine. But then there was choroideremia and degeneration of the retina; in a year his eyesight was tunneled, spattered with rainbow-colored halos. By twelve, when his father took him four thousand miles south, to Florida to see a specialist, his vision had dwindled into darkness.

The ophthalmologist knew the boy was blind as soon as he walked through the door, one hand clinging to his father's belt, the other arm held straight, palm out, to stiff-arm obstacles. Rather than examine him—what was left to examine?—the doctor ushered him into his office, pulled off the boy's shoes and walked him out the back door down a sandy lane onto a spit of beach. The boy had never seen sea and he struggled to absorb it: the blurs that were waves, the smears that were weeds strung over the tideline, the smudged yolk of sun. The doctor showed him a kelp bulb, let him break it in his hands and scrape its interior with his thumb. There were many such discoveries: a small horseshoe crab mounting a larger one in the wavebreak, a fistful of mussels clinging to the damp underside of rock. But it was wading ankle deep, when his toes came upon a small round shell, no longer than a segment of his thumb, that the boy truly was changed. His fingers dug the shell up, he felt the sleek egg of its body, the toothy gap of its aperture. It was the most elegant thing he'd ever held. "That's a mouse cowry," the doctor said. "A lovely find. It has brown spots, and darker stripes at its base, like tiger stripes. You can't see it, can you?"

But he could. He'd never seen anything so clearly in his life. His fingers caressed the shell, flipped and rotated it. He had never felt anything so smooth—had never imagined something could possess such deep polish. He asked, nearly whispering: "Who *made* this?" The shell was still in his hand, a week later, when his father pried it out, complaining of the stink.

Overnight his world became shells, conchology, the phylum *Mollusca.* In Whitehorse, during the sunless winter, he learned Braille, mail-ordered shell books, turned up logs after thaws to root for wood snails. At sixteen, burning for the reefs he had discovered in books like *The Wonders of Great Barrier,* he left Whitehorse for good and crewed sailboats through the tropics: Sanibel Island, St. Lucia, the Batan Islands, Colombo, Bora Bora, Cairns, Mombassa, Moorea. All this blind. His skin went brown, his hair white. His fingers, his senses, his mind—all of him—obsessed over the geometry of exoskeletons, the sculpture of calcium, the evolutionary rationale for ramps, spines, beads, whorls, folds. He learned to identify a shell by flipping it up in his hand; the shell spun, his fingers assessed its form, classified it: *Ancilla, Ficus, Terebra.* He returned to Florida, earned a bachelor's in biology, a Ph.D. in malacology. He circled the equator; got terribly lost in the streets of Fiji; got robbed in Guam and again in the Seychelles; discovered new species of bivalves, a new family of tusk shells, a new *Nassarius,* a new *Fragum.*

Four books, three Seeing Eye shepherds, and a son named Josh later, he retired early from his professorship and moved to a thatch-roofed kibanda just north of Lamu, Kenya, one hundred kilometers south of the equator in a small marine park in the remotest elbow of the Lamu Archipelago. He was fifty-eight years old. He had realized, finally, that he would only understand so much, that malacology only led him downward, to more questions. He had never comprehended the endless variations of design: Why this lattice ornament? Why these fluted scales, these lumpy nodes? Ignorance was, in the end, and in so many ways, a privilege: to find a shell, to feel it, to understand only on some unspeakable level why it bothered to be so lovely. What joy he found in that, what utter mystery.

Every six hours the tides plowed shelves of beauty onto the beaches of the world, and here he was, able to walk out into it, thrust his hands into it, spin a piece of it between his fingers. To gather up seashells—each one an amazement—to know their names, to drop them into a bucket: this was what filled his life, what overfilled it.

Some mornings, moving through the lagoon, Tumaini splashing comfortably ahead, he felt a nearly irresistible urge to bow down.

○

But then, two years ago, there was this twist in his life, this spiral that was at once inevitable and unpredictable, like the aperture in a horn shell. (Imagine running a thumb down one, tracing its helix, fingering its flat spiral ribs, encountering its sudden, twisting opening.) He was sixty-three, moving out across the shadeless beach behind his kibanda, poking a beached sea cucumber with his toe, when Tumaini yelped and skittered and dashed away, galloping downshore, her collar jangling. When the shell collector caught up, he caught up with Nancy, sunstroked, incoherent, wandering the beach in a khaki travel suit as if she had dropped from the clouds, fallen from a 747. He took her inside and laid her on his cot and poured warm chai down her throat. She shivered awfully; he radioed Dr. Kabiru, who boated in from Lamu.

"A fever has her," Dr. Kabiru pronounced, and poured sea water over her chest, swamping her blouse and the shell collector's floor. Eventually her fever fell, the doctor left, and she slept and did not wake for two days. To the shell collector's surprise no one came looking for her—no one called; no water taxis came speeding into the lagoon ferrying frantic American search parties.

As soon as she recovered enough to talk she talked tirelessly, a torrent of personal problems, a flood of divulged privacies. She'd been coherent for a half hour when she explained she'd left a husband and kids. She'd been naked in her pool, floating on her back, when she realized that her life—two kids, a three-story Tudor, an Audi wagon—was not what she wanted. She'd left that day. At some point, traveling through Cairo, she ran across a neo-Buddhist who turned her onto words like inner peace and equilibrium. She was on her way to live with him in Tanzania when she contracted malaria. "But look!" she exclaimed, tossing up her hands. "I wound up here!" As if it were all settled.

The shell collector nursed and listened and made her toast. Every three days she faded into shivering delirium. He knelt by her and trickled seawater over her chest, as Dr. Kabiru had prescribed.

Most days she seemed fine, babbling her secrets. He fell for her, in his own unspoken way. In the lagoon she would call to him and he would swim to her, show her the even stroke he could muster with his sixty-three-year-old arms. In the kitchen he tried making her pancakes and she assured him, giggling, that they were delicious.

And then one midnight she climbed onto him. Before he was fully awake, they had made love. Afterward he heard her crying. Was sex something to cry about? "You miss your kids," he said.

"No." Her face was in the pillow and her words were muffled. "I don't need them anymore. I just need balance. Equilibrium."

"Maybe you miss your family. It's only natural."

She turned to him. "Natural? You don't seem to miss *your* kid. I've seen those letters he sends. I don't see you sending any back."

"Well he's thirty . . ." he said. "And I didn't run off."

"Didn't run off? You're three trillion miles from home! Some retirement. No fresh water, no friends. Bugs crawling in the bathtub."

He didn't know what to say: What did she want anyhow? He went out collecting.

Tumaini seemed grateful for it, to be in the sea, under the moon, perhaps just to be away from her master's garrulous guest. He unclipped her harness; she nuzzled his calves as he waded. It was a lovely night, a cooling breeze flowing around their bodies, the warmer tidal current running against it, threading between their legs. Tumaini paddled to a rock perch, and he began to roam, stooped, his fingers probing the sand. A marlinspike, a crowned nassa, a broken murex, a lined bullia, small voyagers navigating the current-packed ridges of sand. He admired them, and put them back where he found them. Just before dawn he found two cone shells he couldn't identify, three inches long and audacious, attempting to devour a damselfish they had paralyzed.

☽

When he returned, hours later, the sun was warm on his head and shoulders and he came smiling into the kibanda to find Nancy catatonic on his cot. Her forehead was cold and damp. He rapped his knuckles on her sternum and she did not reflex. Her pulse measured at twenty, then eighteen. He radioed Dr. Kabiru, who motored his launch over the reef and knelt beside her and spoke in her ear. "Bizarre reaction to malaria," the doctor mumbled. "Her heart hardly beats."

The shell collector paced his kibanda, blundered into chairs and tables that had been unmoved for ten years. Finally he knelt on the kitchen floor, not praying so much as buckling. Tumaini, who was agitated and confused, mistook despair for playfulness, and rushed to him, knocking him over. Lying there, on the tile, Tumaini slobbering on his cheek, he felt the cone shell, the snail inching its way, blindly, purposefully, toward the door.

Under a microscope, the shell collector had been told, the teeth of certain cones look long and sharp, like tiny translucent bayonets, the razor-edged tusks of a miniature ice-devil. The proboscis slips out the siphonal canal, unrolling, the barbed teeth spring forward. In victims the bite causes a spreading insentience, a rising tide of paralysis. First your palm goes horribly cold, then your forearm, then your shoulder. The chill spreads to your chest. You can't swallow, you can't see. You burn. You freeze to death.

⌒

"There is nothing," Dr. Kabiru said, eyeing the snail, "I can do for this. No antivenom, no fix. I can do nothing." He wrapped Nancy in a blanket and sat by her in a canvas chair and ate a mango with his penknife. The shell collector boiled the cone shell in the chai pot and forked the snail out with a steel needle. He held the shell, fingered its warm pavilion, felt its mineral convolutions.

Ten hours of this vigil, this catatonia, a sunset and bats feeding and the bats gone full-bellied into their caves at dawn and then Nancy came to, suddenly, miraculously, bright-eyed.

"*That,*" she announced, sitting up in front of the dumb-founded doctor, "was the most incredible thing ever." Like she had just finished viewing some hypnotic, twelve-hour cartoon. She claimed the sea had turned to ice and snow blew down around her and all of it—the sea, the snowflakes, the white frozen sky—pulsed. "*Pulsed!*" she shouted. "Sssshhh!" she yelled at the doctor, at the stunned shell collector. "It's still pulsing! *Whump! Whump!*"

She was, she exclaimed, cured of malaria, cured of delirium; she was *balanced.* "Surely," the shell collector said, "you're not entirely recovered," but even as he said this he wasn't so sure. She smelled different, like melt-water, like slush, glaciers softening in spring. She spent the morning swimming in the lagoon, squealing and splashing. She ate a tin of peanut butter, practiced high leg kicks on the beach, cooked a feast, swept the kibanda, sang Neil

Diamond songs in a high, scratchy voice. The doctor motored off, shaking his head; the shell collector sat on the porch and listened to the palms, the sea beyond them.

That night there was another surprise: she begged to be bitten with a cone again. She promised she'd fly directly home to be with her kids, she'd phone her husband in the morning and plead forgiveness, but first he had to sting her with one of those incredible shells one more time. She was on her knees. She pawed up his shorts. "Please," she begged. She smelled so different.

He refused. Exhausted, dazed, he sent her away on a water taxi to Lamu.

☾

The surprises weren't over. The course of his life was diving into its reverse spiral by now, into that dark, whorling aperture. A week after Nancy's recovery, Dr. Kabiru's motor launch again came sputtering over the reef. And behind him were others; the shell collector heard the hulls of four or five dhows come over the coral, heard the splashes as people hopped out to drag the boats ashore. Soon his kibanda was crowded. They stepped on the whelks drying on the front step, trod over a pile of chitons by the bathroom. Tumaini retreated under the shell collector's cot, put her muzzle on her paws.

Dr. Kabiru announced that a mwadhini, the mwadhini of Lamu's oldest and largest mosque, was here to visit the shell collector, and with him were the mwadhini's brothers, and his brothers-in-law. The shell collector shook the men's hands as they greeted him, dhow-builders' hands, fishermen's hands.

The doctor explained that the mwadhini's daughter was terribly ill; she was only eight years old and her already malignant malaria had become something altogether more malignant, something the doctor did not recognize. Her skin had gone mustard-seed yellow, she threw up several times a day, her hair fell out. For the past three days she had been delirious, wasted. She tore at her own skin. Her wrists had to be bound to the headboard. These men, the doctor said, wanted the shell collector to give her the same treatment he had given the American woman. He would be paid.

The shell collector felt them crowded into the room, these ocean Muslims in their rustling kanzus and squeaking flip-flops, each stinking of his work—gutted perch, fertilizer, hull-tar— each leaning in to hear his reply.

"This is ridiculous," he said. "She will die. What happened to Nancy was some kind of fluke. It was not a treatment."

"We have tried everything," the doctor said.

"What you ask is impossible," the shell collector repeated. "Worse than impossible. Insane."

There was silence. Finally a voice directly before him spoke, a strident, resonant voice, a voice he heard five times a day as it swung out from loudspeakers over the rooftops of Lamu and summoned people to prayer. "The child's mother," the mwadhini began, "and I, and my brothers, and my brothers' wives, and the whole island, we have prayed for this child. We have prayed for many months. It seems sometimes that we have always prayed for her. And then today the doctor tells us of this American who was cured of the same disease by a snail. Such a simple cure. Elegant, would you not say? A snail that accomplishes what laboratory capsules cannot. Allah, we reason, must be involved in something so elegant. So you see. These are signs all around us. We must not ignore them."

The shell collector refused again. "She must be small, if she is only eight. Her body will not withstand the venom of a cone. Nancy could have died—she *should* have died. Your daughter will be killed."

The mwadhini stepped closer, took the shell collector's face in his hands. "Are these," he intoned, "not strange and amazing coincidences? That this American was cured of her afflictions and that my child has similar afflictions? That you are here and I am here, that animals right now crawling in the sand outside your door harbor the cure?"

The shell collector paused. Finally he said, "Imagine a snake, a terribly venomous sea snake. The kind of venom that swells a body to bruising. It stops the heart. It causes screaming pain. You're asking this snake to bite your daughter."

"We're sorry to hear this," said a voice behind the mwadhini. "We're very sorry to hear this." The shell collector's face was still in the mwadhini's hands. After long moments of silence, he was pushed aside. He heard men, uncles probably, out at the washing sink, splashing around.

"You won't find a cone out there," he yelled. Tears rose to the corners of his dead sockets. How strange it felt to have his home overrun by unseen men.

The mwadhini's voice continued: "My daughter is my only child. Without her my family will go empty. It will no longer be a family."

His voice bore an astonishing faith, in the slow and beautiful way it trilled sentences, in the way it braided each syllable. The mwadhini was convinced, the shell collector realized, that a snail bite would heal his daughter.

The voice raveled on: "You hear my brothers in your backyard, clattering among your shells. They are desperate men. Their niece is dying. If they must, they will wade out onto the coral, as they have seen you do, and they will heave boulders and tear up corals and stab the sand with shovels until they find what they are looking for. Of course they too, when they find it, may be bitten. They may swell up and die. They will—how did you say it? —have screaming pain. They do not know how to capture such animals, how to hold them."

His voice, the way he held the shell collector's face. All this was a kind of hypnosis.

"You want this to happen?" the mwadhini continued. His

voice hummed, sang, became a murmurous soprano. "You want my brothers to be bitten also?"

"I want only to be left alone."

"Yes," the mwadhini said, "left alone. A stay-at-home, a hermit, a mtawa. Whatever you want. But first, you will find one of these cone shells for my daughter, and you will sting her with it. Then you will be left alone."

◡

At low tide, accompanied by an entourage of the mwadhini's brothers, the shell collector waded with Tumaini out onto the reef and began to upturn rocks and probe into the sand beneath to try to extract a cone. Each time his fingers flurried into loose sand, or into a crab-guarded socket in the coral, a volt of fear would speed down his arm and jangle his fingers. *Conus tessulatus, Conus obscurus, Conus geographus,* who knew what he would find. The waiting proboscis, the poisoned barbs of an expectant switchblade. You spend your life avoiding these things; you end up seeking them out.

He whispered to Tumaini, "We need a small one, the smallest we can," and she seemed to understand, wading with her ribs against his knee, or paddling when it became too deep, but these men leaned in all around him, splashing in their wet kanzus, watching with their dark, redolent attention.

By noon he had one, a tiny tessellated cone he hoped couldn't paralyze a housecat, and he dropped it in a mug with some seawater.

They ferried him to Lamu, to the mwadhini's home, a surfside jumba with marble floors. They led him to the back, up a vermicular staircase, past a tinkling fountain, to the girl's room. He found her hand, her wrist still lashed to the bedpost, and held it. It was small and damp and he could feel the thin fan of her bones through her skin. He poured the mug out into her palm and folded her fingers, one by one, around the snail. It seemed to pulse there, in the delicate vaulting of her hand, like the small dark heart at the center of a songbird. He was able to imagine, in acute detail, the snail's translucent proboscis as it slipped free of the siphonal canal, the quills of its teeth probing her skin, the venom spilling into her.

"What," he asked into the silence, "is her name?"

○

Further amazement: the girl, whose name was Seema, recovered. Completely. For ten hours she was cold, catatonic. The shell collector spent the night standing in a window, listening to Lamu: donkeys clopping up the street, nightbirds squelching from somewhere in the acacia to his right, hammer strokes on metal, far off and the surf, washing into the pylons of the docks. He heard the morning prayer sung in the mosques. He began to wonder if he'd been forgotten, if hours ago the girl had passed gently into death and no one had thought to tell him. Perhaps a mob was silently gathering to drag him off and stone him and wouldn't he have deserved every stone?

But then the cooks began whistling and clucking, and the mwadhini, who had squatted by his daughter nightlong, palms up in supplication, hurried past. "Chapatis," he gushed. "She wants chapatis." The mwadhini brought her them himself, cold chapatis slavered with mango jam.

By the following day everyone knew a miracle had occurred in the mwadhini's house. Word spread, like a drifting cloud of coral eggs, spawning, frenzied; it left the island and lived for a while in the daily gossip of coastal Kenyans. The *Daily Nation* ran a back-page story, and KBC ran a minute-long radio spot featuring sound bites from Dr. Kabiru: "I did not know one hundred percent, that it would work, no. But, having extensively researched, I was confident . . ."

Within days the shell collector's kibanda became a kind of pilgrim's destination. At almost any hour, he heard the buzz of motorized dhows, or the oar-knocking of rowboats, as visitors came over the reef into the lagoon. Everyone, it seemed, had a sickness that required remedy. Lepers came, and children with ear infections, and it was not unusual for the shell collector to blunder into someone as he made his way from the kitchen to the bathroom. His conches were carted off, and his neat mound of scrubbed limpets. His entire collection of Flinder's vase shells disappeared.

Tumaini, thirteen years old and long settled into her routine with her master, did not fare well. Never aggressive, now she became terrified of nearly everything: termites, fire ants, stone crabs. She barked her voice out at the moon's rising. She spent nearly all her hours under the shell collector's cot, wincing at the smells of strangers' sicknesses, and didn't perk up even when she heard her food dish come down upon the kitchen tile.

There were worse problems. People were following the shell collector out into the lagoon, stumbling onto the rocks or the low benches of living coral. A choleric woman brushed up against fire coral and fainted from the pain. Others, thinking she had swooned in rapture, threw themselves on the coral and came away badly welted, weeping. Even at night, when he tried stealing down the path with Tumaini, pilgrims rose from the sand and followed him—unseen feet splashing nearby, unseen hands sifting quietly through his collecting bucket.

It was only a matter of time, the shell collector knew, before something terrible would happen. He had nightmares about finding a corpse bobbing in the wavebreak, bloated with venom. Sometimes it seemed to him that the whole sea had become a tub of poison harboring throngs of villains. Sand eels, stinging corals, sea snakes, crabs, men-of-war, barracuda, mantas, sharks, urchins—who knew what septic tooth would next find skin?

He stopped shelling and found other things to do. He was supposed to send shells back to the university—he had permits to send a boxful every two weeks—but he filled the boxes with old specimens, ceriths or cephalopods he had lying in cupboards or wrapped in newspaper.

And there were always visitors. He made them pots of chai, tried politely to explain that he had no cone shells, that they would be seriously injured or killed, if they were bitten. A BBC reporter came, and a wonderful-smelling woman from the *International Tribune*; he begged them to write about the dangers of cones. But they were more interested in miracles than snails; they asked if he had tried pressing cone shells to his eyes and sounded disappointed to hear he had not.

◡

After some months without miracles the number of visits fell off, and Tumaini slunk out from under the cot, but people continued to taxi in, curious tourists or choleric elders without the shillings for a doctor. Still the shell collector did not shell for fear he would be followed. Then, in the mail that came in by boat twice a month, a letter from Josh arrived.

Josh was the shell collector's son, a camp coordinator in Kalamazoo. Like his mother (who had kept the shell collector's freezer stocked with frozen meals for thirty years, despite being divorced from him for twenty-six), Josh was a goody-goody. At age ten he grew zucchini on his mother's back lawn, then distributed them, squash by squash, to soup kitchens in St. Petersburg. He picked up litter wherever he walked, brought his own bags to the supermarket, and airmailed a letter to Lamu every month, letters that filled half a page of exclamation-laden Braille without employing a single substantial sentence: *Hi Pop! Things are just fabulous in Michigan! I bet it's sunny in Kenya! Have a wonderful Labor Day! Love you tons!*

This month's letter, however, was different.

"Dear Pop!" it read,

> . . . *I've joined the Peace Corps! I'll be working in Uganda for three years! And guess what else? I'm coming to stay with you first! I've read about the miracles you've been working—it's news even here. You got blurbed in* The Humanitarian! *I'm so proud! See you soon!*

Six mornings later Josh splashed in on a water taxi. Immediately he wanted to know why more wasn't being done for the sick people clumped in the shade behind the kibanda. "Sweet Jesus!" he exclaimed, slathering suntan lotion over his arms. "These people are *suffering*! These poor orphans!" He crouched over three Kikuyu boys. "Their faces are covered with tiny flies!"

How strange it was to have his son under his roof, to hear him unzip his huge duffel bags, to come across his Schick razor on the sink. Hearing him chide ("You feed your dog *prawns*?"), chug papaya juice, scrub pans, wipe down counters—who was this person in his home? Where had he come from?

The shell collector had always suspected that he did not know his son one whit. Josh had been raised by his mother; as a boy he preferred the baseball diamond to the beach, cooking to conchology. And now he was thirty. He seemed so energetic, so good . . . so stupid. He was like a golden retriever, fetching things, sloppy-tongued, panting, falling over himself to please. He used two days of fresh water giving the Kikuyu boys showers. He spent seventy shillings on a sisal basket that should have cost him seven. He insisted on sending visitors off with care packages, plantains or House of Mangi tea biscuits, wrapped in paper and tied off with yarn.

"You're doing fine, Pop," he announced, one evening at the table. He had been there a week. Every night he invited strangers, diseased people, to the dinner table. Tonight it was a paraplegic girl and her mother. Josh spooned chunks of curried potato onto their plates. "You can afford it." The shell collector said nothing.

What could he say? Josh shared his blood; this thirty-year-old do-gooder had somehow grown out of him, out of the spirals of his own DNA.

Because he could only take so much of Josh, and because he could not shell for fear of being followed, he began to slip away with Tumaini to walk the shady groves, the sandy plains, the hot, leafless thickets of the island. It was strange moving away from the shore rather than toward it, climbing thin trails, moving inside the ceaseless cicada hum. His shirt was torn by thorns, his skin chewed by insects; his cane struck unidentifiable objects: Was that a fencepost? A tree? Soon these walks became shorter: he would hear rustles in the thickets, snakes or wild dogs, perhaps—who knew what awful things bustled in the thickets of that island? — and he'd wave his cane in the air and Tumaini would yelp and they would hurry home.

One day he came across a cone shell in his path, toiling through dust half a kilometer from the sea. *Conus textile,* a common enough danger on the reef, but to find it so far from water was impossible. How would a cone get all the way up here? And why? He picked the shell from the path and pitched it into the high grass. On subsequent walks he began coming across cones more frequently: his outstretched hand would come across the trunk of an acacia and on it would be a wandering cone; he'd pick up a her-mit crab wandering in the mango grove and find a freeloading cone on its back. Sometimes a stone worked itself into his sandal and he jumped and backpedaled, terrified, thinking it would sting him. He mistook a pine cone for *Conus gloriamaris,* a tree snail for *Conus spectrum.* He began to doubt his previous identifications: maybe the cone he had found in the path was not a cone at all, but a miter shell, or a rounded stone. Maybe it was an empty shell dropped by a villager. Maybe there was no strangely blooming population of cone shells; maybe he had imagined it all. It was ter-rible not to know.

Everything was changing: the reef, his home, poor frightened

Tumaini. Outside the entire island had become sinister, viperous, paralyzing. Inside his son was giving away everything—the rice, the toilet paper, the Vitamin B capsules. Perhaps it would be safest to just sit, hands folded, in a chair, and move as little as possible.

☽

Josh had been there three weeks before he brought it up.

"Before I left the States I did some reading," he said, "about cone shells." It was dawn. The shell collector was at the table waiting for Josh to make him toast. He said nothing.

"They think the venom may have real medical benefits."

"Who are they?"

"Scientists. They say they're trying to isolate some of the toxins and give them to stroke victims. To combat paralysis."

The shell collector wasn't sure what to say. He felt like saying that injecting cone venom into someone already half paralyzed sounded miraculously stupid.

"Wouldn't that be something, Pop? If what you've done winds up helping thousands of people?"

The shell collector fidgeted, tried to smile.

"I never feel so alive," Josh continued, "as when I'm helping people."

"I can smell the toast burning, Josh."

"There are so many people in the world, Pop, who we can *help*. Do you know how lucky we are? How amazing it is just to be healthy? To be able to reach out?"

"The toast, Son."

"Screw the toast! Jesus! Look at you! People are dying on your doorstep and you care about toast!"

He slammed the door on his way out. The shell collector sat and smelled the toast as it burned.

☽

Josh started reading shell books. He'd learned Braille as a Little Leaguer, sitting in his uniform in his father's lab, waiting for his mother to drive him to a game. Now he took books and magazines from the kibanda's one shelf and hauled them out under the palms where the three Kikuyu orphan boys had made their camp. He read aloud to them, stumbling through articles in journals like *Indo-Pacific Mollusca* or *American Conchologist.* "The blotchy ancilla," he'd read, "is a slender shell with a deep suture. Its columella is mostly straight." The boys stared at him as he read, hummed senseless, joyful songs.

The shell collector heard Josh, one afternoon, reading to them about cones. "The admirable cone is thick and relatively heavy, with a pointed spire. One of the rarest cone shells, it is white, with brown spiral bands."

Gradually, amazingly, after a week of afternoon readings, the boys grew interested. The shell collector would hear them sifting through the banks of shell fragments left by the spring tide. "Bubble shell!" one would shout. "Kafuna found a bubble shell!" They plunged their hands between rocks and squealed and shouted and dragged shirtfuls of clams up to the kibanda, identifying them with made-up names: "Blue Pretty! Mbaba Chicken Shell!"

One evening the three boys were eating with them at the table, and he listened to them as they shifted and bobbed in their chairs and clacked their silverware against the table edge like drummers. "You boys have been shelling," the shell collector said.

"Kafuna swallowed a butterfly shell!" one of the boys yelled.

The shell collector pressed forward: "Do you know that some of the shells are dangerous, that dangerous things—bad things—live in the water?"

"Bad shells!" one squealed.

"Bad sheelllls!" the others chimed.

Then they were eating, quietly. The shell collector sat, and wondered.

◡

He tried again, the next morning. Josh was hacking coconuts on the front step. "What if those boys get bored with the beach and go out to the reef? What if they fall into fire coral? What if they step on an urchin?"

"Are you saying I'm not keeping an eye on them?" Josh said.

"I'm saying that they might be looking to get bitten. Those boys came here because they thought I could find some magic shell that will cure people. They're here to get stung by a cone shell."

"You don't have the slightest idea," Josh said, "why those boys are here."

"But you do? You think you've read enough about shells to teach them how to look for cones. You *want* them to find one. You hope they'll find a big cone, get stung, and be cured. Cured of whatever ailment they have. I don't even see anything wrong with them."

"Pop," Josh groaned, "those boys are mentally handicapped. I do *not* think some sea-snail is going to cure them."

◡

So, feeling very old, and very blind, the shell collector decided to take the boys shelling. He took them out into the lagoon, where the water was flat and warm, wading almost to their chests, and worked alongside them, and did his best to show them which animals were dangerous. "Bad sheelllls!" the boys would scream, and cheered as the shell collector tossed a testy blue crab out, over the reef, into deeper water. Tumaini barked too, and seemed her old self, out there with the boys, in the ocean she loved so dearly.

◡

Finally it was not one of the young boys or some other visitor who was bitten, but Josh. He came dashing along the beach, calling for his father, his face bloodless.

"Josh? Josh is that you?" the shell collector hollered. "I was just showing the boys here this girdled triton. A graceful shell, isn't it, boys?"

In his fist, his fingers already going stiff, the back of his hand reddening, the skin distended, Josh held the cone that had bitten him, a snail he'd plucked from the wet sand, thinking it was pretty.

The shell collector hauled Josh across the beach and into some shade under the palms. He wrapped him in a blanket and sent the boys for the radio. Josh's pulse was already weak and rapid and his breath was short. Within an hour his breathing stopped, then his heart, and he was dead.

The shell collector knelt, dumbfounded, in the sand, and Tumaini lay on her paws in the shade watching him with the boys crouched behind her, their hands on their knees, terrified.

☽

The doctor boated in twenty minutes too late, wheezing, and behind him were police, in small canoes with huge motors. The police took the shell collector into his kitchen and quizzed him about his divorce, about Josh, about the boys.

Through the window he heard more boats coming and going. A damp breeze came over the sill. It was going to rain, he wanted to tell these men, these half-aggressive, half-lazy voices in his kitchen. It will rain in five minutes, he wanted to say, but they were asking him to clarify Josh's relationship with the boys. Again (was it the third time? the fifth?) they asked why his wife had divorced him. He could not find the words. He felt as if thick clouds were being shoved between him and the world; his fingers, his senses, the ocean—all this was slipping away. My dog, he wanted to say, my dog doesn't understand this. I need my dog.

"I am blind," he told the police finally, turning up his hands. "I have nothing."

Then the rain came, a monsoon assaulting the thatched roof. Frogs, singing somewhere under the floorboards, hurried their tremolo, screamed into the storm.

○

When the rain let up he heard the water dripping from the roof and a cricket under the refrigerator started singing. There was a new voice in the kitchen, a familiar voice, the mwadhini's. He said, "You will be left alone now. As I promised."

"My son——" the shell collector began.

"This blindness," the mwadhini said, taking an auger shell from the kitchen table and rolling it over the wood, "it is not unlike a shell, is it? The way a shell protects the animal inside? The way an animal can retreat inside it, tucked safely away? Of course the sick came, of course they came to seek out a cure. Well, you will have your peace now. No one will come looking for miracles now."

"The boys——"

"They will be taken away. They require care. Perhaps an orphanage in Nairobi. Malindi, maybe."

○

A month later and these Jims were in his kibanda, pouring bourbon into their evening chai. He had answered their questions, told them about Nancy and Seema and Josh. Nancy, they said, had given them exclusive rights to her story. The shell collector could see how they would write it—midnight sex, a blue lagoon, a dangerous African shell drug, a blind medicine guru with his wolf-dog. There for all the world to peer at: his shell-cluttered kibanda, his pitiful tragedies.

At dusk he rode with them into Lamu. The taxi let them off on a pier and they climbed a hill to town. He heard birds call from the scrub by the road, and from the mango trees that leaned over the path. The air smelled sweet, like cabbage and pineapple. The Jims labored as they walked.

In Lamu the streets were crowded and the street vendors were out, grilling plantains or curried goat over driftwood coals. Pineapples were being sold on sticks, and children moved about yoked with boxes from which they hawked maadazi or chapatis spread with ginger. The Jims and the shell collector bought kebabs and sat in an alley, their backs against a carved wooden door. Before long a passing teenager offered hashish from a water pipe, and the Jims accepted. The shell collector smelled its smoke, sweet and sticky, and heard the water bubble in the pipe.

"Good?" the teenager asked.

"You bet," the Jims coughed. Their speech was slurred.

The shell collector could hear men praying in the mosques, their chants vibrating down the narrow streets. He felt a bit strange, listening to them, as if his head were no longer connected to his body.

"It is Taraweeh," the teenager said. "Tonight Allah determines the course of the world for next year."

"Have some," one of the Jims said, and shoved the pipe in front of the shell collector's face. "More," the other Jim said, and giggled.

The shell collector took the pipe, inhaled.

☽

It was well after midnight. A crab fisherman in a motorized mtepe was taking them up the archipelago, past banks of mangroves, toward home. The shell collector sat in the bow on a crab trap made from chicken wire and felt the breeze in his face. The boat slowed. "Tokeni," the fisherman said, and the shell collector did, the Jims with him, splashing down from the boat into chest-deep water.

The crab boat motored away and the Jims began murmuring about the phosphorescence, admiring the glowing trails blooming behind each other's bodies as they moved through the water. The shell collector took off his sandals and waded barefoot, down off the sharp spines of coral rock, into the deeper lagoon, feeling the hard furrows of intertidal sand and the occasional mats of algal turf, fibrous and ropy. The feeling of disconnectedness had continued, been amplified by the hashish, and it was easy for him to pretend that his legs were unconnected to his body. He was, it seemed suddenly, floating, rising above the sea, feeling down through the water into the turquoise shallows and coral-lined alleys. This small reef: the crabs in their expeditions, the anemones tossing their heads, the tiny blizzards of fish wheeling past, pausing, bursting off . . . he felt it all unfold simply below him. A cowfish, a triggerfish, the harlequin Picasso fish, a drifting sponge—all these lives were being lived out, every day, as they always had been. His senses became supernatural: beyond the breaking combers, the dappled lagoon, he heard terns, and the thrum of insects in the acacias, and the heavy shifting of leaves in avocado trees, the sounding of bats, the dry rasping of bark at the collars of coconut palms, spiky burrs dropping from bushes into hot sand, the smooth seashore roar inside an empty trumpet shell, the rotting smell of conch eggs beached in their black pouches and far down the island, near the horizon—he could walk it down—he knew he would find the finless trunk of a dolphin, rolling in the swash, its flesh already being carted off, piece by piece, by stone crabs.

"What," the Jims asked, their voices far-off and blended, "does it feel like to be bitten by a cone shell?"

What strange visions the shell collector had been having, just now. A dead dolphin? Supernatural hearing? Were they even wading toward his kibanda? Were they anywhere near it?

"I could show you," he said, surprising himself. "I could find some small cones, tiny ones. You would hardly know you'd been bitten. You could write about it."

He began to search for cone shells. He waded, turned in a circle, became slowly disoriented. He moved out to the reef, stepping carefully between the rocks; he was a shorebird, a hunting crane, his beak poised to stab down at any moment, to impale a snail, a wayward fish.

The reef wasn't where he thought it was; it was behind him, and soon he felt the foam of the waves, long breakers clapping across his back, churning the shell fragments beneath his feet, and he sensed the algal ridge just ahead of him, the steep shelf, the rearing, twisting swells. A whelk, a murex, an olive; shells washed past his feet. Here, this felt like a cone. So easy to find. He spun it, balanced its apex on his palm. An arrhythmic wave suckerpunched him, broke over his chin. He spit saltwater. Another wave drove his shin into the rocks.

He thought: God writes next year's plan for the world on this night. He tried to picture God bent over parchment, dreaming, puzzling through the possibilities. "Jim," he shouted, and imagined he heard the big men splashing toward him. But they were not. "Jim!" he called. No answer. They must be in the kibanda, hunkered at the table, folding up their sleeves. They must be waiting for him to bring this cone he has found. He will press it into the crooks of their arms, let the venom spring into their blood. Then they'd know. Then they'd have their story.

He half-swam, half-clambered back toward the reef and climbed onto a coral rock, and fell, and went under. His sunglasses came loose from his face, pendulummed down. He felt for them with his heels, finally gave up. He'd find them later.

Surely the kibanda was around here somewhere. He moved into the lagoon, half-swimming, his shirt and hair soaked through. Where were his sandals? They had been in his hand. No matter.

The water became more shallow. Nancy had said there was a

pulse, slow and loud. She said she could still hear it, even after she woke. The shell collector imagined it as a titanic pulse, the three-thousand-pound heart of an ice whale. Gallons of blood at a beat. Perhaps that was what he heard now, the drumming that had begun in his ears.

He was moving toward the kibanda now, he knew. He felt the packed ridges of lagoon sand under his soles. He heard the waves collapsing onto the beach, the coconut palms above rustling husk on husk. He was bringing an animal from the reef to paralyze some writers from New York, perhaps kill them. They had done nothing to him, but here he was, planning their deaths. Was this what he wanted? Was this what God's plan for his sixty-some years of life led up to?

His chest was throbbing. Where was Tumaini? He imagined the Jims clearly, their damp bodies prone in their sleeping bags, exhaling booze and hashish, tiny siafu biting their faces. These were men who were only doing their jobs.

He took the cone shell and flung it, as far as he could, back into the lagoon. He would not poison them. It felt wonderful to make a decision like this. He wished he had more shells to hurl back into the sea, more poisons to rid himself of. His shoulder seemed terribly stiff.

Then, with a clarity that stunned him, a clarity that washed over him like a wave, he knew he'd been bitten. He was lost in every way: in this lagoon, in the shell of his private darkness, in the depths and convolutions of the venom already crippling his nervous system. Gulls were landing nearby, calling to each other, and he had been poisoned by a cone shell.

The stars rolled up over him in their myriad shiverings. His life had made its final spiral, delving down into its darkest whorl, where shell tapered into shadow. What did he remember, as he faded, poisoned finally, into the tide? His wife, his father, Josh? Did his childhood scroll by first, like a film reel, a boy under the northern lights, clambering into his father's Bell 47 helicopter? What was there, what was the hot, hard kernel of human experience at his center—a dreamy death in water, poison, disappearing, dissolution, the cold sight of his arctic origins or fifty years of blindness, the thunder of a caribou hunt, lashing bullets into the herd from the landing strut of a helicopter? Did he find faith, regret, a great sad balloon of emptiness in his gut, his unseen, unknown son, just one of Josh's beautiful unanswered letters?

No. There was no time. The venom had spread to his chest. He remembered this: blue. He remembered how that morning one of the Jims had praised the blue body of a reef fish. "That *blue*," he'd said. The shell collector remembered seeing blue in ice fields, in Whitehorse, as a boy. Even now, fifty-five years later, after all his visual memories had waned, even in dreams—the look of the world and his own face long faded—he remembered how blue looked at the bottom pinch of a crevasse, cobalt and miraculous. He remembered kicking snow over the lip, tiny slivers disappearing into an icy cleft.

Then his body abandoned him. He felt himself dissolve into that most extravagantly vivid of places, into the clouds rising darkly at the horizon, the stars blazing in their lightless tracts, the trees sprouting up from the sand, the ebbing, living waters. What he must have felt, what awful, frigid loneliness.

☽

The girl, Seema, the mwadhini's daughter, found him in the morning. She was the one who had come, every week since her recovery, to stock his shelves with rice and dried beef, to bring him toilet paper and bread and what mail he had and Uhu milk in paper cartons. Rowing there from Lamu with her nine-year-old arms, out of sight of the island, of other boats, with only the mangroves to see, sometimes she would unpin her black wraparound and let the sun down on her shoulders, her neck, her hair.

She found him awash, faceup, on a stretch of white sand. He

was a kilometer from his home. Tumaini was with him, curled around his chest, her fur sopped, whining softly.

He was barefoot; his left hand was badly swollen, the fingernails black. She took him up, his body that smelled so much like the sea, of the thousands of boiled gastropods he had tweezered from shells, and heaved him into her little boat. She fitted the oarlocks and rowed him to his kibanda. Tumaini raced alongside, bounding along the shore, pausing to let the boat catch up, yelping, galloping off again.

When they heard the girl and the dog come clattering up to the door, the Jims burst from their sleeping bags, their hair matted, eyes red, and helped in the best ways they knew. They carried the shell collector in and with the girl's help radioed Dr. Kabiru. They wiped the shell collector's face with a washcloth and listened to his heart beating shallowly and slowly. Twice he stopped breathing and twice one of those big writers put his mouth on the shell collector's and blew life into his lungs.

☽

He was numb forever. What clockless hours passed, what weeks and months? He didn't know. He dreamed of glass, of miniature glassblowers making cone teeth like tiny snow-needles, like the thinnest bones of fish, vanes on the arms of a snowflake. He dreamed of the ocean glassed over with a thick sheet and him skating out on it, peering down at the reef, its changing, perilous sculpture, its vast, miniature kingdoms. All of it—the limp tentacles of a coral polyp, the chewed floating body of a clownfish—was gray and lonesome, torn down. A freezing wind rushed down his collar, and the clouds, stringy and ragged, poured past in a terrible hurry. He was the only living thing on the whole surface of the earth and there was nothing to meet, nothing to see, no ground to stand on.

Sometimes he woke to chai pouring into his mouth. He felt his body freeze it, ice chunks rattle through his guts.

⌣

It was Seema who warmed him, finally. She visited every day, rowing from her father's jumba to the shell collector's kibanda, under the white sun, over the turquoise waters. She nursed him out of bed, shooed the siafu from his face, fed him toast. She began walking him outside and sitting with him in the sun. He shivered endlessly. She asked him about his life, about shells he had found and about the cone shell that saved her life. Eventually she began to hold his wrists and walk him out into the lagoon and he shivered whenever air touched his wet skin.

⌣

The shell collector was wading, feeling for shells with his toes. It had been a year since he'd been bitten.

Tumaini perched on a rock and sniffed at the horizon where a line of birds threaded along beneath stacks of cumulus. Seema was on the reef with them, as she had been nearly every day, her shoulders free of her wraparound. Her hair, usually bound back, hung across her neck and reflected the sun. What comfort it was to be with a person who could not see, who did not care anyway.

Seema watched as a school of fish, tiny and spear-shaped, flashed just below the surface of the water. They stared up at her with ten thousand round eyes, then turned lazily. Their shadows glided over the rutted sand, over a fern-shaped colony of coral. Those are needlefish, she thought, and that is Xenia soft coral. I know their names, how they rely on each other.

The shell collector moved a few meters, stopped and bent. He had come across what he thought was a bullia—a blind snail with a grooved, high-spired shell—and he kept his hand on it, two fingers resting lightly on the apex. After a long moment, waiting, tentative, the snail brought its foot from the aperture and resumed hauling itself over a ridge of sand. The shell collector, using his fingers, followed it for a while, then stood. "Beautiful," he murmured. Beneath his feet the snail kept on, feeling its way forward, dragging the house of its shell, fitting its body to the sand, to the private unlit horizons that whorled all around it.

The Hunter's Wife

It was the hunter's first time outside of Montana. He woke, stricken still with the hours-old vision of ascending through rose-lit cumulus, of houses and barns like specks deep in the snowed-in valleys, all the scrolling country below looking December—brown and black hills streaked with snow, flashes of iced-over lakes, the long braids of a river gleaming at the bottom of a canyon. Above the wing the sky had deepened to a blue so pure he knew it would bring tears to his eyes if he looked long enough.

Now it was dark. The airplane descended over Chicago, its galaxy of electric lights, the vast neighborhoods coming clearer as the plane glided toward the airport—streetlights, headlights, stacks of buildings, ice rinks, a truck turning at a stoplight, scraps of snow atop a warehouse and winking antennae on faraway hills, finally the long converging parallels of blue runway lights, and they were down.

He walked into the airport, past the banks of monitors. Already he felt as if he'd lost something, some beautiful perspective, some lovely dream fallen away. He had come to Chicago to see his wife, whom he had not seen in twenty years. She was there to perform her magic for a higher-up at the state university. Even universities, apparently, were interested in what she could do.

Outside the terminal the sky was thick and gray and hurried by wind. Snow was coming. A woman from the university met him and escorted him to her Jeep. He kept his gaze out the window.

They were in the car for forty-five minutes, passing first the tall, lighted architecture of downtown, then naked suburban oaks, heaps of ploughed snow, gas stations, power towers and telephone wires. The woman said, So you regularly attend your wife's performances?

No, he said. Never before.

She parked in the driveway of an elaborate and modern mansion with square balconies suspended at angles over two trapezoidal garages, huge triangular windows in the facade, sleek columns, domed lights, a steep shale roof.

Inside the front door about thirty name tags were laid out on a table. His wife was not there yet. No one, it seemed, was there yet. He found his tag and pinned it to his sweater. A silent girl in a tuxedo appeared and disappeared with his coat.

The foyer was all granite, flecked and smooth, backed with a grand staircase that spread wide at the bottom and tapered at the top. A woman came down. She stopped four or five steps from the bottom and said, Hello, Anne, to the woman who had driven him there and, You must be Mr. Dumas, to him. He took her hand, a pale bony thing, weightless, like a featherless bird.

Her husband, the university's chancellor, was just knotting his bow tie, she said, and laughed sadly to herself, as if bow ties were something she disapproved of. Beyond the foyer spread a vast parlor, high-windowed and carpeted. The hunter moved to a bank of windows, shifted aside the curtain and peered out.

In the poor light he could see a wooden deck encompassing the length of the house, angled and stepped, never the same width, with a low rail. Beyond it, in the blue shadows, a small pond lay encircled by hedges, with a marble birdbath at its center. Behind the pond stood leafless trees—oaks, maples, a sycamore white as bone. A helicopter shuttled past, winking a green light.

It's snowing, he said.

Is it? asked the hostess, with an air of concern, perhaps false. It was impossible to tell what was sincere and what was not. The woman who drove him there had moved to the bar where she cradled a drink and stared into the carpet.

He let the curtain fall back. The chancellor came down the staircase. Other guests fluttered in. A man in gray corduroy, with BRUCE MAPLES on his name tag, approached him. Mr. Dumas, he said, your wife isn't here yet?

You know her? the hunter asked. Oh no, Maples said, and shook his head. No I don't. He spread his legs and swiveled his hips as if stretching before a foot race. But I've read about her.

The hunter watched as a tall, remarkably thin man stepped through the front door. Hollows behind his jaw and beneath his eyes made him appear ancient and skeletal—as if he were visiting from some other leaner world. The chancellor approached the thin man, embraced him, and held him for a moment.

That's President O'Brien, Maples said. A famous man, actually, to people who follow those sorts of things. So terrible, what happened to his family. Maples stabbed the ice in his drink with his straw.

The hunter nodded, unsure of what to say. For the first time he began to think he should not have come.

Have you read your wife's books? Maples asked.

The hunter nodded.

In her poems her husband is a hunter.

I guide hunters. He was looking out the window to where snow was settling on the hedges.

Does that ever bother you?

What?

Killing animals. For a living, I mean.

The hunter watched snowflakes disappear as they touched the window. Was that what hunting meant to people? Killing animals? He put his fingers to the glass. No, he said. It doesn't bother me.

☽

The hunter met his wife in Great Falls, Montana, in the winter of 1972. That winter arrived immediately, all at once—you could watch it come. Twin curtains of white appeared in the north, white all the way to the sky, driving south like the end of all things. They drove the wind before them and it ran like wolves, like floodwater through a cracked dyke. Cattle galloped the fence-lines, bawling. Trees toppled; a barn roof tumbled over the high-way. The river changed directions. The wind flung thrushes screaming into the gorge and impaled them on the thorns in grotesque attitudes.

She was a magician's assistant, beautiful, sixteen years old, an orphan. It was not a new story: a glittery red dress, long legs, a traveling magic show performing in the meeting hall at the Central Christian Church. The hunter had been walking past with an armful of groceries when the wind stopped him in his tracks and drove him into the alley behind the church. He had never felt such wind; it had him pinned. His face was pressed against a low window, and through it he could see the show. The magician was a small man in a dirty blue cape. Above him a sagging banner read THE GREAT VESPUCCI. But the hunter watched only the girl; she was graceful, young, smiling. Like a wrestler the wind held him against the window.

The magician was buckling the girl into a plywood coffin that was painted garishly with red and blue bolts of lightning. Her neck and head stuck out one end, her ankles and feet the other. She beamed; no one had ever before smiled so broadly at being locked into a coffin. The magician started up an electric saw and brought it noisily down through the center of the box, sawing her in half. Then he wheeled her apart, her legs going one way, her torso another. Her neck fell back, her smile waned, her eyes showed only white. The lights dimmed. A child screamed. Wiggle your toes, the magician ordered, flourishing his magic wand, and she did; her disembodied toes wiggled in glittery high-heeled pumps. The audience squealed with delight.

The hunter watched her pink fine-boned face, her hanging hair, her outstretched throat. Her eyes caught the spotlight. Was she looking at him? Did she see his face pressed against the window, the wind slashing at his neck, the groceries—onions, a sack of flour—tumbled to the ground around his feet? Her mouth flinched; was it a smile, a flicker of greeting?

She was beautiful to him in a way that nothing else had ever been beautiful. Snow blew down his collar and drifted around his boots. The wind had fallen off but the snow came hard and still the hunter stood riveted at the window. After some time the magician rejoined the severed box halves, unfastened the buckles, and fluttered his wand, and she was whole again. She climbed out of the box and curtsied in her glittering slit-legged dress. She smiled as if it were the Resurrection itself.

Then the storm brought down a pine tree in front of the courthouse and the power winked out, streetlight by streetlight, all over town. Before she could move, before ushers began escorting the crowd out with flashlights, the hunter was slinking into the hall, making for the stage, calling for her.

He was thirty years old, twice her age. She smiled at him, leaned over from the dais in the red glow of the emergency exit lights and shook her head. Show's over, she said. In his pickup he trailed the magician's van through the blizzard to her next show, a library fund-raiser in Butte. The next night he followed her to Missoula. He rushed to the stage after each performance. Just eat dinner with me, he'd plead. Just tell me your name. It was hunting by persistence. She said yes in Bozeman. Her name was plain, Mary Roberts. They had rhubarb pie in a hotel restaurant.

I know how you do it, he said. The feet in the sawbox are dummies. You hold your legs against your chest and wiggle the dummy feet with a string.

She laughed. Is that what you do? she asked. Follow a girl to four towns to tell her her magic isn't real?

No, he said. I hunt.

You hunt. And when you're not hunting?

I dream about hunting. She laughed again. It's not funny, he said.

You're right, she said, and smiled. It's not funny. I'm that way with magic. I dream about it. I dream about it all the time. Even when I'm not asleep.

He looked into his plate, thrilled. He searched for something he might say. They ate. But I dream bigger dreams, you know, she said afterward, after she had eaten two pieces of pie, carefully, with a spoon. Her voice was quiet and serious. I have magic inside of me. I'm not going to get sawed in half by Tony Vespucci all my life.

I don't doubt it, the hunter said.

I knew you'd believe me, she said.

☽

But the next winter Vespucci brought her back to Great Falls and sawed her in half in the same plywood coffin. And the winter after that. After both performances the hunter took her to the Bitterroot Diner where he watched her eat two pieces of pie. The watching was his favorite part: a hitch in her throat as she swallowed, the way the spoon slid cleanly out from her lips, the way her hair fell over her ear.

Then she was eighteen, and after pie she let him drive her to his cabin, forty miles from Great Falls, up the Missouri, then east into the Smith River valley. She brought only a small vinyl purse. The truck skidded and sheered as he steered it over the unploughed roads, fishtailing in the deep snow, but she didn't seem afraid or worried about where he might be taking her, about the possibility that the truck might sink in a drift, that she might freeze to death in her pea coat and glittery magician's-assistant dress. Her breath plumed out in front of her. It was twenty degrees below zero. Soon the roads would be snowed over, impassable until spring.

At his one-room cabin with furs and old rifles on the walls, he unbolted the crawlspace and showed her his winter hoard: a hundred smoked trout, skinned pheasant and venison quarters hanging frozen from hooks. Enough for two of me, he said. She scanned his books over the fireplace, a monograph on grouse habits, a series of journals on upland game birds, a thick tome titled simply *Bear*. Are you tired? he asked. Would you like to see something? He gave her a snowsuit, strapped her boots into a pair of leather snowshoes, and took her to hear the grizzly.

She wasn't bad on snowshoes, a little clumsy. They went creaking over wind-scalloped snow in the nearly unbearable cold. The bear denned every winter in the same hollow cedar, the top of which had been shorn off by a storm. Black, three-fingered and huge, in the starlight it resembled a skeletal hand thrust up from the ground, a ghoulish visitor scrabbling its way out of the underworld.

They knelt. Above them the stars were knife points, hard and white. Put your ear here, he whispered. The breath that carried his words crystallized and blew away, as if the words themselves had taken on form but expired from the effort. They listened, face-to-face, their ears over woodpecker holes in the trunk. She heard it after a minute, tuning her ears into something like a drowsy sigh, a long exhalation of slumber. Her eyes widened. A full minute passed. She heard it again.

We can see him, he whispered, but we have to be dead quiet. Grizzlies are light hibernators. Sometimes all you do is step on twigs outside their dens and they're up.

He began to dig at the snow. She stood back, her mouth open, eyes wide. Bent at the waist, he bailed snow back through his legs. He dug down three feet and then encountered a smooth icy crust covering a large hole in the base of the tree. Gently he dislodged plates of ice and lifted them aside. The opening was dark, as if he'd punched through to some dark cavern, some netherworld. From the hole the smell of bear came to her, like wet dog, like wild mushrooms. The hunter removed some leaves. Beneath was a shaggy flank, a brown patch of fur.

He's on his back, the hunter whispered. This is his belly. His forelegs must be up here somewhere. He pointed to a place higher on the trunk.

She put one hand on his shoulder and knelt in the snow above the den. Her eyes were wide and unblinking. Her jaw hung open. Above her shoulder a star separated itself from the galaxy and melted through the sky. I want to touch him, she said. Her voice sounded loud and out of place in that wood, under the naked cedars.

Hush, he whispered. He shook his head no. You have to speak quietly.

Just for a minute.

No, he hissed. You're crazy. He tugged at her arm. She removed the mitten from her other hand with her teeth and reached down. He pulled at her again but lost his footing and fell back, clutching an empty mitten. As he watched, horrified, she turned and placed both hands, spread-fingered, in the thick shag of the bear's chest. Then she lowered her face, as if drinking from the snowy hollow, and pressed her lips to the bear's chest. Her entire head was inside the tree. She felt the soft, silver tips of its fur brush her cheeks. Against her nose one huge rib flexed slightly. She heard the lungs fill and then empty. She heard blood slug through veins.

Want to know what he dreams? she asked. Her voice echoed up through the tree and poured from the shorn ends of its hollowed branches. The hunter took his knife from his coat. Summer, her voice echoed. Blackberries. Trout. Dredging his flanks across river pebbles.

◡

I'd have liked, she said later, back in the cabin as he built up the fire, to crawl all the way down there with him. Get into his arms. I'd grab him by the ears and kiss him on the eyes.

The hunter watched the fire, the flames cutting and sawing, each log a burning bridge. Three years he had waited for this. Three years he had dreamed this girl by his fire. But somehow it had ended up different from what he had imagined; he had thought it would be like a hunt—like waiting hours beside a wallow with his rifle barrel on his pack to see the huge antlered head of a bull elk loom up against the sky, to hear the whole herd behind him inhale, then scatter down the hill. If you had your opening you shot and walked the animal down and that was it. All the uncertainty was over. But this felt different, as if he had no choices to make, no control over any bullet he might let fly or hold back. It was exactly as if he was still three years younger, stopped outside the Central Christian Church and driven against a low window by the wind or some other, greater force.

Stay with me, he whispered to her, to the fire. Stay the winter.

◡

Bruce Maples stood beside him jabbing the ice in his drink with his straw.

I'm in athletics, Bruce offered. I run the athletic department here.

You mentioned that.

Did I? I don't remember. I used to coach track. Hurdles.

Hurdles, the hunter repeated.

You bet.

The hunter studied him. What was Bruce Maples doing here? What strange curiosities and fears drove him, drove any of these people filing now through the front door, dressed in their dark suits and black gowns? He watched the thin, stricken man, President O'Brien, as he stood in the corner of the parlor. Every few minutes a couple of guests made their way to him and took O'Brien's hands in their own.

You probably know, the hunter told Maples, that wolves are hurdlers. Sometimes the people who track them will come to a snag and the prints will disappear. As if the entire pack just leaped into a tree and vanished. Eventually they'll find the tracks again, thirty or forty feet away. People used to think it was magic—flying wolves. But all they did was jump. One great coordinated leap.

Bruce was looking around the room. Huh, he said. I wouldn't know about that.

○

She stayed. The first time they made love, she shouted so loudly that coyotes climbed onto the roof and howled down the chimney. Her rolled off her, sweating. The coyotes coughed and chuckled all night, like children chattering in the yard, and he had nightmares. Last night you had three dreams and you dreamed you were a wolf each time, she whispered. You were mad with hunger and running under the moon.

Had he dreamed that? He couldn't remember. Maybe he talked in his sleep.

In December it never got warmer than fifteen below. The river froze—something he'd never seen. Christmas Eve he drove all the way to Helena to buy her figure skates. In the morning they wrapped themselves head to toe in furs and went out to skate the river. She held him by the hips and they glided through the blue dawn, skating hard up the frozen coils and shoals, beneath the leafless alders and cottonwoods, only the bare tips of creek willow showing above the snow. Ahead of them vast white stretches of river faded on into darkness. An owl hunkered on a branch and watched them with its huge eyes. Merry Christmas, Owl! she shouted into the cold. It spread its huge wings, dropped from the branch and disappeared into the forest.

In a wind-polished bend they came upon a dead heron, frozen by its ankles into the ice. It had tried to hack itself out, hammering with its beak first at the ice entombing its feet and then at its own thin and scaly legs. When it finally died, it died upright, wings folded back, beak parted in some final, desperate cry, legs rooted like twin reeds in the ice.

She fell to her knees and knelt before the bird. Its eye was frozen and cloudy. It's dead, the hunter said, gently. Come on. You'll freeze too.

No, she said. She slipped off her mitten and closed the heron's beak in her fist. Almost immediately her eyes rolled back in her head. Oh wow, she moaned. I can *feel* her. She stayed like that for whole minutes, the hunter standing over her, feeling the cold come up his legs, afraid to touch her as she knelt before the bird. Her hand turned white and then blue in the wind.

Finally she stood. We have to bury it, she said. He chopped the bird out with his skate and buried it in a drift.

That night she lay stiff and would not sleep. It was just a bird, he said, unsure of what was bothering her but bothered by it himself. We can't do anything for a dead bird. It was good that we buried it, but tomorrow something will find it and dig it out.

She turned to him. Her eyes were wide; he remembered how they had looked when she put her hands on the bear. When I touched her, she said, I saw where she went.

What?

I saw where she went when she died. She was on the shore of a lake with other herons, a hundred others, all facing the same direction, and they were wading among stones. It was dawn and they watched the sun come up over the trees on the other side of the lake. I saw it as clearly as if I was there.

He rolled onto his back and watched shadows shift across the ceiling. Winter is getting to you, he said. In the morning he resolved to make sure she went out every day. It was something he'd long believed: go out every day in winter or your mind will slip. Every winter the paper was full of stories about ranchers' wives, snowed in and crazed with cabin fever, who had dispatched their husbands with cleavers or awls.

The next night he drove her all the way north to Sweetgrass, on the Canadian border, to see the northern lights. Great sheets of violet, amber and pale green rose from the distances. Shapes like the head of a falcon, a scarf and a wing rippled above the mountains. They sat in the truck cab, the heater blowing on their knees. Behind the aurora the Milky Way burned.

That one's a hawk! she exclaimed.

Auroras, he explained, occur because of Earth's magnetic field. A wind blows all the way from the sun and gusts past the earth, moving charged particles around. That's what we see. The yellow-green stuff is oxygen. The red and purple at the bottom there is nitrogen.

No, she said, shaking her head. The red one's a hawk. See his beak? See his wings?

☽

Winter threw itself at the cabin. He took her out every day. He showed her a thousand ladybugs hibernating in an orange ball hung in a riverbank hollow; a pair of dormant frogs buried in frozen mud, their blood crystallized until spring. He pried a globe of honeybees from its hive, slow-buzzing, stunned from the sudden exposure, each bee shimmying for warmth. When he placed the globe in her hands she fainted, her eyes rolled back. Lying there she saw all their dreams at once, the winter reveries of scores of worker bees, each one fiercely vivid: bright trails through thorns to a clutch of wild roses, honey tidily brimming a hundred combs.

With each day she learned more about what she could do. She felt a foreign and keen sensitivity bubbling in her blood, as though a seed planted long ago was just now sprouting. The larger the animal, the more powerfully it could shake her. The recently dead were virtual mines of visions, casting them off with a slow-fading strength like a long series of tethers being cut, one by one. She pulled off her mittens and touched everything she could: bats, salamanders, a cardinal chick tumbled from its nest, still warm. Ten hibernating garter snakes coiled beneath a rock, eyelids sealed, tongues stilled. Each time she touched some frozen insect, some slumbering amphibian, anything just dead, her eyes rolled back and its visions, its heaven, went shivering through her body.

Their first winter passed like that. When he looked out the cabin window he saw wolf tracks crossing the river, owls hunting from the trees, six feet of snow like a quilt ready to be thrown off. She saw burrowed dreamers nestled under the roots against the long twilight, their dreams rippling into the sky like auroras.

With love still lodged in his heart like a splinter, he married her in the first muds of spring.

☽

Bruce Maples gasped when the hunter's wife finally arrived. She moved through the door like a show horse, demure in the way she kept her eyes down but assured in her step; she brought each tapered heel down and struck it against the granite. The hunter had not seen his wife for twenty years, and she had changed— become refined, less wild, and somehow, to the hunter, worse for it. Her face had wrinkled around the eyes, and she moved as if avoiding contact with anything near her, as if the hall table or closet door might suddenly lunge forward to snatch at her lapels.

She wore no jewelry, no wedding ring, only a plain black suit, double-breasted.

She found her name tag on the table and pinned it to her lapel. Everyone in the reception room looked at her then looked away. The hunter realized that she, not President O'Brien, was the guest of honor. In a sense they were courting her. This was their way, the chancellor's way—a silent bartender, tuxedoed coat girls, big icy drinks. Give her pie, the hunter thought. Rhubarb pie. Show her a sleeping grizzly.

They sat for dinner at a narrow and very long table, fifteen or so high-backed chairs down each side and one at each head. The hunter was seated several places away from his wife. She looked over at him finally, a look of recognition, of warmth, and then looked away again. He must have seemed old to her—he must always have seemed old to her. She did not look at him again.

The kitchen staff, in starched whites, brought onion soup, scampi, poached salmon. Around the hunter guests spoke in half whispers about people he did not know. He kept his eyes on the windows and the blowing snow beyond.

☽

The river thawed and drove huge saucers of ice toward the Missouri. The sound of water running, of release, of melting, clucked and purled through the open windows of the cabin. The hunter felt that old stirring, that quickening in his soul, and he would rise in the wide pink dawns, take his fly rod and hurry down to the river. Already trout were rising through the chill brown water to take the first insects of spring. Soon the telephone in the cabin was ringing with calls from clients, and his guiding season was on.

Occasionally a client wanted a lion or a trip with dogs for birds, but late spring and summer were for trout. He was out every morning before dawn, driving with a thermos of coffee to pick up a lawyer, a widower, a politician with a penchant for native cutthroat. After dropping off clients he'd hustle back out to scout for the next trip. He scouted until dark and sometimes after, kneeling in willows by the river and waiting for a trout to rise. He came home stinking of fish gut and woke her with his eager stories, cutthroat trout leaping fifteen-foot cataracts, a stubborn rainbow wedged under a snag.

By June she was bored and lonely. She wandered through the woods, but never very far. The summer woods were dense and busy, nothing like the quiet graveyard feel of winter. You couldn't see twenty feet in the summer. Nothing slept for very long; everything was emerging from cocoons, winging about, buzzing, multiplying, having litters, gaining weight. Bear cubs splashed in the river. Chicks screamed for worms. She longed for the stillness of winter, the long slumber, the bare sky, the bone-on-bone sound of bull elk knocking their antlers against trees. In August she went to the river to watch her husband cast flies with a client, the loops lifting from his rod like a spell cast over the water. He taught her to clean fish in the river so the scent wouldn't linger. She made the belly cuts, watched the viscera unloop in the current, the final, ecstatic visions of trout fading slowly up her wrists, running out into the river.

In September the big-game hunters came. Each client wanted something different: elk, antelope, a bull moose, a doe. They wanted to see grizzlies, track a wolverine, even shoot sandhill cranes. They wanted the heads of seven-by-seven royal bulls for their dens. Every few days he came home smelling of blood, with stories of stupid clients, of the Texan who sat, wheezing, too out of shape to get to the top of a hill for his shot. A bloodthirsty New Yorker claimed only to want to photograph black bears, then pulled a pistol from his boot and fired wildly at two cubs and their mother. Nightly she scrubbed blood out of the hunter's coveralls, watched it fade from rust to red to rose in the river water.

He was gone seven days a week, all day, home long enough only to grind sausage or cut roasts, clean his rifle, scrub out his meat pack, answer the phone. She understood very little of what he did, only that he loved the valley and needed to move in it, to watch the ravens and kingfishers and herons, the coyotes and bobcats, to hunt nearly everything else. There is no order in that world, he told her once, waving vaguely toward Great Falls, the cities that lay to the south. But here there is. Here I can see things I'd never see down there, things most folks are blind to. With no great reach of imagination she could see him fifty years hence, still lacing his boots, still gathering his rifle, all the world to see and him dying happy having seen only this valley.

She began to sleep, taking long afternoon naps, three hours or more. Sleep, she learned, was a skill like any other, like getting sawed in half and reassembled, or like divining visions from a dead robin. She taught herself to sleep despite heat, despite noise. Insects flung themselves at the screens, hornets sped down the chimney, the sun angled hot and urgent through the southern windows; still she slept. When he came home each autumn night, exhausted, forearms stained with blood, she was hours into sleep. Outside, the wind was already stripping leaves from the cottonwoods—too soon, he thought. He'd lie down and take her sleeping hand. Both of them lived in the grips of forces they had no control over—the November wind, the revolutions of the earth.

◡

That winter was the worst he could remember: from Thanksgiving on they were snowed into the valley, the truck buried under six-foot drifts. The phone line went down in December and stayed down until April. January began with a chinook followed by a terrible freeze. The next morning a three-inch crust of ice covered the snow. On the ranches to the south cattle crashed through and bled to death kicking their way out. Deer punched through with their tiny hooves and suffocated in the deep snow beneath. Trails of blood veined the hills.

In the mornings he'd find coyote tracks written in the snow around the door to the crawlspace, two inches of hardwood between them and all his winter hoard hanging frozen now beneath the floorboards. He reinforced the door with baking sheets, nailing them up against the wood and over the hinges. Twice he woke to the sound of claws scrabbling against the metal, and charged outside to shout the coyotes away.

Everywhere he looked something was dying ungracefully, sinking in a drift, an elk keeling over, an emaciated doe clattering onto ice like a drunken skeleton. The radio reported huge cattle losses on the southern ranches. Each night he dreamt of wolves, of running with them, soaring over fences and tearing into the steaming, snow-matted bodies of cattle.

Still the snow fell. In February he woke three times to coyotes under the cabin, and the third time mere shouting could not send them running; he grabbed his bow and knife and dashed out into the snow barefoot, already his feet going numb. This time they had gone in under the door, chewing and digging the frozen earth under the foundation. He unbolted what was left of the door and swung it free.

A coyote hacked as it choked on something. Others shifted and panted. Maybe there were ten. Elk arrows were all he had, aluminum shafts tipped with broadheads. He squatted in the dark entryway—their only exit—with his bow at full draw and an arrow nocked. Above him he could hear his wife's feet pad silently over the floorboards. A coyote made a coughing sound. He began to fire arrows steadily into the dark. He heard some bite into the foundation blocks at the back of the crawlspace, others sink into flesh. He spent his whole quiver: a dozen arrows. The yelps of speared coyote went up. A few charged him, and he lashed at them with his knife. He felt teeth go to the bone of his arm, felt hot breath on his cheeks. He lashed with his knife at ribs, tails, skulls. His muscles screamed. The coyote were in a frenzy. Blood bloomed from his wrist, his thigh.

Upstairs she heard the otherwordly screams of wounded coyotes come through the floorboards, his grunts and curses as he
fought. It sounded as if an exit had been tunneled all the way up
from hell to open under their house, and what was now pouring
out was the worst violence that place could send up. She knelt
before the fireplace and felt the souls of coyote as they came
through the boards on their way skyward.

ℑ

He was blood-soaked and hungry and his thigh had been badly
bitten but he worked all day digging out the truck. If he did not
get food, they would starve, and he tried to hold the thought of
the truck in his mind. He lugged slate and tree bark to wedge
under the tires, excavated a mountain of snow from the truck bed.
Finally, after dark, he got the engine turned over and ramped the
truck up onto the frozen, wind-crusted snow. For a brief, wonderful moment he had it careening over the icy crust, starlight washing through the windows, tires spinning, engine churning, what
looked to be the road unspooling in the headlights. Then he
crashed through. Slowly, painfully, he began digging it out again.

It was hopeless. He would get it up and then it would crash
through a few miles later. Hardly anywhere was the sheet of ice
atop the snow thick enough to support the truck's weight. For
twenty hours he revved and slid the truck over eight-foot drifts.
Three more times it broke through and sank to the windows.
Finally he left it. He was ten miles from home, thirty miles from
town.

He made a weak and smoky fire with cut boughs and lay beside
it and tried to sleep but couldn't. The heat from the fire melted
snow and trickles ran slowly toward him but froze solid before
they reached him. The stars twisting in their constellations above
had never seemed farther or colder. In a state that was neither
fully sleep nor fully waking, he watched wolves lope around his

fire, just outside the reaches of light, slavering and lean. A raven dropped through the smoke and hopped to him. He thought for the first time that he might die if he did not get warmer. He managed to kneel and turn and crawl for home. Around him he could feel the wolves, smell blood on them, hear their nailed feet scrape across the ice.

He traveled all that night and all the next day, near catatonia, sometimes on his feet, more often on his elbows and knees. At times he thought he was a wolf and at times he thought he was dead. When he finally made it to the cabin, there were no tracks on the porch, no sign that she had gone out. The crawlspace door was still flung open and shreds of the siding and door frame lay scattered about as though some wounded devil had clawed its way out of the cabin's foundation and galloped into the night.

She was kneeling on the floor, ice in her hair, lost in some kind of hypothermic torpor. With his last dregs of energy he constructed a fire and poured a mug of hot water down her throat. As he fell into sleep, he watched himself as from a distance, weeping and clutching his near-frozen wife.

☽

They had only flour, a jar of frozen cranberries, and a few crackers in the cupboards. He went out only to split more wood. When she could speak her voice was quiet and far away. I have dreamt the most amazing things, she murmured. I have seen the places where the coyotes go when they are gone. I know where spiders go, and geese. . . .

Snow fell incessantly. He wondered if some ice age had befallen the entire world. Night was abiding; daylight passed in a breath. Soon the whole planet would become a white and featureless ball hurtling through space, lost. Whenever he stood up his eyesight fled in slow, nauseating streaks of color.

Icicles hung from the cabin's roof and ran all the way to the porch, pillars of ice barring the door. To exit he had to hack his way out with an axe. He went out with lanterns to fish, shoveled down to the river ice, drilled through with a hand auger and shivered over the hole jigging a ball of dough on a hook. Sometimes he brought back a trout, frozen stiff in the short snowshoe from the river to the cabin. Other times they ate a squirrel, a hare, once a famished deer whose bones he cracked and boiled and finally ground into meal, or only a few handfuls of rose hips. In the worst parts of March he dug out cattails to peel and steam the tubers.

She hardly ate, sleeping eighteen, twenty hours a day. When she woke it was to scribble on notebook paper before plummeting back into sleep, clutching at the blankets as if they gave her sustenance. There was, she was learning, strength hidden at the center of weakness, ground at the bottom of the deepest pit. With her stomach empty and her body quieted, without the daily demands of living, she felt she was making important discoveries. She was only nineteen and had lost twenty pounds since marrying him. Naked she was all rib cage and pelvis.

He read her scribbled dreams but they read like senseless poems and gave him no clues to her: *Snail,* she wrote,

sleds down blades in the rain.
Owl: fixed his eyes on hare, dropping as if from the moon.
Horse: rides across the plains with his brothers . . .

Eventually he hated himself for bringing her there, for quarantining her in a cabin winterlong. This winter was making her crazy—making them both crazy. All that was happening to her was his fault.

⌒

In April the temperature rose above zero and then above twenty. He strapped the extra battery to his pack and went to dig out the truck. Its excavation took all day. He drove it slowly back up the slushy road in the moonlight, went in and asked if she'd like to go to town the next morning. To his surprise, she said yes. They heated water for baths and dressed in clothes they hadn't worn in six months. She threaded twine through her belt loops to keep her trousers up.

Behind the wheel his chest filled up to have her with him, to be moving out into the country, to see the sun above the trees. Spring was coming; the valley was dressing up. Look there, he wanted to say, those geese streaming over the road. The valley lives. Even after a winter like that.

She asked him to drop her off at the library. He bought food— a dozen frozen pizzas, potatoes, eggs, carrots. He nearly wept at seeing bananas. He sat in the parking lot and drank a half gallon of milk. When he picked her up at the library, she had applied for a library card and borrowed twenty books. They stopped at the Bitterroot for hamburgers and rhubarb pie. She ate three pieces. He watched her eat, the spoon sliding out of her mouth. This was better. This was more like he dreamed it would be.

Well, Mary, he said. I think we made it.

I love pie, she said.

⌣

As soon as the lines were repaired the phone began to ring. He took his fishing clients down the river. She sat on the porch, reading, reading.

Soon her appetite for books could not be met by the Great Falls Public Library. She wanted other books, essays about sorcery, primers on magic-working and conjury that had to be mail-ordered from New Hampshire, New Orleans, even Italy. Once a week the hunter drove to town to collect a parcel of books from the post office: *Arcana Mundi, The Seer's Dictionary, Paragon of Wizardry, Occult Science Among the Ancients*. He opened one to a random page and read, *bring water, tie a soft fillet around your altar, burn it on fresh twigs and frankincense.* . . . .

She regained her health, took on energy, no longer lay under furs dreaming all day. She was out of bed before him, brewing coffee, her nose already between pages. With a steady diet of meat and vegetables her body bloomed, her hair shone; her eyes and cheeks glowed. After supper he'd watch her read in the firelight, blackbird feathers tied all through her hair, a heron's beak hanging between her breasts.

In November he took a Sunday off and they cross-country skied. They came across a bull elk frozen to death in a draw, ravens shrieking at them as they skied to it. She knelt by it and put her palm on its leathered skull. Her eyes rolled back in her head. There, she moaned. I feel him.

What do you feel? he asked, standing behind her. What is it?

She stood, trembling. I feel his life flowing out, she said. I see where he goes, what he sees.

But that's impossible, he said. It's like saying you know what I dream.

I do, she said. You dream about wolves.

But that elk's been dead at least a day. It doesn't go anywhere. It goes into the crops of those ravens.

How could she tell him? How could she ask him to understand such a thing? How could anyone understand? The books she read never told her that.

More clearly than ever she could see that there was a fine line between dreams and wakefulness, between living and dying, a line so tenuous it sometimes didn't exist. It was always clearest for her in winter. In winter, in that valley, life and death were not so different. The heart of a hibernating newt was frozen solid but she could warm and wake it in her palm. For the newt there was no line at all, no fence, no River Styx, only an area between living and dying, like a snowfield between two lakes: a place where lake denizens sometimes met each other on their way to the other side, where there was only one state of being, neither living nor dead, where death was only a possibility and visions rose shimmering to the stars like smoke. All that was needed was a hand, the heat of a palm, the touch of fingers.

◡

That February the sun shone during the days and ice formed at night—slick sheets glazing the wheat fields, the roofs and roads. He dropped her off at the library, the chains on the tires rattling as he pulled away, heading back up the Missouri toward Fort Benton.

Around noon Marlin Spokes, a snowplough driver the hunter knew from grade school, slid off the Sun River Bridge in his plough and dropped forty feet into the river. He was dead before they could get him out of the truck. She was reading in the library a block away and heard the plough crash into the riverbed like a thousand dropped girders. When she got to the bridge, sprinting in her jeans and T-shirt, men were already in the water—a telephone man from Helena, the jeweler, the butcher in his apron, all of them scrambling down the banks, wading in the rapids, prying the door open. She careened down the snow-covered slope beneath the bridge and splashed to them. The men lifted Marlin from the cab, stumbling as they carried him. Steam rose from their shoulders and from the crushed hood of the plow. Her hand on the jeweler's arm, her leg against the butcher's leg, she reached for Marlin's ankle.

When her finger touched Marlin's body, her eyes rolled immediately back and a single vision leapt to her: Marlin Spokes pedaling a bicycle, a child's seat mounted over the rear tire with a helmeted boy—Marlin's own son—strapped into it. Spangles of light drifted over the riders as they rolled down a lane beneath giant sprawling trees. The boy reached for Marlin's hair with one small fist. Fallen leaves turned over in their wake. In the glass of a storefront window their reflection flashed past. This quiet vision—like a ribbon of rich silk—ran out slowly and fluidly, with great power, and she shook beneath it. It was she who pedaled the bike. The boy's fingers pulled through her hair.

The men who were touching her or touching Marlin saw what she saw, felt what she felt. They tried not to talk about it, but after the funeral, after a week, they couldn't keep it in. At first they spoke of it only in their basements, at night, but Great Falls was not a big town and this was not something one kept locked in a basement. Soon they talked about it everywhere, in the super-market, at the gasoline pumps. People who didn't know Marlin Spokes or his son or the hunter's wife or any of the men in the river that morning soon spoke of the event like experts. All you had to do was *touch* her, a barber said, and you saw it too. The most beautiful lane you've ever dreamed, raved a deli owner. Giant trees bigger'n you've ever imagined. You didn't just pedal his son around, movie ushers whispered, you *loved* him.

☽

He could have heard anywhere. In the cabin he built up the fire, flipped idly through a stack of her books. He couldn't understand them—one of them wasn't even in English.

After dinner she took the plates to the sink.

You read Spanish now? he asked.

Her hands in the sink stilled. It's Portuguese, she said. I only understand a little.

He turned his fork in his hands. Were you there when Marlin Spokes was killed?

I helped pull him out of the truck. I don't think I was much good.

He looked at the back of her head. He felt like driving his fork through the table. What tricks did you play? Did you hypnotize people?

Her shoulders tightened. Her voice came out furious: Why

can't you——, she began, but her voice fell off. It wasn't tricks, she muttered. I helped carry him.

When she started to get phone calls, he hung up on the callers. But they were relentless: a grieving widow, an orphan's lawyer, a reporter from the *Great Falls Tribune*. A blubbering father drove all the way to the cabin to beg her to come to the funeral parlor, and finally she went. The hunter insisted on driving her. It wasn't right, he declared, for her to go alone. He waited in the truck in the parking lot, engine rattling, radio moaning.

I feel so alive, she said afterward as he helped her into the cab. Her clothes were soaked through with sweat. Like my blood is fizzing through my body. At home she lay awake, far away, all night.

She got called back and called back, and each time he drove her. Some days he'd take her after a whole day of scouting for elk and he'd pass out from exhaustion while he waited in the truck. When he woke she'd be beside him, holding his hand, her hair damp, her eyes wild.

You dreamt you were with the wolves and eating salmon, she said. They were washed up and dying on the shoals. It was right outside the cabin.

It was well after midnight and he'd be up before four the next day. The salmon used to come here, he said. When I was a boy. There'd be so many you could stick your hand in the river and touch one. He drove them home over the dark fields. He tried to soften his voice. What do you do in there? What really?

I give them solace. I let them say good-bye to their loved ones. I help them know something they'd never otherwise know.

No, he said. I mean what kind of tricks? How do you do it?

She turned her hands palm up. As long as they're touching me they see what I see. Come in with me next time. Go in there and hold hands. Then you'll know.

He said nothing. The stars above the windshield seemed fixed in their places.

Families wanted to pay her; most wouldn't let her leave until they did. She would come out to the truck with fifty, a hundred—once four hundred—dollars folded into her pocket. She grew her hair out, obtained talismans to dramatize her performances: a bat wing, a raven's beak, a fistful of hawk's feathers bound with a sprig of cheroot. A cardboard box full of candle stubs. Then she went off for weekends, disappearing in the truck before he was up, a fearless driver. She stopped for roadkill and knelt by it—a crumpled porcupine, a shattered deer. She pressed her palm to the truck's grille where a hundred husks of insects smoked. Seasons came and went. She was gone half the winter. Each of them was alone. They never spoke. On longer drives there were times she was tempted to keep the truck pointed away and never return.

In the first thaws he would go out to the river, try to lose himself in the rhythm of casting, in the sound of pebbles driven downstream, clacking together. But even fishing had gone lonely for him. Everything, it seemed, was out of his hands—his truck, his wife, the course of his own life.

As hunting season came on his mind wandered. He was botching opportunities—getting upwind of elk or telling a client to call it quits thirty seconds before a pheasant burst from cover and flapped slowly, untroubled, into the sky. When a client missed his mark and pegged an antelope in the neck, the hunter berated him for being careless, knelt over its tracks and clutched at the bloody snow. Do you understand what you've done? he shouted. How the arrow shaft will knock against the trees, how the animal will run and run, how the wolves will trot behind it to keep it from resting? The client was red-faced, huffing. Wolves? the client said. There haven't been wolves here for twenty years.

She was in Butte or Missoula when he discovered her money in a boot: six thousand dollars and change. He canceled his trips and stewed for two days, pacing the porch, sifting through her things, rehearsing his arguments. When she saw him, the sheaf of bills jutting from his shirt pocket, she stopped halfway to the door, her bag over her shoulder, her hair brought back. The light came across his shoulders and fell onto the yard.

It's not right, he said.

She walked past him into the cabin. I'm helping people. I'm doing what I love. Can't you see how good I feel afterward?

You take advantage of them. They're grieving, and you take their money.

They *want* to pay me, she shrieked. I help them see something they desperately want to see.

It's a grift. A con.

She came back out on the porch. No, she said. Her voice was quiet and strong. This is real. As real as anything: the valley, the river, the trees, your trout hanging in the crawlspace. I have a talent. A gift.

He snorted. A gift for hocus-pocus. For swindling widows out of their savings. He lobbed the money into the yard. The wind caught the bills and scattered them over the snow.

She hit him, once, hard across the mouth. How dare you? she cried. You, of all people, should understand. You who dream of wolves every night.

◡

He went out alone the next evening and she tracked him through the snow. He was up on a deer platform under a blanket. He was wearing white camouflage; he'd tiger-striped his face with black paint. She crouched a hundred yards away, for four hours or more, damp and trembling in the snow behind his tree stand. She thought he must have dozed off when she heard an arrow sing down from the platform and strike a doe she hadn't even noticed in the chest. The doe looked around, wildly surprised, and charged off, galloping through the trees. She heard the aluminum shaft of the arrow knocking against branches, heard the deer plunge through a thicket. The hunter sat a moment, then climbed down from his perch and began to follow. She waited until he was out of sight, then followed.

She didn't have far to go. There was so much blood she thought he must have wounded other deer, which must all have come charging down this same path, spilling out the quantities of their lives. The doe lay panting between two trees, the thin shaft of the arrow jutting from her shoulder. Blood so red it was almost black pulsed down its flank. The hunter stood over the animal and slit its throat.

Mary leapt forward from where she squatted, her legs all pins and needles, dashed across the snow in her parka and, lunging, grabbed the doe by its still-warm foreleg. With her other hand she seized the hunter's wrist and held on. His knife was still inside the deer's throat and as he pulled away blood spread thickly into the snow. Already the doe's vision was surging through her body—fifty deer wading a sparkling brook, their bellies in the current, craning their necks to pull leaves from overhanging alders, light pouring around their bodies, a buck raising its antlered head like a king. A silver bead of water hung from its muzzle, caught the sun, and fell.

What?—the hunter gasped. He dropped his knife. He was pulling away, pulling from his knees with all his strength. She held on; one hand on his wrist, the other clamped around the doe's foreleg. He dragged them across the snow and the doe left her blood as she went. Oh, he whispered. He could feel the world—the grains of snow, the stripped bunches of trees—falling away. The taste of alder leaves was in his mouth. A golden brook rushed under his body; light spilled onto him. The buck was raising its head, meeting his eyes. All the world washed in amber.

The hunter gave a last pull and was free. The vision sped away. No, he murmured. No. He rubbed his wrist where her fingers had been and shook his head as if shaking off a blow. He ran.

Mary lay in the blood-smeared snow a long time, the warmth of the doe running up her arm until finally the woods had gone cold and she was alone. She dressed the doe with his knife and quartered the carcass and ferried it home over her shoulders. Her husband was in bed. The fireplace was cold. Don't come near me, he said. Don't touch me. She built the fire and fell asleep on the floor.

In the months that followed she left the cabin more frequently and for longer durations, visiting homes, accident sites and funeral parlors all over central Montana. Finally she pointed the truck south and didn't turn back. They had been married five years.

꙳

Twenty years later, in the Bitterroot Diner, he looked up at the ceiling-mounted television and there she was, being interviewed. She lived in Manhattan, had traveled the world, written two books. She was in demand all over the country. Do you commune with the dead? the interviewer asked. No, she said, I help people. I commune with the living. I give people peace.

Well, the interviewer said, turning to speak into the camera, I believe it.

The hunter bought her books at the bookstore and read them in one night. She had written poems about the valley, written them to the animals: you rampant coyote, you glorious bull. She had traveled to Sudan to touch the backbone of a fossilized stegosaur, and wrote of her frustration when she divined nothing from it. A TV network flew her to Kamchatka to embrace the huge shaggy forefoot of a mammoth as it was airlifted from the permafrost—she had better luck with that one, describing an entire herd slogging big-footed through a slushy tide, tearing at sea grass and bringing it to their mouths with their trunks. In a handful of poems there were even vague allusions to him—a brooding, blood-soaked presence that hovered outside the margins, like storms on their way, like a killer hiding in the basement.

The hunter was fifty-eight years old. Twenty years was a long time. The valley had diminished slowly but perceptibly: roads came in, and the grizzlies left, seeking higher country. Loggers had thinned nearly every accessible stand of trees. Every spring runoff from logging roads turned the river chocolate-brown. He had given up on finding a wolf in that country although they still came to him in dreams and let him run with them, out over frozen flats under the moon. He had never been with another woman. In his cabin, bent over the table, he set aside her books, took a pencil, and wrote her a letter.

A week later a Federal Express truck drove all the way to the cabin. Inside the envelope was her response on embossed stationery. The handwriting was hurried and efficient. *I will be in Chicago,* it said, *day after tomorrow. Enclosed is a plane ticket. Feel free to come. Thank you for writing.*

‿

After sherbet the chancellor rang his spoon against a glass and called his guests into the reception room. The bar had been dismantled; in its place three caskets had been set on the carpet. The caskets were mahogany, polished to a deep luster. The one in the center was larger than the two flanking it. A bit of snow that had fallen on the lids—they must have been kept outside—was melting, and drops ran onto the carpet where they left dark circles. Around the caskets cushions had been placed on the floor. A dozen candles burned on the mantel. There were the sounds of staff clearing the dining room. The hunter leaned against the entryway and watched guests drift uncomfortably into the room, some cradling coffee cups, others gulping at gin or vodka in deep tumblers. Eventually everyone settled onto the floor.

The hunter's wife came in then, elegant in her dark suit. She knelt and motioned for O'Brien to sit beside her. His face was pinched and inscrutable. Again the hunter had the impression that he was not of this world but of a slightly leaner one.

President O'Brien, his wife said. I know this is difficult for you. Death can seem so final, like a blade dropped through your center. But the nature of death is not at all final; it is not some dark cliff off which we leap. I hope to show you it is merely a fog, something we can peer into and out of, something we can know and face and not necessarily fear. By each life taken from our collective lives we are diminished. But even in death there is much to celebrate. It is only a transition, like so many others.

She moved into the circle and unfastened the lids of the caskets. From where he sat the hunter could not see inside. His wife's hands fluttered around her waist like birds. Think, she said. Think hard about something you would like resolved, some matter, gone now, which you wish you could take back—perhaps with your daughters, a moment, a lost feeling, a desperate wish.

The hunter lidded his eyes. He found himself thinking of his wife, of their long gulf, of dragging her and a bleeding doe through the snow. Think now, his wife was saying, of some wonderful moment, some fine and sunny minute you shared, your wife and daughters, all of you together. Her voice was lulling. Beneath his eyelids the glow of the candles made an even orange wash. He knew her hands were reaching for whatever—whoever—lay in those caskets. Somewhere inside him he felt her extend across the room.

His wife said more about beauty and loss being the same thing, about how they ordered the world, and he felt something happening—a strange warmth, a flitting presence, something dim and unsettling like a feather brushed across the back of his neck. Hands on both sides of him reached for his hands. Fingers locked around his fingers. He wondered if she was hypnotizing him, but it didn't matter. He had nothing to fight off or snap out of. She was inside him now; she had reached across and was poking about.

Her voice faded, and he felt himself swept up as if rising toward the ceiling. Air washed lightly in and out of his lungs; warmth pulsed in the hands that held his own. In his mind he saw a sea emerging from fog. The water was broad and flat and glittered like polished metal. He could feel dune grass moving against his shins, and wind coming over his shoulders. The sea was very bright. All around him bees shuttled over the dunes. Far out a shorebird was diving for crabs. He knew that a few hundred yards away a pair of girls were building castles in the sand; he could hear their song, soft and lilting. Their mother was with them, reclined under an umbrella, one leg bent, the other straight. She was drinking iced tea and he could taste it in his mouth, sweet and bitter with a trace of mint. Each cell in his body seemed to breathe. He became the girls, the diving bird, the shuttling bees; he was the mother of the girls and the father; he could feel himself flowing outward, richly dissolving, paddling into the world like the very first cell into the great blue sea. . . .

When he opened his eyes he saw linen curtains, women in gowns kneeling. Tears were visible on many people's cheeks— O'Brien's and the chancellor's and Bruce Maples's. His wife's head was bowed. The hunter gently released the hands that held his and walked out into kitchen, past the sudsy sinks, the stacks of dishes. He let himself out a side door and found himself on the long wooden deck that ran the length of the house, a couple inches of snow already settled on it.

He felt drawn toward the pond, the birdbath and the hedges. He walked to the pond and stood at its rim. The snow was falling easily and slowly and the undersides of the clouds glowed yellow with reflected light from the city. Inside the house the lights were all down and only the dozen candles on the mantel showed, trembling and winking through the windows, a tiny, trapped constellation.

Before long his wife came out onto the deck and walked through the snow and came down to the pond. There were things he had been preparing to say: something about a final belief, about his faithfulness to the idea of her, an expression of gratitude for providing a reason to leave the valley, if only for a night. He wanted to tell her that although the wolves were gone, may always have been gone, they still came to him in dreams. That they could run there, fierce and unfettered, was surely enough. She would understand. She had understood long before he did.

But he was afraid to speak. He could see that speaking would be like dashing some very fragile bond to pieces, like kicking a dandelion gone to seed; the wispy, tenuous sphere of its body would scatter in the wind. So instead they stood together, the snow fluttering down from the clouds to melt into the water where their own reflected images trembled like two people trapped against the glass of a parallel world, and he reached, finally, to take her hand.

So Many Chances

Dorotea San Juan, a fourteen year old in a brown cardigan. The janitor's daughter. Walks with her head down, wears cheap sneakers, never lipstick. Picks at salads during lunch. Tacks maps to her bedroom walls. Holds her breath when she gets nervous. Years of being the janitor's daughter teach her to blend in, look down, be nobody. Who's that? Nobody.

Dorotea's dad is fond of saying this: A man only gets so many chances. He says it now, after dark, in Youngstown, Ohio, as he sits on Dorotea's bed. And says this also: This is a real opportunity for us. His hands open and close. He grabs at air. Dorotea wonders about "us."

Shipbuilding, he says. A man only gets so many chances, he says. We're moving. To the sea. To Maine. Place called Harpswell. Soon as school's out.

Shipbuilding? Dorotea asks.

Mama's all for it, he says. Least I think she is. Who wouldn't be all for it?

Dorotea watches the door shut behind him and thinks that her mother's never been all for anything. That her father has never once owned, rented or mentioned any kind of boat.

She snatches up her world atlas. Studies the markless blue that means Atlantic Ocean. Her eye traces ragged coastlines. Harpswell: a tiny green finger pointing at blue. She tries to imagine ocean and conjures petal-blue water packed with fish gill-to-gill. Imagines herself transformed into Maine Dorotea, barefoot girl with a coconut necklace. New house, new town, new life. Nueva Dorotea. New Dorothy. She holds her breath, counts to twenty.

◡

Dorotea tells nobody and nobody asks. They leave on the last day of school. That afternoon. Like sneaking out of town. The wood-paneled Wagoneer splashes across wet asphalt: Ohio, Pennsylvania, New York, Massachusetts, into New Hampshire. Her father drives empty-eyed, knuckles white on the wheel. Her mother sits stern and sleepless behind tracking wipers, lips curled above her chin like two rain-drowned earthworms, her small frame tensed as if bound in a hundred iron bands. As if crushing rocks in her bony fists. Slicing a pepper on her lap. Passing back dry tortillas painfully bound in plastic.

They see Portland at sunrise, after miles of pine bending over blacktop. The sun leers up behind slabs of cloud the color of salmon filets.

Dorotea trembles at the idea of ocean nearing. Fidgets in her seat. The energy of a caged fourteen-year-old piling up like marbles on a dinner plate. Finally the highway bends and Casco Bay shines before them. From across the bay the sun flings a trail of spangles to her. She lowers her nose to the window frame, feels certain there will be porpoises. Watches the glitter carefully for fins, flukes.

She glances at the back of her mother's neck to see if she

notices, if she feels it too, to see if her mother can be touched by a shimmering expanse of sea. Her mother who hid under onions for four days in a train car to Ohio. Who met her husband in a city built over a swamp, cracked sidewalks, train whistles, slushy winter. Her mother who made a home, who never left it. Who must be boiling at the sight of unbounded water. Dorotea sees no sign that it is so.

⌒

Harpswell. Dorotea stands in the doorway of the rented house. This threshold of paradise. The sea a misty backdrop behind soft-rustling pines and coils of blackberry bush.

Her father stands in the tiny kitchen among shell ornaments hanging by strings from cabinet knobs, faded bottles on the windowsill, pushes up his glasses, opens and closes his fists. As if he expected to find shipbuilding manuals, polished brass, portholes. As if he hadn't figured on this part of it: this kitchen with clamshells on the cabinets. Her mother stands in the living room like a bolt balanced on end. Stares down at boxes, bags and suitcases unloaded from the truck. Hair yarded into a big knot.

Dorotea stretches her arms, stands on her toes. She takes off her brown cardigan. Gulls screech in a wheel just past the pines, an osprey-shadow glides.

Her mother says, Ponte el sueter, Dorotea. No estás en puesta al sol.

As if the sun here was a different sun altogether. Dorotea walks a sandy path through brown grass to the sea. The path ends at rock, rust-colored, crenellated, heaved up from the earth long ago. The rock stretches into a haze at both ends. Nothing else but ocean and wind-bent pines and morning fog. At the sea's lip she watches tiny green waves flop onto a slick slope of rock, nudge forward a receding ribbon of foam. Come, retreat. Come, retreat.

She turns and glimpses the small white house through the

pine trunks. Heavy-headed dandelions, sandy yard, paint flaking. The house slumped and wet on its foundation. Her father talking in the doorway, pointing at her mother, at the truck, at the rented house. Arguing. Sees her father's hands open, close. Sees her mother climb into the truck, slam the door, sit in the passenger's seat and stare straight ahead. Her father retreats into the house.

Dorotea turns back, shades her eyes, sees the mist breaking. To her left, a gliding green current, a river mouth. To the right, trees lining the sea edge. Five hundred yards or so down the coast she sees a rocky point.

She walks to it; her sneakers bend to steep rock. Occasionally she has to step into the sea, water eddying around her knees, cold salt stinging thighs. Sea mud sliding underfoot. A rag of mist descends and she loses sight of the point. In a place the rock is steep and she wades to get around it. The water rises above her waist, shocks her belly. Finally the rock climbs back on an upslope, her feet dig in, and she climbs up, mud in her fingers and salt drying already on her skin, legs lifting her dripping out onto the shelf of rock. The point still half-obscured in mist.

She shades her eyes, again takes in the ocean. Are there dolphins out there? Sharks? Sailboats? She sees no sign of them. Of anything. Is ocean merely rock and weed and water? Mud? She had not expected emptiness, flittery light, a blotted horizon. Waves march in from some obscure haze. For a terrifying moment she can imagine herself the only organism on the planet. And she is about to go back.

Then she sees the fisherman. Just to her left. Wading. As if he came from nowhere. From nothing. From the sea itself.

She watches him. Feels lucky to watch. The world peeled back and left with only this vision. This silent flying wizardry. The rod seems an extension of his arm, an extra and perfect appendage, his shoulder pivoting, his bare brown chest, his legs tapering to calves buried in the sea. So this is Maine, this is how it can be, she thinks. This fisherman. This grace.

He rears back with his fishing rod and swings his line in great unrolling loops, far behind, then far in front. When the line unfurls so it is horizontal with the sea, he brings his rod tip back, and the line shoots in the opposite direction, over the rocks, almost to the trees, as if it surely must wrap around some low branch, but before it can the fisherman flings it forward again, out over the sea. Then slings it back. Each subsequent cast longer, more desperately close to the trees. Finally, when it seems his back cast is yards into the scrub, he shoots the line straight out, over the wave tops, into the sea. Then he wedges the butt end of his pole in his armpit and strips in the line with both hands. Then casts again, those hypnotic loops of line swinging back and forth like the wave-break itself and finally shooting out over the sea where it settles across the tiny swell. And strips it in again.

She stands on the rock, feels the packed rows of fossil beneath her feet. Holds her breath. Counts to twenty. And then splashes from her shelf of rock into the sea, her sneakers again on barnacle and slippery weed. She walks a hundred yards, head up. Toward the fisherman.

☾

Turns out he's a boy, sixteen maybe. Skin like calf leather. A string of small white shells on his throat. Looks at her through brick-colored hair. Eyes like green medicine.

He says, Funny to be wearing a sweater on a morning like this.

What?

Warm for a sweater.

He casts again. She watches the line, watches him feed it into the cast from the neat coils floating around his ankles. Watches the line swing back and forth and back and forth and finally shoot into the sea. He strips it in, says, Tide's turned. Be coming in soon.

Dorotea nods, not sure what this information means.

She asks, What kind of fishing pole is that? I've never seen a pole like that.

Pole? Poles are for bait fishermen. This is a rod. A fly rod.

You don't fish with bait?

Bait, he says. No . . . Never bait. Bait makes it easy.

Makes what easy?

The fisherboy hauls in his line, casts again. This. Casting to fish. A'course a striper or a blue will bite on a hunk of squid. A'course a mackerel will take a bloodworm. What's that? It's a game with the rules removed. No elegance.

Elegance. Dorotea considers this. Had no idea that elegance had something to do with fishing. But watch him cast! See the mist tear away from the pines.

The boy continues, Bait fishermen toss a herring out there, move it around a bit. Drag in a striper. That's not fishing. That's criminal.

Oh. Dorotea struggles to understand the coarseness of bait-fishing.

He hauls in his line, pinches the leader. Holds the fly in front of Dorotea. White hair tied with neat wraps of thread to a steel hook. A tiny painted wooden head. Two round eyes.

Is that a lure?

A streamer. Bucktail streamer. That white hair there's dyed buck's tail.

Dorotea holds the fly gently in her palm. The neck wrapped with perfect tiny wraps. Did you paint this? The eyes?

Sure. Tied the whole thing. He reaches in his pocket, removes a paper bag. Pours its contents onto her palm. Dorotea sees three more flies, yellow, blue, brown. Imagines how they must look in the water, to a fish. Long and thin. Like little fish. Like a snack. Perfect. Marvelous. Soft beauty lashed to sharp steel.

He is casting again, splashing down the coast.

Dorotea follows. The water higher on her shins than before.

Wait, she says. Your hooks. Your streamers.

You keep them, he says. I'll tie more.

She refuses. But does not take her eyes from them.

He casts. Sure, he says. A gift.

She shakes her head but puts them in her pocket. The wave-break laps her knees. She studies the sea, looks for signs of sealife. Fins bending? Sea creatures leaping? She sees only the sun laying gold coins across the waves, the ever-retreating fog. When she looks up the fisherboy has nearly rounded the point. She splashes after. Watches him cast. The waves sough as they collapse.

Hey, she says, there's fish out there, right? Or you wouldn't be fishing.

The boy smiles. Sure. It's the ocean.

Somehow, I thought there would be more. More stuff in the ocean. More fish. Where I'm from there's nothing and I hoped that maybe here there would be and I thought there was but now it just seems huge and empty.

The boy turns to look at her. Laughs. Lets his line drop, bends and reaches into the water at his feet. Digs into the mud, brings up a fistful.

Look here, he says.

In the dark clump Dorotea sees nothing at first. Mud clots dripping. Shell fragments. Water droplets. Then she notices microscopic movement, translucent flecks squirming. Hopping like fleas. The boy shakes his hand. A tiny clam appears on his palm, its foot half-clamped in the shell like a bitten tongue. Also a snail clinging upside-down, its minute unicorn horn shell pointing at the earth. And a tiny translucent crab. Some kind of eel squirming.

Dorotea pokes the mud with her finger. The boy laughs again, washes his hand in the sea.

He casts. Says, You haven't been here before.

No. She looks out at the sea. Thinks of all the creatures that must be under her feet. Thinks how much she has to learn. Looks at the boy. Asks his name.

After dark Dorotea stands in her tiny new room and looks around. She tacks a map to the wall. Sits on her sleeping bag and traces the state of Maine with her eye. The land with its borders and capitals and names. Her eye is drawn continually back to the blue that stretches into the fringes.

A moth hurls itself at her window. In the trees outside insects rasp and scream. Dorotea thinks she can hear the sea. She pulls the bucktail streamers from her pocket to admire them.

Her father stands in the doorway, knocks softly on the door frame, says hey, sits on the floor beside her. He looks caved in by sleeplessness. His back and shoulders are round.

Hi, Daddy.

What do you think?

It's so new, Daddy. It'll take some time. To get used to it.

She doesn't talk to me.

She hardly ever talks to anybody. That's her way.

Her father slumps. Gestures with his chin towards the streamers in Dorotea's hand. What are those?

Flies. For fishing. Streamers.

Oh. He does not bother to conceal that he is elsewhere.

I want to fly-fish, Daddy. Can I tomorrow?

Her father's hands open and close. His eyes are open but not seeing. Sure, Dorotea. You can go fishing. Fishing. Claro que sí.

The door closes behind him. Dorotea holds her breath. Counts to twenty. Hears her dad inhaling slowly in the other room. As if each breath taken summons barely enough courage to take the next.

She pulls on her brown cardigan, slides open her window and climbs out. She stands in the wet yard. Exhales. The galaxy wheels above the pines.

The bonfire is in a grove near the point. The wind is clean, the grass drowned with dew. Clouds slide in ranks below the stars. Her sneakers are soaked. Forest mulch clings to her cardigan. She crouches in pine needles outside the circle of firelight, sees dark figures shifting, their warped shadows thrown up into the pines. They sit on logs, stumps. They laugh. She hears the clink of bottles.

She sees the boy among them, sitting on a log. His smile orange in the firelight. His necklace white. He laughs, tips back a bottle. She holds her breath a long time, almost a minute. She stands, turns to go, steps on a stick and it snaps.

The laughter fades. She does not move.

Hey, the boy says. Dorothy?

Dorotea turns from the shadows, steps out into the firelight, walks with her head down, sits next to the boy.

Dorothy. Everybody, this is Dorothy.

The firelit faces look at her, look away. Conversation starts up again.

Knew you'd come, the boy says.

Did you.

Sure I did.

How did you know?

Just knew. Felt it. Like I told you, we have these fires every night, just about. I said to myself, you just wait. The girl will come. Dorothy will come. And here you are.

Did you catch anything today? After I saw you?

Got a few. I let them go.

My dad got hired at the ironworks. He designs the hulls of ships.

Is that right?

Well, he will. He will do that.

He holds her hand and her palm is damp with sweat but she holds on and they lock fingers and she can feel his strong hand, rough fingertips. They sit like that a bit and she sits as still as she can. They do not talk. The fire sends smoke high into the trees. The stars wink and gutter. It feels nice being the daughter of a shipbuilder.

Later he tries to kiss her. Leans across clumsily and his breath is hot on her chin and she clamps her eyes shut. She thinks of her mother, her tiny mother under onions in a train car. She pulls away from the boy, stands and hurries home, head down, through the low-bending pines. She climbs through her bedroom window. Takes off her wet sneakers, hangs her brown cardigan. Listens for the ocean. Thinks of eyes like green medicine. She boils inside.

☽

In the morning she drags her mother to the sea by the wrist. To confront her with the sea dressed in fog. To show her that this place is not empty. Wings of mist drag through the treetops. The fog shreds everywhere; flashes of pure blue wink above. The sea undressing. A wide-brimmed hat crammed over her mother's hair. Gulls turn in a high noisy wheel above the gliding tide. Cormorants dive for breakfast.

They stand on the rocks. Dorotea studies her mother, searches her face for signs of change. Of awakening. Dorotea holds her breath. Counts to twenty. Her mother stands closed and rigid.

Mentiras, her mother says. Your father doesn't know a thing about ships. He worked as a janitor all his life. He lied to everybody. Even himself. He'll be fired today, or tomorrow.

No, Mama. Daddy's smart. He'll find a way. He'll learn as he goes. He has to. He saw a chance and took it. We'll make it. Lookit how nice it is. Lookit this place.

Life can turn out a million ways, Dorotea. Her mother speaks English like she is spitting rocks. But the one way life will not turn out is the way you dream it. You can dream anything, but it's never what will be. It's never the way it is. The only thing that can't come true is your dream. Everything else . . .

She shuts her mouth, shrugs.

Dorotea looks at her wet sneakers. The leather is coming apart. She clambers down the steep rocks, grabs hold of weed for balance. Plunges her hand into the mud beneath the water. Holds it up.

Lookit, Mama. Lookit all the things that live here. In just one handful.

Mother squints at her daughter. Her daughter holding ocean mud to the sky like some offering.

And then through the mist a green canoe glides. A lone fisherman, paddling, his rod across the stern. A fisherman with a white necklace on his throat.

The boy stops in mid-paddle. His oar drips. He studies the two figures on the rocks, the thin and brittle mother with a hand on her hat like she is holding herself to the rock. And the girl, wet to her waist, holding up part of the sea.

He raises his hand. Smiles. Shouts Dorotea's name.

☽

They sell fishing gear in the back of the hardware store in Bath. A giant with a beard and huge round knees sits on a stool tying leaders. Her father looks up at the rack of fishing rods, thumbs up his glasses.

The giant says, I help you folks?

My daughter here would like a fishing pole.

The giant reaches into a cupboard, pulls out a Zebco all-in-one spinning kit. Hands it to Dorotea, says, This'll be perfect for just about anything you'd ever need. Comes with spinners and everything.

Dorotea holds the package at arm's length, studies the reel, the blunt two-piece rod. Chrome-plated guides. The plastic wrap. On the tag a cartoon bass curls out of a cartoon pond to devour a treble-hooked lure. Her dad puts his hand on her head, asks Dorotea how she likes the looks of it.

She doesn't like the looks of it at all: it's blunt, clumsy-looking. No coils of fly line. No elegance. She imagines chunks of flesh glommed on her hook, her reel rusting, the boy laughing at her.

Daddy, she says. I want a fly rod. This is for bait-fishermen.

The giant roars. Her father rubs his jaw.

‿

The giant rings up Dorotea's fly rod on a black cash register. His huge fingers count change.

Don't know a single girl that fly-fishes, the giant says. Never heard of girls fly-fishing, really. He says it kindly. Eyes on Dorotea. Fingers like fat pink cigars.

I've flung a fly myself, he continues. I'm still learning it. I suppose we're all still learning. You learn and learn and then you die and you haven't learned half of it.

He shrugs his hilly shoulders, hands her father change.

You're new here. He talks only to Dorotea.

We just moved to Harpswell, she says. Daddy's working at Bath Iron Works. He designs ships. It was his first day today.

The giant nods, glances down at her father. Her father's hands open, close.

We lived in Ohio, he mutters. I did hullwork on lake freighters. Thought we'd come up here, give it a shot. A man only gets so many chances is what I figure.

The giant offers another shrug. Smiles. Says to Dorotea, Maybe we could fish together sometime. We could try down by Popham Beach. They been getting into some nice cows down there. Schoolies race the shallows at slack tide. Get one of those on your little rod there and look out.

The giant smiles, sits back on his stool. Dorotea and her father leave the store, drive past the ironworks, the shipyard and the vast iron warehouses, a high chain-link fence, cranes swinging, a green-hulled tug at dry dock dripping rust. From the top of Mill

Street Dorotea can see the Kennebec River rolling heavily into the Atlantic.

꙳

In the evening Dorotea sits on her sleeping bag and fits her rod together. Two pieces join together, screw on the plastic reel, feed fly line through the guides. Tie on a leader.

Her dad in the door frame.

You like the rod, Dorotea?

It's beautiful, Daddy. Thank you.

You going to fish in the morning?

In the morning.

Your mother say anything?

Dorotea shakes her head. She thinks he will say more but he doesn't.

After he leaves she holds her breath, takes her new fly rod, and climbs out her window. She walks beneath the dark pines, feels her way in the moonless night. She reaches the firelight, hears a guitar and singing, sees the boy on his log. She crouches under the pines and watches. Thinks of her father saying a man only gets so many chances. Puts her hand in her pocket. Feels the three streamers there, their hook points, their feathers. She shuts her eyes. Her hands shake. A hook pricks her finger.

She stands, balks, turns around, walks to her left, to the ocean. She clambers over rocks, shadows among shadows. Stands at the sea's fringe, sucks a drop of blood from her fingertip. She has the shakes. Holds her breath to fight them.

She holds the air in her lungs and stands very still and listens. The silence of Harpswell rises up in her ear like a wave and breaks into a rainbow of tiny sounds: an owl calling, the faint sound of laughter at the bonfire, the pines creaking, cicadas screeching, resting, screeching. Rodents rustling in blackberry brambles. Pebbles clinking. Leaves shifting. Even clouds marching. And beneath, the murmuring sea benched in fog. This is indeed a full world, Dorotea. It overspills. She breathes, tastes the salty ocean cycle of rot and birth. Takes up her rod and feeds the line clumsily through the guides. Whips it behind her. It snags on something. She turns.

The boy is there. His fingertips on her shoulders, the sleeves of her cardigan. His eyes on hers.

◡

Her mother stands in Dorotea's room in the dark. Her hands on her hips like she is trying to crush her own pelvis. Her black shoes planted firmly. Dorotea straddles the window frame, one leg in, one out. Her fly rod half into her room. Her dew-soaked sneaker stuck all over with pine needles.

I thought I told you not to see that boy.

What boy?

Who called you Dorothy.

The boy in the canoe?

You know what boy.

You don't. You don't know him. I don't either.

Her mother stares. Her body quakes, tendons in her throat stand out. Dorotea holds her breath. Holds it so long she feels sick.

I wasn't with him, Mama. I was fishing. Or trying to. I got a terrible tangle in my line. I wasn't with him.

Pescador. Pescadora.

I went out fishing.

◡

From then on Dorotea is imprisoned after dark. Her mother does it herself: she screws long bolts into Dorotea's window, hammers it shut. Dorotea's door locked at night. She stares at her maps.

The summer rolls forward in silence. The rented house

cramped and creaky. Every day her father leaves at dawn, comes home late. Dinners are eaten silently. Her mother's face retreats inside itself like a poked sea anemone. Silverware clinking, a platter on the table. Beans with the life boiled out of them. Tortillas wrung dry. Please pass the peppers, Mama. The house creaks. The pines whisper. I went fishing today, Daddy. Found a lobster claw long as my foot. Really.

Dorotea leaves the house just after her father does and she stays out all day. Fishing. Telling herself she is fishing and not looking for the boy. She tramps all the way to South Harpswell, muddy-ankled, walking the sea edge, turning over shells, jabbing anemones with sticks, learning the tiny tricks of shore life. Don't squeeze a sea cucumber. Scallop shells break easily. Stone crabs hide under driftwood. Check periwinkles for hermit crabs. Snails stay tucked inside murex shells. Stepping on horseshoe crabs doesn't do anybody any good. Barnacles are good traction. From a hundred feet up a cormorant can hear you split open a sea clam and will turn and dive and land and beg for it. The sea, Dorotea learns, blooms. She learns and relearns it.

But mostly she fishes. Learning the knots, catching a barbed streamer in her hair, crouching on driftwood to pull out wind-knots or undo massive tangles of leader. Gets her line caught on brambles, on branches, one time on a floating detergent bottle. Learns to walk with her rod, guide it through brush, over rocks. Didn't even know she needed a tippet. The cork handle on her rod goes dark with salt and sweat. Her brown shoulders go the color of old pennies. Her sneakers rot off her feet. She walks the sea's edge barefoot, head up. This new Dorotea. This seaside Dorothy.

She catches nothing. She tries Popham Beach, the long faded spit of sand there, the estuary at ebb tide, at slack tide. She casts from rocky points, from a wooden dock; she wades to her neck and casts. And nothing. Sees men in boats haul in twenty, thirty stripers. Beautiful striped bass with charcoal stripes and translucent mouths gasping. And nothing for her own streamer hooks but greenweed or flotsam. And those awful tangles of leader; line wraps itself around her ankles; knots from nowhere spoil her tippets.

Never a sign of the boy.

She sees fish out of the water, sturgeon leaping. Sees the ocean violence. Sees a pack of bluefish snarl out of a wave, curl through a panicked cloud of herring, drive half-bitten, quivering smelt onto the sand. Sees a dead cod turn over white and fat in the swash. Sees a tide-beached skate picked apart by gannets, an osprey pluck a whiting from a wavetop.

One noon she hikes to where they light the bonfires. The sky is gray and low, skimming the treetops. Rain plunks slow and warm. The fire pit black and wet and flat. Beer bottles rolled up against logs, standing on stumps. She walks out to the point, takes off her sweater, wades into the sea. Waves lap at her neck. Her hair floats beside her. She thinks of the boy, his hot breath. His rough fingertips. Those green eyes gone black in the dark.

Daylong she talks to no one. Each time she rounds a bend, she prays the boy will be there, enwombed in fog, casting, casting for fish, casting for her. But there is only rock and weed and sometimes boats trolling downriver.

⊃

A July night arrives, hangs heavier and wetter than any night Dorotea can remember. The air heavy all day, waiting for a storm that won't begin. The ocean pewter and flat. The horizon erased in a smear of gray and the sky hung so low it seems to rest on top of the rented house; any moment it might collapse the roof. Night comes but does not break the heat.

Dorotea sits in her bedroom and sweats. She feels the sky threatening to bury her.

Her father stands in the door frame. Sweat circles under his arms. He used to get those when he mopped floors. Her dad the shipbuilder.

Hiya Dorotea.

Daddy it's hot.

Only thing for it is to wait.

Can't we get her to open the window? Just for tonight. I'll never sleep. I'm sweating through my sleeping bag.

I don't know, Dorotea.

Please, Daddy. It's so hot.

Maybe we could leave the door open.

The window, Daddy. Mama's asleep. She'll never know. Just for tonight.

Her father breathes. His shoulders slumped, rounded. Comes back with a screwdriver. Quietly unbolts the window, pries the nails loose.

The boy is not there.

Dorotea sweats outside the firelight. Pine needles stick to her knees. Mosquitoes loop, alight, bite. She smears them on her skin. The smoke from the bonfire rises into a windless sky. She holds her breath so long that her eyes lose focus and her chest stings. She goes over the soft smeary faces once more, orange firelit kids around a bonfire on Harpswell Point. His face is not among them. He is nowhere.

She walks around to the point, a place she has learned so well, the small and secret coves, a deep pool where she saw a white lobster one morning. All the secrets she feels she owes to him. She knows she will see him there, fishing and laughing that she wore her sweater on the hottest night ever. He will be there and he will show her things about the sea. He will lift this cargo that has settled on her.

He is not on the point either.

She goes back to the bonfire, walks right to it, this fourteen-year-old girl wound up and strong. The Harpswell kids stare at her. She feels the heat of it. Smoke rolls into her eyes. She says the boy's name.

He's gone, someone says. They look at her, then look away. They stare at the fire.

Back to Boston. A week ago. His whole family went back.

He's summer people.

◡

Dorotea walks away. She walks blind; pine boughs scrape her face. She trips, falls into wet grass. Her knees grass-stained, muddy, scratched. She comes to a gravel road. Her head is down. Her insides churn. She passes driveways, a house with windows lit television blue. A dog barks. She hears an owl. Turns down a paved road. Passes a lumberyard. A part of her realizes she is lost. She feels cold very far inside and the sky could not hang lower.

She walks and runs and she is barefoot and cannot shake the cold inside and could not say which direction the ocean is. She walks a mile, more maybe. The road turns from gravel to pavement. She sits a while and shivers. An hour goes by, then another. The sky turns pink. A truck rattles along the road, fenders sagging, one headlight burned out. It slows beside her. A man in glasses leans across, pushes open the door. She gets in, asks him to the ironworks.

He lets her off at the high chain-link gate. Her legs are scratched red and muddy, her hair hangs in clumps. Men in caps carry lunchboxes, hurry past her; a Mercedes rolls by, tinted windows and tires crunching gravel. She follows the men through the gate. There is a sign that reads OFFICE. A fat man with a badge in a booth. Beyond him a great corrugated warehouse, a crane swinging. Stacks of culvert pipes on a barge.

She knocks on the man's window; he looks up from a clipboard.

My father, she says. Santiago San Juan. He forgot his lunch. I would like to bring it to him.

The fat man pushes up his glasses, studies her, her brown and scraped feet. Her shaking fingers. Looks down at the clipboard. Flips through sheets. Glances through time cards.

What did you say the name was?

San Juan.

The fat man studies her again. And finally looks back at the clipboard. San Juan, he says. Here he is. Dock C-Four. Around back.

She follows arrows to C-4, a concrete pier with a heavy crane hanging above and bordered by boxcars in high stacks. Men in suits and ties and hard hats walk past, rolled plans under their arms. A beeping forklift wheels; the driver gives her a hard look.

She finds her father at the pier's edge by a big blue Dumpster, where the river rolls past dirty. Stryofoam cups bob in the current. Gulls screech around the Dumpster, a flurry of white and gray feather. Her father wears tan and grimy coveralls. He holds a broom. Waves it weakly at the gulls. The gulls scream, dive-bomb his head.

He turns, sees her. Their eyes meet. He looks away.

Dorotea.

Daddy. All this time. All these months. You said you were building ships. She cannot say more. She shakes with cold. Stands beside him. He leans on his broom. They watch the river roil out to sea. They stand and Dorotea shivers and her father holds her and still she shivers.

A destroyer is towed in from the horizon. A throbbing of the tug's engines, behind it the quiet gray behemoth rolls a giant wake and Dorotea sees the numbers painted on the sides and ship-sinking cannons that look so calm and clean. Its hull is big as an apartment building; she wonders how she could ever believe her father could learn about something so big. How anyone could learn about something so big.

⌣

Dorotea stays cold. She can't shake it and she gets sick. She lies in her sleeping bag all day. Her fly rod leans against the wall of her room. She can't look at it. The ocean in her ears makes her sick. The whole world's turning makes her sick. She feels frost creep up from somewhere between her legs and it climbs all the way to her neck. She holds her breath as long as she can, and then longer, until her vision goes splotchy, until at last a switch inside she can't control throws itself and the air pours out and back in and her vision straightens a bit.

She curls in her sleeping bag and shivers and dreams of winter blowing in. The sea cement gray and the horizon burying the sun before it ever gets a chance to get going. Nights winterlong. Stars like the points of hooks. Snow creaking under her bare feet. In her dream she crouches on Harpswell Point and watches the wind blow down the wavetops. The boy is nowhere. There is nobody anywhere, no birds, no fish. The fish have fled, left the river, darted into the widening sea in schools. The ocean and river emptied. The rocks scoured of limpets, barnacles, weed. There are horrible tangles of lines around her ankles, thick ropes, coiled spider webs. She becomes a fish flailing in a net. She becomes her father. His whole world a nasty tangle.

Her mother is there when she wakes. She brings Dorotea hot water. Her mother now a fraction softer with this role to play. Her mother with Dorotea back, still half-believing her husband is somehow managing to design hulls of ships. Dorotea looks at her mother by her side, at the tight and narrow cords in her mother's neck. Dorotea has cords like that in her own neck. She lies half-asleep and listens to her mother move through the house, hears her wash pans in the sink.

○

Early August. A knock on the door at dawn. A rapping so loud and out of place that Dorotea jumps from her sleeping bag. She is at the door before her mother has left the kitchen. Heat crackling inside her. She squints into the morning. A massive figure in the door frame. The giant from the hardware store. In his giant hand a sleek fly rod.

His voice is so loud the tiny house can't hold it. Morning, morning, he booms. Thought you might like to do a bit of fishing this morning. If you have the time.

He looks only at Dorotea and Dorotea stands in her sleeping clothes and smells the giant who smells like sea and pine. Her mother peers out from the kitchen, wiping her hands on a towel.

☽

They walk along Popham Beach, the giant's huge strides eating up yards. She half-jogs to keep up. The day blue and true all the way to the horizon. They wade out to fish side by side. Dorotea feels the ocean tugging at her legs. The giant fishes with a cigarette bobbing from his lip. Occasionally watches her cast, smiles at her tangles, praises her when she lays it out nicely.

The giant fishes ugly. His line does not dance beautifully; he does not bother with the false casting the boy did. He just flings it back once, then sends it singing over the wavetops. Strips it in with one giant pink hand. Casts again.

Fishing is about time, he tells Dorotea. It's about how much time you can keep your line in the water. Can't catch fish if your line isn't in the water.

They fish until noon and catch nothing and they sit on a piece of driftwood. The giant has raisins in a plastic bag and they eat those. She asks him questions and he answers and she feels the sun straight overhead touch a spot inside her.

In the afternoon the giant begins to catch striped bass, one after another, his line shooting way out there, and each time his rod tip bends into a steep parabola and he fights the fish in and knocks one over the head with a rock and puts it in a plastic shopping bag and leaves it on the beach.

In the evening Dorotea stands beside him and watches the giant gut his striper, his quick belly cut, loops of viscera swinging into the surf. This is Maine, too, she thinks, this fisherman cleaning a fish on the sand and she realizes that new or old she is Dorotea, will always be Dorotea, that there are still plenty of chances left in this world.

⟝

When the giant leaves with his fish, he looks at Dorotea and smiles and tells her she is a fine fisherwoman and wishes her luck. Buena suerte, he says, which is funny because he sounds like a giant gringo from Maine when he says it, but it is nice all the same.

Dorotea casts still and the horizon slowly fixes itself down around the sun. Her arm burns from the effort, but she is making nice casts now, she is laying it out there, presenting her streamer like the giant showed her, and she is reading the water too, seeing how a fish might sit in a cove, hole up. She watches for passing bait fish or the birds that might be feeding on them. Her arm goes leaden. Her legs numb. Her legs feel more connected to the ocean than to her.

The sunset, a furnace of light, paints the clouds with color. And it sends, too, submerged wedges of light into the cove where Dorotea strips in her streamer and for a miraculous moment she sees her streamer flit through a haft of blue and that is when a striped bass takes it.

The fish is strong and she fights it and her rod bends more than she ever imagined it could and she swallows panic by slowly walking the fish backward to the beach. The fish thrashes, fights her treachery. Dorotea clings. Feels its strength come through the line. Such noble fight. Such fighting for its life. She fights too.

When finally she lands it, she drags it gasping and flopping onto the sand and stands over it and works the hook out of its mouth. This big striped translucent fish in the near-dark. She pinches it by the lower jaw, holds it up and stares into its big unintelligent eyes.

She cradles the fish in her arms and wades out into the sea. To her shoulders. Takes a deep breath, holds it in her lungs. She holds the fish beside her. Feels its muscles, its packed columns of flesh. Feels her own muscles, sore and ragged and strong. She lowers herself into the sea. Counts to twenty. Lets the fish swim.

For a Long Time This Was Griselda's Story

In 1979 Griselda Drown was a senior volleyballer at Boise High, a terrifically tall girl with trunky thighs, slender arms and a volleyball serve that won an Idaho State Championship despite T-shirts claiming it was a team effort. She was a gray-eyed growth spurt, orange-haired, an early bloomer, and there were rumors about how she took boys two at a time in the dusty band closet where the dented tubas and ruptured drums were kept, about how she straddled the physics teacher, about her escapades during study hall with ice cubes. They were rumors; whether they were true or not didn't matter. We all knew them. They might as well have been true.

Griselda's father was long gone; her mother worked two shifts at Boise Linen Supply. Her younger sister, Rosemary, too short and plump to play, was equipment manager for the team. She sat on a fold-up chair and flipped scoreboard switches, penciled statistics, occasionally pumped air into flat volleyballs while the coach made the team run windsprints.

It began on an August afternoon, after practice, with Griselda on the sidewalk, in the shadow of the bricked gymnasium, a social studies book slipped under one long arm, listening to the air-brakes of school buses and the wind rasping in a thin school-front stand of aspens. Her sister, curly-headed, eyes just clearing the dash, pulled up in the rust-pocked Toyota the girls shared with their mother. They headed for the Idaho Fairgrounds, the Great Western Fair, Griselda in the front seat with her big knees wedged against the glove box, leaning her long face out the window to catch the wind. Rosemary drove slowly, stopped completely at stop signs, was clumsy with the clutch. They didn't speak.

At the fairgrounds we saw them in the parking lot inhaling the effluvium of carnival, the smells of fried dough, caramel and cinnamon, the flap-flapping of tents, a carousel plinking out music-box songs, voluptuous sounds bouncing down tent ropes and along the trampled dust of the midway. Wind-curled handbills staple-gunned to telephone poles, the hum of gas-powered generators and the gyro truck, the lemonade truck, pretzels and popcorn, baked potatoes, the American flag, the rumblings of rides and the disconnected screams of riders—all of it shimmered before them like a mirage, something not quite real.

Griselda strode to the rope-gate entrance, the ticket seller's cage, where a dwarfish ticket taker stood on a stool, and Rosemary plodded behind, the foothills of Boise lifting beyond the tent peaks, brown and hazed, into a pale sky. Griselda dug a pair of wrinkled singles from her pocket and passed them through.

This is how we told Griselda's story, later, in check-out lanes or in the bleachers during volleyball games: two sisters strolling the midway, single file, Griselda in the lead and Rosemary behind. They bought cotton candy for a quarter, moved about with faces half-wrapped in a pink cumulus of sugar, plodding through the catcalls of game operators: Squirt the gun in the clown's mouth!

Break the balloon, now, girls! They paid quarters to sling rings over Coke bottlenecks. Rosemary pulled a rubber ducky from a water trough with a fishing pole and won a small and smudgy panda with plastic button eyes and a scowl made of thread.

The sunlight went long and orange. The sisters drifted among the booths and rides, feeling vaguely sick, cotton candy dissolving in their mouths. Finally, in the purpling dusk, they arrived at the metal eater's tent, at the far corner of the fairgrounds. A crowd had gathered, men mostly, in jeans and boots. Griselda stopped, hipped herself a place between them, easily saw over the capped and hatted heads. There was a card table at the back of the tent, set up from the ground on risers, spotlit yellow. She smelled the rubber tent-smell, saw the lazy lift of insects in the spotlight, heard the men around her discuss the impossibility and strangeness of metal eating.

Rosemary couldn't see. She shifted from foot to foot. She mentioned that they should go—it was getting late. The crowd filled in behind them. Griselda tore off a puff of cotton candy and pressed it into the roof of her mouth with her tongue. She studied her sister, the panda hanging from her fist. I could lift you, she offered. Rosemary blushed, shook her head. It's a metal eater, Griselda whispered. I've never seen one. I don't even know what one is. It'll be fake, Rosemary said. It won't be real. This kind of stuff is never real. Griselda shrugged.

The sisters looked at each other. I want to see it, Griselda insisted. I *can't* see it, Rosemary whined. Now it was Griselda's turn to shake her head. Then don't, she said. Rosemary's face went stern and hurt. She clumped off toward the car, the panda against her chest like a rueful child. Griselda watched the stage.

Soon the metal eater came out, and the men in the tent quieted, and there was only the whispering of the crowd and the slow looping of insects in the yellow spotlight and, far off, the plink-plinking of the carousel. The metal eater was a tidy-looking man in a business suit, trim and small and mannered. Griselda stood transfixed. What a man he was, what glinty spectacles, what shiny shoes, what a neatness to his construction, what pinstripes and cufflinks to wear to eat metal in Boise, Idaho. She had never seen a man like him.

He seated himself at the raised-up table, moving with a delicacy and tidiness that made Griselda want to charge the stage, throw herself upon him and smother him, consume him, flail her body against his. He was madly different, significant, endlessly captivating; she must have discerned something deep beneath his surface, something less acutely evident to the rest of us.

He produced a razor blade from a vest pocket and slit a sheet of paper lengthwise with it. Then he swallowed it. He kept his eyes on hers without blinking. His Adam's apple jerked furiously. He swallowed a half dozen razors, then bowed and disappeared behind the tent. The crowd clapped politely, almost confusedly. Griselda's blood boiled over.

When Rosemary returned to that place after dusk, indignant and frizz-haired, the metal-eating show was long done and Griselda was long gone, leaning over a plate of sausage patties in the Galaxy Diner on Capitol. Her eyes were still on the gray eyes of the metal eater and his were still on hers. By midnight she was gone from Boise altogether, lying across the bench seat of a Ryder truck, the metal eater crossing into Oregon and Griselda's head in his lap, his thin fingers in her hair, his little feet stretching for the pedals.

꙳

In the morning Mrs. Drown made Rosemary tell her story to a traffic cop who yawned, thumbs through his belt loops. But you aren't even writing it down, Mrs. Drown stammered. Griselda was eighteen, he told her, what should he be writing down. By law she was a woman. He pronounced woman loudly and carefully. Woman. He said to have hope. He'd heard the same story a thousand times. She'd come home eventually. They always did.

Around school the stories about Griselda took on teeth and venom, even left the school and lived for a while in produce sections and movie queues. She'll be back soon, we told each other, and boy will she be sorry, dashing off with a carnival freak twice her age, a bad seed anyway, you wouldn't believe the things she'd do. Probably knocked up by now. Or worse.

Mrs. Drown went sour immediately. We'd see her in Shaver's Supermarket after work, shrunken, embittered, a basket of celery hung on an arthritic forearm, a handkerchief knotted around her neck. She imagined herself moving at the center of a pocket of formalities—Why, Mrs. Drown, this rain is something, isn't it?—while her daughter's story spun all around her, circulating in the town's whispers, just outside her hearing.

Within a month she refused to leave home. She got fired. Her friends stopped coming by. They talk too much anyhow, is what she told Rosemary, who had dropped out of school to take her job at Boise Linen. Who talks too much, Mom? Everybody. Everybody talks behind your back. You turn your back and off they go, talking at you, telling each other stories they don't know the first thing about.

Of course, it wasn't long before we stopped talking about Griselda. She didn't come back. There was nothing new or interesting about a portly sister who worked fourteen hours a day or a mother made bitter by a lost daughter. There were new bodies in the high school, new fodder for rumors. Griselda's story was scrapped for lack of new material.

Unfortunately for her, Mrs. Drown never stopped believing that the gossip lived just one breath beyond earshot. She shouted at us when we strolled past the bungalow on our way into the hills. Stop blabbing, she'd yell from a window. Rumormongers! She moved into Griselda's room, slept in Griselda's bed. Her skin went sallow, yellow. She didn't go out, even for the mail. Dust mounded up. The yard went brown. The gutters clogged with mulch. The house looked as if it were about to sink into the earth.

All this time Griselda sent letters home. Rosemary found them in the mail, one every month, lying between bills, envelopes addressed with tiny printing beneath a wild series of stamps and postmarks. The letters were short, misspelled things:

Dear Mom and Sis—this city we're in has an acre reserved for dead people. They are kept in tall stacks of things like white cupboards with drawers inside. There are grass aisles to walk between. It is lovely. Our show is going well. The riots are on the other side of the island. Like you, we hardly know they are there.

They never explained, never betrayed a guilty twitch or regretful pause. Rosemary sat on her bed mouthing the names on the stamps and postmarks: Molokai, Belo Horizonte, Kinabalu, Damascus, Samara, Florence. They were names from anywhere and everywhere, each envelope stamped with some euphony like Sicilia, Mazatlán, Nairobi, Fiji or Malta, names that invoked for her imagination the great unknown tracts of land and ocean that lay beyond Boise. She would sit on her bed, holding a letter for hours, imagining the hands that had moved it along its path, all the hands between her sister and Boise, between herself and the cloud-pink alpen-glow of Nepal, the millennial gardens of Kyoto, the black tide of the Caspian Sea. There was a world glimmering beyond Boise Linen, Shaver's Supermarket, outside the cracked and sinking bungalow in the North End. It was another world altogether. Here was the proof. Her sister was out in it.

Rosemary never showed the letters to her mother. She decided it was best for her mother if Griselda was gone permanently, gone for good.

☽

Life for Rosemary yawned around the letters, her mother and work: dull, heavy-footed, tasteless. At Boise Linen she supervised dyed cloth as it rolled onto bobbins, back stinging daylong, sitting behind safety goggles and listening to the grind and groan of spooling machines. She gained weight; her feet wore down the soles of shoes. She took meticulous grocery lists to Shaver's, balanced her checkbook with a nubbed pencil, fed soup to her crumbling mother. She did not bother to clean the house or buy makeup. The curtains went gray; Twinkie wrappers sprouted from couch cushions; ants roved in the metal mouths of soda cans stuck to windowsills.

Eventually she gave her virginity and ring finger to Duck Winters, the timid and overweight butcher at Shaver's who smelled permanently of ground beef. He moved into the sinking bungalow. He helped in a sheepish kind of way, tinkering around the yard, beer can in one hand, flushing out the lopsided gutters, replacing the screen door and the cracked sections of the front walk. He tolerated Mrs. Drown—her inane mutterings about gossipmongers, her insistence on sleeping in Griselda's room and forgetting to flush the toilet—by keeping himself half-drunk on watery beer. He was sincere and big and fell asleep while Rosemary did the Find-A-Word beside him. Occasionally they grappled together at awkward sex. It never took.

And still the letters from Griselda came, each month, missives from all over the world, mishandled prose tucked inside envelopes stamped with heart-pulling names, Katmandu, Auckland, Reykjavík.

◡

Ten years after Griselda ran off with the metal eater, Duck Winters found his mother-in-law dead in the bathroom. Natural causes. Rosemary sprinkled her mother's ashes in the backyard. It was raining and the ashes clumped together undramatically; what was left of Mrs. Drown pooled on the leaves of the pachysandra or ran in mucky trickles under the fence into the neighbor's yard.

When he came home from Shaver's that evening, Duck drudged into the bedroom and found Rosemary splayed on the bed, her thick legs stuck out straight, tears shining on her cheeks, a tidily tied bundle of envelopes on her knee, a ragged stuffed panda in her lap. Duck lay down beside her and put a hand on her neck. Rosemary looked at him from tear-rimmed eyes. You should know, she blubbered, my sister has been sending letters all this time. I didn't want Mom to find out. I know, whispered Duck. She's been everywhere, all over the world. All these places with the same man. Duck pulled her to him, held her head against his belly and rocked her. She told Duck the story—Griselda's story— while he shushed her and kissed the teardrops sliding over her cheeks. I know, he whispered. Everyone knows.

Rosemary sobbed, buried herself into him. They held on, Duck kissing the top of her head, the smell of her hair in his nose. They began to move together in a salty, careful sweetness, moving patiently and tenderly. He kissed her all over. After, Rosemary lay in Duck's big arms and whispered, Those are my sister's stories. Those are for her. We have our own stories now. Right, Duck? He said nothing. He might have been asleep.

In the morning Duck woke late and when he came into the kitchen Rosemary was burning the last envelope from her carefully preserved bundle. Together they watched it burn black and then flake apart in the sink. Duck took her by the wrist and walked her out under a gleaming sky, the trees and grass greened from rain the day before. They climbed past the neighborhood into a nameless gulch, huffing and wheezing through the sagebrush in their weight-tortured Reeboks, wading through prairie star, peppergrass, sunflower, the gossamery spores of plants kicked free and floating. They stopped on a high ridge, panting, the town stretched out below them, the capitol dome, the arbor-lined streets, the slim neighborhoods of the North End in rows and, far off, the glittering Owyhee Mountains. Duck took off his flannel shirt, laid it down over the wildflowers, and they made love, among the moaning crickets, the drifting schools of spores, under the sky, in the foothills above the town of Boise.

○

From then on they lived with a measure of contentment, learning each other finally, imperceptibly. Duck whitewashed the bungalow; Rosemary planted a backyard stone for her mother. They shined up the doors and windows, carted out boxes and bags of old clothes, volleyball trophies, high school notebooks. They tried diets; we'd even see them out walking, hand-holding in a lazy lap around Camel's Back Park. Griselda's monthly letters went into the kitchen trash without so much as a glance at the postmark.

Then, one day, years later, the ad appeared. It was in the funnies section of the Sunday *Idaho Statesman,* an ad for the Metal Eater's World Tour, a kind of cultish extravaganza, selling out all over the globe, coming to the gym at Boise High in January. It was extravagant, a full newspaper page, featuring ludicrous fonts dripping into one another, a barely dressed cartoon girl proclaiming outrageous things, that the metal eater never consumed the same thing twice, that he had eaten a Ford Ranger just two weeks before at his tour stop in Philadelphia.

Rosemary, Duck said over bran cereal and doughnuts, you're not going to believe this.

○

Everybody wanted tickets. We wouldn't miss it. It sold out in four hours, the telephones blitzed over at the high school, people clamoring for a bigger venue. But Rosemary wouldn't go. She wouldn't hear of it, wouldn't dream of it. Twenty-five dollars a person, she moaned. You've got to be kidding me. Can't we move on, Duck? Can't we forget? A letter from Griselda arrived a week later, a Tampa postmark. Rosemary shredded it and dropped the pieces into the trash.

On the afternoon before the metal eater was to appear in the gym, the management at Shaver's declared that the supermarket would close its doors on the last of the month. It had been losing money for years, they said. Everyone shopped at the Albertson's on State. They would be letting people go immediately.

Duck slogged out to the loading dock in his bloodied apron and sat on a milk crate. It was snowing. Clumps of flakes were melting in the alley. The produce manager tapped Duck on the back and held up a case of beer. They drank and talked a little about where they could find work. They peed in the snow. The produce manager got a call from his wife. She couldn't go to the metal-eating show with him tonight. He offered the ticket to Duck.

My wife, mumbled Duck. She wouldn't let me go. She says it's a waste of money. Duck, groaned the produce manager, we just lost our jobs! You think we don't deserve a night to ourselves? Duck shrugged. Look, the produce manager said, tonight this guy is going to eat *metal*. I heard he might eat a snowmobile.

Besides, he went on, Griselda Drown might be there.

☽

Someone had built a stage in the high school gym, blocked it off with a maroon curtain and surrounded it with fold-up chairs. Twenty-five dollars a head and the place was packed. A half hour late, the curtain groaned upwards and there was the metal eater, seated behind a table. He was little, a well-kept fifty-something in a black suit, white shirt, black necktie. He sat at the table, prim, a halo of gray hair beneath a pink shiny head like a half egg. His eyes were gray, drawn back and too big. He sat complacently, wrists crossed in his lap. Behind him, a sequined blue curtain shifted briefly, then hung still.

We waited, shuffled our snow boots at this plain spectacle, this unimpressive man seated before a bare table in the plain glow of gymnasium lights. We whispered, shifted, sweated. Upon us sat the great steam of a congregated people in parkas.

The snow fell outside, onto minivans and wagons in the school lot, and the air had taken on the smell of slush and impatience. A baby began to howl. The rubber-capped legs of the fold-up chairs creaked on the hardwood. Snow boots squeaked on the three-point line.

We studied our handbills, the drastic fonts, letters bleeding and spilling into one another, claiming impossible and remarkable things: See the Metal Eater who eats scrapped tin, an entire out-board motor, never the same act twice. It was difficult to believe that the little man at the table was going to do anything. Duck came in with the produce manager and found seats near the back, their big thighs sagging over the edges of their chairs.

Then the sequined back curtain floated aside and out came a woman who could only have been Griselda Drown. She was all thighs and calves in a shiny slit-legged dress, heels ridiculously high, tapering down to minuscule points—how did she walk on those shoes, how could she even stand in them?—those long calves scissoring and her dress sparkling madly. A few men whis-tled. She moved like a giraffe, tall but appropriately graceful, unimpeded by her body. Her hair was yarded back in rows like someone had clamped it in a vise, eyes like whirlpools, long-fin-gered hands wheeling a cart over the uneven boards of the stage toward the table where the little man sat.

She dwarfed the metal eater, her breasts strapped into that glittering dress, the line between them soft and dark. She took a white napkin from her cart, held it above the metal eater's bald and shining head, snapped it, lowered it, and knotted it behind his neck. In turn she took a butter knife, a fork, and a tin plate from her cart, dinging the knife and fork—to prove they were made of metal—and then dinging them against the plate—that's metal, too. She laid them down, setting the table. Fork, knife, plate.

The metal eater sat, implacable, in front of his table setting. Griselda turned, a flourish of sparkle, and rolled her cart back the way she came. Her thighs flashed under the slit gown, long and thick and suntanned. Her cart rattled, stopped. She disappeared behind the sequined back curtain. The metal eater sat alone at the table under the raw light of humming gym bulbs.

What would he eat? Was Griselda going to wheel out some awful metal repast, a chainsaw or an office chair? The papers claimed that the metal eater had eaten a lawnmower, swallowed down the wing of a Cessna. How could something like that be possible? What would she put on his plate? A nail? A razor blade? A measly thumbtack? We had not paid twenty-five bucks to sit hip to hip and watch a tiny man swallow a thumbtack. The produce manager announced he would ask for his money back if they didn't bring back Duck's sister-in-law in the next ten minutes.

The metal eater sat smugly, napkin around his neck. He took the knife and fork in his little pink fists. He held them against the table, upright, ends down, like a petulant child awaiting supper. Then, with a certainty and casualness that was almost appalling, he took the knife and slid it down his throat and closed his mouth behind it. He sat, natty, unruffled, staring at the crowd, some of whom missed the feat entirely and were only now swinging their heads around as brothers or uncles tugged their sleeves. The metal eater had a fraction of a smile on his lips. His Adam's apple was the only part of him that moved. It jerked freakishly up and down and side to side, like a muscled and angry monkey chained by one ankle.

He followed the knife with the fork, nudging it down. While he swallowed the fork, he folded the plate into quarters, his throat straining wildly, his shoulders perfectly still, and put that into his mouth, and poked it down with one finger. His Adam's apple jerked, seized, thrashed. After a half minute or so, it slowed, then restored itself to its original, sedated state. The little metal eater unknotted the napkin, dabbed at the corners of his mouth, stood up from the table, and bowed. He tossed the napkin into the first rows of the crowd.

Applause started slowly, just the produce manager and some others in the back bringing their hands together, and then others joined in, and it mounted and soon we were beside ourselves, hooting and hollering and pounding the floor with our boot heels. How about that? the produce manager was shouting. How about that?

When the ovation began to subside, three large men in utility belts hustled out, lifted the table and hefted it offstage. The applause faded. The great overhead dome lights in the gym went out, one by one, ticking as they cooled in the growing silence. Over the doors, red exit signs cast the only light.

Finally one blue spotlight switched on, a single shaft of light falling from the ceiling to illuminate the center of the stage where a tall figure had appeared in a suit of plated armor, complete with visored helmet, an ostrich plume canting off the peak. Another spotlight came on, yellow, and shone on the metal eater, stationed like a tiny well-dressed peasant beside the armored figure. He held a stool, which he set down and squatted on, facing the crowd. He withdrew a ball-peen hammer from his suit pocket and twirled it in his palm. Then he removed the shin legging from one foot of the armored figure and folded it and banged it flat against the floor of the stage. He folded it again and banged it flat again. Then he pushed it down his throat, swallowing contentedly on his stool, his Adam's apple flailing madly. Beneath the removed armor, in the ray of blue, we could see one long calf, a bare foot.

It took the metal eater less than a minute to swallow down the legging. He promptly moved to the other. How about *that,* whispered the produce manager. Is *that* for real? He was shaking Duck's shoulder. The crowd began to get into it, clapping as the metal eater removed each subsequent piece of armor, the thigh pieces next, and when it was clear that the thick, suntanned legs belonged to Griselda, we stood and pounded the floor and chanted and cheered and everyone was grinning and enjoying the show. The metal eater swallowed on, his frenetic Adam's apple riveting each swallow home.

Within twenty minutes the metal eater had done most of his work. He was standing beside the stool and tenderly sliding off the second gauntlet. All that remained to eat were the helmet and massive chest piece. Griselda held her arms out from her body, palms to the sky, had in fact held them there during the entire spectacle. We stomped the floor to match the rhythm of the metal eater's swallowing.

When he had choked down the last gauntlet, the metal eater slid his stool behind Griselda and climbed onto it. The boots pounded the floor. The metal eater brought his arms above both his head and hers and gently tugged the ostrich plume free, letting it float to the stage in front of them. Then, with a flourish of wrists and fingers, he removed her helmet. Her hair, orange and long, slipped free, and we were rapturous, screaming and cheering and whistling. The metal eater climbed off his stool, took the helmet and flattened it under one dazzling wing tip. He folded it and banged it flat again. Then he lit into it with his teeth. It took him over two minutes to eat it and we were at frenzy pitch by the time he finished, one great and frothing roar quaking the rafters of that old gym. The produce manager was hugging Duck and tears were on his cheeks. If that isn't something, he shouted. If that isn't something.

The metal eater climbed back on the stool, stretched as widely as he could and ran his hands along both of Griselda's arms, over her biceps and onto her shoulders and under the chestpiece. He dislodged it, held it in front of her for an unbearably long moment, and finally raised it high over their heads into the trembling blue spotlight, and we beheld Griselda, her broad and flat belly, her navel, her breasts and her outstretched arms—a masterpiece of a woman, a marble column fixed in a blade of light, a golden-blue monument. Amid salvos of ovations, the metal eater folded and flattened the final piece until he could fit his mouth around it. He gulped it down. The big men in utility belts appeared and wrapped Griselda in a red kimono and carried her offstage.

‿

In the aftermath—the pandemonium subsided, bows demanded and demanded again, the gymnasium lights burning once more at full, lacerating power, the men in utility belts already dismantling the stage—Duck sat shaken and sweat-damped. He gathered himself into his big puffy coat, stood, and tottered into the head-light-swept parking lot, shuffling through the new snow, over the slushy curbs.

Rumbling at the back of the parking lot was an eighteen-wheeler, its wipers sliding slowly over the windshield, running lights glowing yellow across the top of the cab and down the lines of the trailer. From bumper to bumper the truck was painted an extravagant green, the metal eater's logo laid lustily across it and before Duck knew what he was doing he walked past his car, to the end of the lot, and rapped on the window of the cab.

Griselda herself answered, leaning through the open door, one foot on the running board, stooped so she could push her head out, orange hair framing her face. She looked like a very tall Rosemary, squinting at him like Rosemary did when she was try-ing to figure something out. I'm Duck Winters, Duck said. I know all about you. He stammered, he smiled, he asked if she would like to come over the house for tea, or beer, or whatever. I think you should see your sister, he said. It might be good. I lost my job today. He tried for a smile that was more like a shrug. Griselda smiled back. Okay, she said. Once the truck gets loaded.

So that's how it came to be that Duck Winters drove through the snowy and quiet residential streets of Boise's North End, steering slowly and cautiously home, after midnight, with a lurid eighteen-wheeler inches from his rear bumper, its roof knocking snow from overhanging branches.

⌣

Rosemary woke to airbrakes sighing in the street. She heard boots on the front walk, low voices, and the refrigerator door unstick as it opened. She pushed herself up in bed. Duck appeared, prancing down the hall, tracking snow along the rug. His hair was slicked down with sweat, his cheeks flushed. He put his mittened hands on her shoulders. Rosie, he hissed, you awake? You're not going to believe it. He was bursting over. You're just not go-ing to be-lieve it.

He took her by the wrists, pulled her out of bed, her hair frizzed, wearing only a tight T-shirt and green sweatpants. He hauled her down the hall, through the melting tracked-in snow, to stand in the kitchen doorway and behold her sister, seated at the kitchen table, towering and radiant and glittering in a red kimono, holding hands with a little man in a black tweed suit with an awkward look on his face. On the table, in front of each of them, stood an unopened can of beer.

Rosemary found it impossible to look at Griselda—her presence was too solar for this kitchen with its cracked countertops and veneered cabinets, a box of stale doughnuts, a wilted amaryllis slumped out of its plastic pot, a porcelain Santa on the windowsill that should have been put away weeks ago. Moonlight fell in parallelograms through the kitchen window. In the basin of the sink sat a bowl half full of sludgy cereal.

Duck squeezed past her, fussing, twitching about with little jumps, his belly quivering under his jacket. This is your sister, he gushed, and her husband, Gene. You should have seen them tonight, Rosie, the *show* they put on. It was incredible! Incredible! You'd never believe it! You guys should talk, Rosie, you and your sister, is what I was thinking, it's her first time home in twenty years! She said she wrote a letter. It was nice of them to come, wasn't it? Their truck's outside. They actually *live* in their truck! We have tea if you guys don't like that beer.

Out the kitchen window Rosemary saw many of us—maybe two dozen neighbors—laboring across the lawn, figures examining the cab of the metal eater's truck, faces peering in the living room window. Griselda asked Rosemary if she'd been getting the letters and Rosemary managed to nod her head. Griselda said something about the new light fixture above the sink, about how it was nice. Rosemary watched a slushy bootprint turning to water on the kitchen floor.

Duck was toddling around the kitchen, rummaging through the fridge. He offered the guests summer sausage, noodle salad, pushed a can of beer into Rosemary's hand and announced that the metal eater had an entire suit of armor inside his stomach, right here, Rosie, in our very own kitchen. Isn't it something?

Rosemary stood rigid and barefoot in the doorway. Her sister, the men, the peeping neighbors and the eighteen-wheeler outside—all this loomed in the outskirts of her vision. She blinked her eyes several times. The beer can in her hand was cold. The bootprint of snow on the kitchen tile was turning to water.

She moved through the kitchen, set the beer on the table and tore a paper towel from the rack under the sink. She swabbed at the bootprint on the floor, watched the paper absorb the gray slush. Duck and me, she said, we've been married fifteen years. You know that, Griselda? Her voice didn't shake and she was glad for it.

She stood and leaned on the table, the damp and crumpled paper towel in her fist. You know Mom would go to sleep with one of your volleyball trophies in her arms? You know that after she died we poured out her ashes in the backyard? Did you know that? At work I dye giant sheets of linen and guide them onto spools all day. That's what Mom used to do; she used to do that while we were at school. Every day.

She took Duck's hand and held it. I used to want to leave, she said. I used to want to get out of Boise so bad. But this—she gestured at the kitchen, the bowl of abandoned cereal, the amaryllis and the porcelain Santa—this is a life at least. This is a place to come home to.

Griselda had begun to cry, quiet sobs like whispers. Rosemary stopped. A moment like this—the four of them around the table under the sad, dusty kitchen lamp—could never accommodate all the things she had to say. She went to the metal eater and took him by the wrist and led him out the door, into the snow. Hey, she yelled, at the eighteen-wheeler, at the foothills standing up white under the moon, at all of us standing there on her lawn. Here he is! I want you all to get a good look. Look at him! She was screaming. You think eating metal is any harder than what I do, than what each of you do? You think this man is amazing? Look at him!

But—and this is what we remembered later—she was the one we looked at: her hair trembling on her head like flames, her shoulders back, her chest quaking—an image of power and fury. She burned, magnificent, in the snow, barefoot, in a T-shirt and green sweatpants, shouting at us. Griselda appeared and took the metal eater by the arm and led him out to their truck. Duck brought Rosemary inside and shut the door and the lights in the house went off and the curtains snapped shut. We watched the big truck labor into gear and rumble past the drive and each of us filed through the snow back to our homes and the sounds of the night finally faded until there was nothing to hear but snow coming down from the hills and pressing against the windows of our houses.

◡

A shouting in the streets. The heart wavers, surges to life, wavers again. Griselda's letters still came once a month and Rosemary and Duck went on living their lives; Duck found work as a grill cook at a steakhouse; Rosemary inherited a beagle from a deceased coworker. This was when Boise was growing like mad and there were always new people around, people building mansions in the hills, people who didn't know there had ever been a Shaver's Supermarket.

Sometimes, in the spring, we'd stroll past the bungalow and see Rosemary on the front step, doing the Find-A-Word in the *Statesman,* Duck dozing in the chair beside her, the beagle watching us from between their feet. Rosemary would be chewing the end of her pencil, thinking hard, and we'd begin to tell whoever was with us the story and we'd hike up into the hills, gesticulating as we talked, up the steep paths to a place where we could see the mountains beyond the hills, jagged and endless, illuminated under the sun, folding back on each other all the way to the horizon.

JULY FOURTH

By July fourth it was all but over. The Americans went to
fish the River Neris one last time. They boarded a trolleybus outside the Balatonas Hotel, squeezed shoulder to shoulder with
grim Lithuanians—whiskered old ladies, sullen-faced men in thin
ties, a miniskirted girl with a cluster of nose rings—and stood in
their rubber waders, holding their bamboo poles out the windows
to keep them from being snapped. The trolley rolled past the
green market stalls and awning-fronted shops on Pilies Street, past
the cathedral and belfry below the castle on the promontory. It
rattled to a stop at the Zaliasis Bridge and the Americans pushed
off and slumped down the slick grassless slope underneath the
arches where the river slogged between concrete banks. They
spread out along the cobbles, impaled cubes of bread on their
hooks, and pitched them into the current.

At noon they laid down their poles and brooded on the sidewalk stones, not talking. Before long the slim-legged school-

teacher brought her students to the river, as she had done every noon that week, to point at the Americans and call them fools.

◡

But the story gets ahead of itself. First, the beginning.

For that we need to be in America, Manhattan, in the leather armchairs of an uptight anglers' club with mounted marlin, brass urns and hushed speaking. The Americans, retired industrialists, angling members all, sat in a row at the bar, picking at platters of tempura and sipping vodka martinis. Behind them a gang of British sportfishermen were guzzling margaritas and insulting the Americans' fishing prowess. Things progressed. Soon the Brits were clog-dancing around the billiards tables and hollering indelicate and anti-American boasts of recent shark-fishing successes. The Americans kept dipping their tempura, but eventually took offense.

There were the standard provocations: tequila, reminders of the Marshall Plan, rudely phrased questions about the queen's gender and the president's bedside fancies. It mounted to a challenge, as these things do, and a contest was born. Limeys vs. Yanks. Old World vs. New.

The contest would consist of this: the first side to land the largest freshwater fish on each of the continents won. A month per continent. The losers had to parade naked through Times Square waving We Can't Fish placards. Europe would be first. The contest would begin immediately.

◡

In the morning the hungover Americans conferred over sausage and Bloody Marys. There was parley about where to fish. Hemingway had fished Spain, someone offered, but another argued Papa had fished Germany, not Spain, and in any case had caught nothing. Someone else declared that Teddy Roosevelt once pulled a fifteen-pound bluegill from a Venetian canal, and after that the group grew silent, picturing stout Teddy muscling a panfish the size of a manhole cover into a wobbling gondola, sun blazing in one spectacle lens. Finally they were brought a telephone and a teenager at L.L. Bean told them to try the Finnish Reindeerlands. Two weeks, he raved, in the Reindeerlands and you'll get your fish.

So they began it with a pair of nights in Helsinki drinking cognac, placing enormously expensive phone calls to America and flirting with hotel maids. They provided the concierge with a list for provisions: Swedish muesli bars (13 cases) and Norwegian vodka (3 dozen jars).

Then a train north; then an antique motorbus upholstered with violet velvet; then a wet cabin cruiser forty miles up a black river into the silver moorlands of Lapland. The boat motored on into serious wilderness, silent and soggy, the river flanked by impenetrable-looking thickets. A pair of shaggy bears padded over riverside moraine. The Americans stood at the bow rail looking sick.

The captain backed the boat beside a rotten dock. Behind it sagged an abandoned gold panner's hut with wire windows and a leaning chimney. He tossed the Americans' duffels and rod cases ashore and roared off. The Americans stood on the swaying dock and slapped at mosquitoes. Above them rain came crawling in from the fjords and descended on the river, dull and somber.

They were wet for two weeks. Each evening, shivering, swabbing their noses with their Gore-Tex sleeves, they splashed to the wind-battered hut, peeled down their waders and pulled fleece jerseys over their wet chests. Fourteen days of this for dinner: fire-blackened chunks of salmon flesh on skewers, muesli bars, and jar after jar of Norwegian vodka, crystal, painful. Outside the river rose cold and tea-colored beneath the ceaseless drizzle.

They reeled in hundreds of foot-long salmon—nothing bigger. Soggy and headachy, grim-faced, the Americans fished on, into the long dusks and drawn-out dawns, wrapped in shrouds of mosquitoes. Their two weeks expired. The largest fish they hooked was a thirteen-inch salmon they photographed and promptly eviscerated.

The captain who boated them out brought along a reindeer farmer in furs and a Tartan-plaid scarf who could speak a tortured English. He said if they wanted big fish they ought to fish Poland, a bison reserve called Bialowieza. Huge trouts, he said, and showed them how huge with his hands.

⌣

Back in Helsinki the Americans regrouped over diamond-bone sirloins and Doritos. The waiter brought an envelope: inside was a Polaroid of the Brits beaming over a string of rainbow trout, each more than twenty-four inches, silver bodies shining in the camera flash. In the background the Eiffel Tower shimmered, brilliant and unmistakable in June light.

Fourteen days to go.

Two overbooked Lufthansa flights later the undaunted Americans tramped through customs in Warsaw. A savage-looking cabdriver accosted them outside, herded them into a Japanese taxi-van. Ah, he nodded, the bison reserve. Bialowieza. He leaned over his seat and winked. It is risky, you know, this place. Risky-risky.

He winked more, switched off his meter, then stomped the gas and they went hurtling over a dizzying labyrinth of dirt roads. Wet forests hurtled in and out of view, spindly white birch and giant oaks, and between the forests lay fields or clusters of gray cottages. It was near dark when the minivan skidded to a stop beneath a stand of leafy hornbeams. The driver slid open the door, threw down their gear, announced he'd be back in a week. Once they had their big fish. Wink-wink. Hush-hush. His taxi-van spat gravel on its way out.

The Americans hiked in. Peat moss country: flat, flooded, lush, bogs between copses of spruce, rotted logs and mucky footing. The forest floated before them, a green and black sponge; insects swirled in gray spires between fungus-chewed trunks.

Munching muesli bars, the Americans clambered over a series of fences, the first split-rail and the last chain-link. At dark they reached a river, its black riffles barely visible beneath clouds of gnats, and pitched tents under a stand of rattling limes. Their dreams were decorated with the leaps of trophy trout.

They woke to the black noses of bison snorting rosemary-scented breath through the tents' mesh windows. A shaggy and horned herd had stalled on the riverbanks, ruminating, drooling green saliva. When the Americans unzipped their way out, they found a bison herder in shorts rooting through their duffels.

○

The bison herder had an automatic rifle and wanted nothing to do with bribes. She waited on a bench outside a Belorussian border station eating confiscated muesli bars while helmeted police unscrewed the Americans' rod cases, peered into their fly boxes and upended their duffels. As a kind of interrogation, a tiny police captain in pump-up basketball shoes asked the dumbfounded Americans a series of questions about pro basketball. Did Patrick Ewing have a wife? How carefully did American refs call the three-second rule? How much did Americans pay for basketball shoes with built-in pumps?

When he seemed satisfied he nodded, then deflated and repumped one of his sneakers. All this will have to go, he finally said, sweeping his arm over their fishing gear.

But we only wanted to fish, the Americans insisted. For trout.

Oh yes, he nodded, repumping the other shoe. Oh yes. There

are trouts, big trouts in the Biebzra. He said something to his men and they repeated, Big trouts, and showed the Americans how big with their hands.

But you see, the little chief shook his head, Americans must not fish here. It is illegal. The czars shot boars here. And before them, Polish kings. Lithuanian princes. All shooting boars.

We didn't shoot boars, the Americans said. We didn't even fish. We were sleeping. We thought we were in Poland.

Nonetheless, said the chief, removing his helmet, you must play us in basketball for your things.

There was a dirt court behind the border station: chain nets, plywood backboards. The Belorussians unclipped their police belts and leapt into a series of pregame drills. When the game started they executed backdoor cuts, shot rainbow jumpers, ran the pick and roll to perfection. They beat the befuddled Americans by forty. Afterward the Belorussians hoisted their small chief onto their shoulders and sang to him. The bison herder on her bench unwrapped another muesli bar and cheered placidly.

The sweaty Americans were ushered onto a motorbus with cracks in the windshield. You will go to Lodz, the chief told them, picking at a thread on his newly won Gore-Tex pullover. Back to Poland. It is lovely there.

Halfway to Lodz the windshield fell onto the driver and the motorbus plunged into a drainage culvert and rolled onto its side. The passengers climbed out hatches in the roof and squatted by the roadside in a field of buckthorn. It began to rain. The Americans sat in a soggy cluster, mud seeping through their socks.

Hours later they were shivering on a speeding flatbed between plastic crates of meat chickens heading south to a Slovakian slaughterhouse. They watched southern Poland scroll past, crumbling apartment blocks, buckled roads, rusted cisterns, weathered steeples, haystacks, the skeleton of a Soviet tank grown over with sawgrass—all the unkempt, haphazard Polish gloom. By the time they got to Kraków they were drenched and ravenous

and the swarthy Poles in velour jogging suits who smoked cigarettes on street corners shot them wary scowls.

The Americans were badly discouraged. Twelve days to go,
stripped of their gear, sniffling, they huddled in a Kraków McDon-
ald's and invoked middle-school platitudes about Cornwallis's
surrender and Valley Forge, about pitching crates of tea into
Boston Harbor and bloody-soled snow marches for the good of
the Republic. We must not quit now, they mumbled, and dipped
their chicken nuggets into a tasteless sauce.

〇

The morning broke blue and the Americans, having dreamed of
Washington and Wayne, Bunyan and Balboa, found themselves
hopeful: eleven days seemed like enough time to beat some boor-
ish Brits. They cash-advanced their MasterCards and bought rubber waders, bamboo poles, Japanese hooks, three spools of thick
monofilament. A Pole at the sporting goods shop insisted they fish
a place called Lake Popradské, only an hour away. It's *the* place to
fish, he gushed. *Insane* fishing—muskie imported from Minnesota.
He demonstrated the impressive length of the lake muskie with
his hands.

By afternoon the Americans were stepping off a bus in the
Carpathian Mountains, jaggy summits collared in peacock greens
and mustard yellows. Falcons soared above the sprucetops and
breezes brought the scent of glacial carnations. The Americans
exchanged smiles, felt a renewed cheer as they descended a comfortable, craggy trail that wound deliberately down to a lodge
cozied up against a lake.

This—they thumped each other on the backs—was the place
to fish all right: a deluxe mountain hotel with a stuffed lynx above
the fireplace, gentians in crystal vases, smiling Slovakian hostesses
in white aprons who escorted them to carpeted rooms. They
shaved, showered, clinked glasses on the canopied deck. Above

them, on surround-sound speakers, the delicate staccato of a string quartet. On a massive RCA home theater, a taped replay of the Super Bowl.

In the twilight the Americans brought gin and tonics to the beach and rented pedal-boats shaped like giant swans. They trolled night crawlers from their bamboo poles, sipped their drinks and nodded to the lovers who paddled among them, spell-bound, all of them, in the tangerine dusk.

☽

For three days they pedaled their swan-boats and caught sunfish. Huge sunfish, to be sure, but the sunfish at their largest got no big-ger than a dinner plate, and the Americans unhooked them and let them slap along the fiberglass breasts of their swans until they reached the water and were free. The Americans knew there were muskie in Lake Popradské because the hostesses had shown them photos, but the muskie were not cooperating.

On June twenty-seventh they got their first muskie in a shal-low shoal on a Rapala they had run through that water fifty times or more. It was big, probably thirty-five inches, with faded green gills and mahogany fins. The Americans cheered, brained it with the butt of a wine bottle and resumed their angling with a renewed verve.

With a week left the Americans were gleefully boating a forty-one-inch muskie when a FedEx van came gliding over a pass into the valley. They watched it park at the hotel. A purple jumpsuited driver jogged to the beach and waved them in where he had them sign for a videotape.

When the Americans pushed the tape into the hotel VCR, they watched the oversized screen where the Brits bobbed into view, unshaven and bug-bitten, crowded around what looked like the stern of a rusty pontoon boat. The picture zoomed and focused on a crouching Brit who withdrew from the dark water a colossal salmon. His hand entirely disappeared inside the fish's gill slot. It was overlarge; it disgusted the Americans, its outsized jaw, black-button eyes, sagging belly and massive tail. It was, one American stammered, the size of a first-grader.

Offscreen the Brits spouted gloats. The image zoomed, fixed on the bloated salmon for an unbearable moment. Finally the camera panned, and with horror the Americans recognized the rotten dock, wire windows and leaning chimney of the gold panner's hut in the Reindeerlands, unmistakable, rendered before them in crude and superreal clarity. They sat, boggled, while the surround-sound speakers assaulted them with exultant and decidedly anti-American yelps.

◡

This time no Boston Tea Party speeches were offered up. The Americans sat under a pall of defeat and could not shake the searing image of that overgrown salmon, more real than anything around them now, the dusty lynx above the fireplace or the lake beyond the windows. For the first time they began to contemplate the realities of a naked parade through Times Square, the goose bumps on their white thighs, the foul slickness of that pavement under their soles, the giggles of ogling Europeans come to New York to photograph the New World. What horrible ignominy, what raw disgrace. There wasn't a muskie in all of Poland as big as that salmon. They would have to return to Finland, maybe take a train into Norway, slog into the wilderness. It was almost too much to stomach.

Downhearted, dispirited, the Americans returned to Kraków and haggled on a pay phone with a Lufthansa man. There was weather in Helsinki, he explained, thunderstorms, planes weren't flying near it. He said he could get them to Vilnius, Lithuania. Vilnius was as close as they could get.

So they flew to Lithuania. They checked into a hotel at midnight and ordered potato chips from the bar, which were delivered to their rooms on fine china. At daybreak they rephoned the Lufthansa man: no flights to Helsinki today. The desk girl spoke a timid English, produced a *Lithuania in Your Pocket* and showed them the River Neris on a cartoon map. You want to fish, she said, fish here. Right in Vilnius.

So they took a trolleybus to Vingis Park, past concrete apartment blocks and the drab spaces between them—overgrown weedlot, cracked pavement and bits of shiny trash, Kit Kat wrappers, Pepsi cans. In the park the grass was wet from rain and the air was heavy and the trees were still. A woman with her head wrapped in a gray scarf bent to tear weeds from cracks in the sidewalk.

The river was hopeless: a stagnant silt-bottomed canal swirling through the heart of the city, slow and shallow and sullied, populated by schools of plastic bags. The Americans impaled hunks of bread on their hooks, pitched them into the brown current and dragged in carp minnows, one after another. They were slimy runt-fish, dark green with red-fringed fins. Scowling, the Americans pitched them back.

All morning they worked upstream, into the gut of Vilnius, fishing among buildings, below people crossing a great stone plaza, beside a weathered cathedral, beneath torrents of cars rumbling over a bridge.

Each hour churchbells chimed all through the city, dissonant, a low and sad cacophony. At twelve bells the Americans smoked Marlboros and sat on the smooth stones of the cobbled banks. A class of girls came tramping crisply toward them, little girls in double file. The girls wore saddle shoes and white socks to the knee and T-shirts adorned with the Lion King or Mickey or Bugs. As they walked they slapped the pleats of their skirts with composition books. They followed on the heels of their teacher, a speed-walking slim-legged beauty in sandals, tan slacks, and a blue blazer with brass buttons, a black hair ribbon trailing behind.

They were naming things. The teacher threw an arm toward the bridge, her wrist shooting from her brass-buttoned cuff, and the schoolgirls named it in octaves only schoolgirls can reach, gleefully shouting their English, BRIDGE. She threw her arm at the river, RIVER, and at the traffic, AUTOBUS, CAR, MOTOR-BIKE. The teacher pointed at a Marlboro billboard pasted across the side of a building and the girls shouted, AMERICAN CAN-CER, NO THANK YOU.

As the class whirled past the Americans with their bamboo poles in their laps, sweating in their waders and smiling at the little procession, the teacher aimed her bony finger at *them,* and the girls cheerily called out, FOOLS. Giggling, they marched down-river.

In the evening the Americans climbed into their undersized beds and had ghastly nightmares about British whaling vessels. The next day there were no flights into Helsinki (terrible flooding, chirped the Lufthansa man) and the Americans returned to the River Neris, despondent, clumping off the trolleybus at the Zalia-sis Bridge.

Again at noon the English class came parading downriver behind their teacher, her pointer finger itemizing surroundings. The girls emitted piercing shrieks: RIVER, TREES, TRAFFIC, SIDEWALK, FOOLS. The Americans, feeling vaguely guilty, waded into the mucky current so the class could pass.

◡

There would be no flights to Helsinki; they gave up trying to get there. They would finish it fishing the River Neris. Each hour the churchbells clanged through the city, mirthless knells. The Americans fished on, not hoping for much anymore, perhaps for a miracle, searching for small things to be happy about, because they were Americans and this was what their upbringings had taught them to do. They found a brief happiness, for example, in the potato chips that came to their rooms on expensive china and in the genuinely hopeful way the hotel girl asked if they'd had any luck. They took pleasure in their morning calls to the Lufthansa man, his wriggly explanations for the canceled flights to Norway. They smiled at the way a church had been built so the setting sun hit it high and perfect and orange, and the way they could follow the river to a park where miniskirted women lay in the grass with headphones clamped over their ears, and even at the way the little student-girls came filing down at noon behind their English-teaching beauty to call them fools.

⌣

Finally there was only one day left, July fourth. Morning bells clanged in the haze above the rooftops. The Americans filed off the trolleybus to fish. By noon they had caught nothing; the water was murky and brown, their casting hopeless.

The little class came tramping along the riverbank, screeching English and slapping their composition books in rhythm: RIVER, CHURCH, FOOLS, WALL, STONES, yapping and promenading cheerily behind their teacher. She led them up the grassless slope to the avenue and marched them onto the Zaliasis Bridge where they stopped to lean over the railing, still naming in their shrill voices: SIDEWALK, STATUES, FLOWERS, FOOLS, BILLBOARD, AMERICAN CANCER, NO THANK YOU.

The Americans groaned to their feet, waded in and cast their soggy squares of bread into the current. And as the girls shrieked, as the brassy river flowed through the city, as the Americans held their poles in a last, hopeless hope, one of their poles quivered, then bent into a steep parabola. Monofilament dragged from the reel. The pole bent and continued to bend; the tip strained unbearably close to the handle. The Americans thought the line must have snagged on some cinderblock or tire or rusty sink, or

worse, had lodged itself into the canal bottom, onto some umbil-
ical iron strut plugged into the underworks of the entire city.
You've hooked Vilnius, they joked. Try pulling that up.

But the little girls, their pale faces leaning over the bridge railing, began to shout excitedly in Lithuanian, pointing and nodding.
The American with the straining pole let out a fierce cheer, and
the other Americans splashed around him and watched. The line
began to wander between the channel banks, patiently, almost
indifferently, cutting broad S shapes. Eventually it crossed to the
near bank and hung there, motionless, a dead weight.

The American with the rod strained and grunted and finally
grappled it into the shallows between his feet. Then he set down
the pole and gaped and the Americans around him shook their
heads and gaped too. The girls on the bridge began to shout more
loudly, leaping as they shouted, and soon they were racing down
from the bridge and sprinting beside the canal. They stopped at a
distance of a few yards, panting, staring wide-eyed at the Americans who heaved a great homely fish onto the cobbled banks
where it lay gulping.

It was a carp: grayish-ocher, as if it had absorbed the color of
the city at its most dismal. Some of its scales had come loose and
lay on the stones like translucent half-dollars. Its tattered fins
were fringed with red, and its lidless eyes were twice as big as the
Americans' eyes, and the curl of its whiskers made it look like a
sullen and venerable Spaniard, lying wounded, gasping.

The Americans stood staring sheepishly down, arms slack.
Above them traffic rumbled along the bridge. The fish was huge,
surely bigger than the Brits' salmon, surely one of the biggest carp
ever caught. It waved its pectoral fin slowly, raising it, lowering it,
an awful gesture.

One of the Americans lifted the fish, cradled its sagging mass in
his arms, and proclaimed it fifty or so pounds. Sixty, maybe. He
held it, not knowing what to do. Its belly sagged between his

hands. A string of excrement trailed from its anus. The sun weighed down heavily through the haze. The teacher arrived frowning and huffing behind her students.

The carp shifted, a small shrug, no more than a slight leaning, but it was enough to slip the grasp of the arms that held it. It thudded jaw-first onto the bank and slid a little on its side, leaving the stones it had slid across wet with slime. It came to a stop and lay there, flexing its tail. The Americans produced a disposable travel camera, but when they went to click the button, the camera stuck. They fumbled with it; it fell into the river, and sank.

The carp sucked and gasped, its round mouth and four barbell whiskers making feeble O's in the air and a line of blood, barely visible against the scales, went trickling from one gill. The girls began to cry. The teacher sniffled.

The Americans looked over at this gaggle of girls in saddle shoes, standing openmouthed, with fingers laced in front of their composition books, little girls with gold crucifixes around their necks and a few with bruises on their knees, bangs coiled against their foreheads, knee socks sagging in July fourth heat, tears on their chins. Behind them their teacher had her fingers on her temples, elbows against her chest, one trembling lip between her teeth.

Fools, she said. You fools.

◡

What a fish. What schoolgirls, what Americans to let that carp go, its fins dappling the surface of the river, lazy, ugly, wandering into the whorling depths of city current. Churchbells sounded, and at some point the Americans decided they would do better on the next continent. They would research and avoid risks, not fish in illegal places, not drink so much, not heed the advice of every stranger, they would carry two sets of everything, two rods and two fleece jerseys per man, next time they wouldn't have to wait until the last day, they would map out routes and make contingency plans, and the boundless resources of America, its endless undulant swale, its nodding wheat and white silos gone lavender in the twilight, its vast warehouses and deft craftsmen, would unfurl to help them.

They would not lose, they could not lose; they were Americans, they had already won.

THE CARETAKER

For his first thirty-five years, Joseph Saleeby's mother makes his bed and each of his meals; each morning she makes him read a column of the English dictionary, selected at random, before he is allowed to set foot outside. They live in a small collapsing house in the hills outside Monrovia in Liberia, West Africa. Joseph is tall and quiet and often sick; beneath the lenses of his oversized eyeglasses, the whites of his eyes are a pale yellow. His mother is tiny and vigorous; twice a week she stacks two baskets of vegetables on her head and hikes six miles to sell them in her stall at the market in Mazien Town. When the neighbors come to compliment her garden, she smiles and offers them Coca-Cola. "Joseph is resting," she tells them, and they sip their Cokes, and gaze over her shoulder at the dark shuttered windows of the house, behind which, they imagine, the boy lies sweating and delirious on his cot.

Joseph clerks for the Liberian National Cement Company, transcribing invoices and purchase orders into a thick leatherbound ledger. Every few months he pays one more invoice than he should, and writes the check to himself. He tells his mother the extra money is part of his salary, a lie he grows comfortable making. She stops by the office every noon to bring him rice—the cayenne she heaps onto it will keep illness at bay, she reminds him, and watches him eat at his desk. "You're doing so well," she says. "You're helping make Liberia strong."

In 1989 Liberia descends into a civil war that will last seven years. The cement plant is sabotaged, then transformed into a guerilla armory, and Joseph finds himself out of a job. He begins to traffic in goods—sneakers, radios, calculators, calendars—stolen from downtown businesses. It is harmless, he tells himself, everybody is looting. We need the money. He keeps it in the cellar, tells his mother he's storing boxes for a friend. While his mother is at the market, a truck comes and carries the merchandise away. At nights he pays a pair of boys to roam the townships, bending window bars, unhinging doors, depositing what they steal in the yard behind Joseph's house.

He spends most of his time squatting on the front step watching his mother tend her garden. Her fingers pry weeds from the soil or cull spent vines or harvest snap beans, the beans plunking regularly into a metal bowl, and he listens to her diatribes on the hardships of war, the importance of maintaining a structured lifestyle. "We cannot stop living because of conflict, Joseph," she says. "We must persevere."

Spurts of gunfire flash on the hills; airplanes roar over the roof of the house. The neighbors stop coming by; the hills are bombed, and bombed again. Trees burn in the night like warnings of worse evil to come. Policemen splash past the house in stolen vans, the barrels of their guns resting on the sills, their eyes hidden behind mirrored sunglasses. Come and get me, Joseph wants to yell at them, at their tinted windows and chrome tailpipes. Just you try. But he does not; he keeps his head down and pretends to busy himself among the rosebushes.

In October of 1994 Joseph's mother goes to the market in the morning with three baskets of sweet potatoes and does not return. He paces the rows of her garden, listening to the far-off thump-thump of artillery, the keening of sirens, the interminable silences between. When finally the last hem of light drops behind the hills, he goes to the neighbors. They peer at him through the rape gate across the doorway to their bedroom and issue warnings: "The police have been killed. Taylor's guerillas will be here any minute."

"My mother . . ."

"Save yourself," they say and slam the door. Joseph hears chains clatter, a bolt slide home. He leaves their house and stands in the dusty street. At the horizon columns of smoke rise into a red sky. After a moment he walks to the end of the paved road and turns up a muddy track, the way to Mazien Town, the way his mother traveled that morning. At the market he sees what he expected: fires, a smoldering truck, crates hacked open, teenagers plundering stalls. On a cart he finds three corpses; none is his mother's, none is familiar.

No one he sees will speak to him. When he collars a girl running past, cassettes spill from her pockets; she looks away and will not answer his questions. Where his mother's stall stood there is only a pile of charred plywood, neatly stacked, as if someone had already begun to rebuild. It is light before he returns home.

The next night—his mother does not return—he goes out again. He sifts through remains of market stalls; he shouts his mother's name down the abandoned aisles. In a place where the market sign once hung between two iron posts, a man has been suspended upside-down. His insides, torn out of him, swing beneath his arms like black infernal ropes, marionette strings cut free.

In the days to come Joseph wanders farther. He sees men leading girls by chains; he stands aside so a dumptruck heaped with corpses can pass. Twenty times he is stopped and harassed; at makeshift checkpoints soldiers press the muzzles of rifles into his chest and ask if he is Liberian, if he is a Krahn, why he is not helping them fight the Krahns. Before they let him go they spit on his shirt. He hears that a band of guerillas wearing Donald Duck masks has begun eating the organs of its enemies; he hears about terrorists in football cleats trampling the bellies of pregnant women.

Nowhere does anyone claim to know his mother's whereabouts. From the front step he watches the neighbors raid the garden. The boys he paid to loot stores no longer come by. On the radio a soldier named Charles Taylor brags of killing fifty Nigerian peacekeepers with forty-two bullets. "They die so easily," he boasts. "It is like sprinkling salt onto the backs of slugs."

After a month, with no more information about his mother than he had the night she disappeared, Joseph takes her dictionary under his arm, stuffs his shirt, pants and shoes with money, locks the cellar—stocked with stolen notepads, cold medicine, boom boxes, an air compressor—and leaves the house for good. He travels awhile with four Christians fleeing to the Ivory Coast; he falls in with a band of machete-toting kids roving from village to village. The things he sees—decapitated children, drugged boys tearing open a pregnant girl, a man hung over a balcony with his severed hands in his mouth—do not bear elaboration. He sees enough in three weeks to provide ten lifetimes of nightmares. In Liberia, in that war, everything is left unburied, and anything once buried is now dredged up: corpses lie in stacks in pit latrines, wailing children drag the bodies of their parents through the streets. Krahns kill Manos; Gios kills Mandingoes; half the travelers on the highway are armed; half the crossroads smell of death.

Joseph sleeps where he can: in leaves, under bushes, on the floorboards of abandoned houses. A pain blooms inside his skull. Every seventy-two hours he is rocked with fever—he burns, then freezes. On the days when he is not feverish, it hurts to breathe; it takes all his energy to continue walking.

Eventually he comes to a checkpoint where a pair of jaundiced soldiers will not let him pass. He recites his story as well as he can—the disappearance of his mother, his attempts to gather information about her whereabouts. He is not a Krahn or a Mandingo, he tells them; he shows them the dictionary, which they confiscate. His head throbs steadily; he wonders if they plan to kill him. "I have money," he says. He unbuttons his collar, shows them the bills in his shirt.

One of the soldiers talks on a radio for a few minutes, then returns. He orders Joseph into the back of a Toyota and takes him up a long, gated drive. Rubber trees run out in seemingly endless rows beneath a plantation house with a tiled roof. The soldier leads him behind the house and through a gate onto a tennis court. On it are a dozen boys, perhaps sixteen years old, lounging on lawn furniture with assault rifles in their laps. White sunlight reflects off the concrete. They sit, and Joseph stands, and the sun bears down upon them. No one speaks.

After several minutes, a sweating captain hauls a man from the back door of the house, down the breezeway to the tennis court, and throws him onto the center line. The man wears a blue beret; his hands are tied behind his back. When they turn him over, Joseph sees his cheekbones have been broken; the face sags inward. "This parasite," the captain says, toeing the man's ribs, "piloted an airplane which bombed towns east of Monrovia for a month."

The man tries to sit up. His eyes drift obscenely in their sockets. "I am a cook," he says. "I am traveling from Yekepa. They tell me to go by road to Monrovia. So I try to go. But then I am arrested. Please. I cook steaks. I have bombed nobody."

The boys in the lawn furniture groan. The captain takes the beret from the man's head and flings it over the fence. The pain in Joseph's head sharpens; he wants to crumple; he wants to lie down in the shade and go to sleep.

"You are a killer," the captain says to the prisoner. "Why not come clean? Why not own up to what you have done? There are dead mothers, dead girls, in those towns. You think you had no hand in their deaths?"

"Please! I am a cook! I grill steaks in the Stillwater Restaurant in Yekepa! I have been traveling to see my fiancée!"

"You have been bombing the countryside."

The man tries to say more but the captain presses his sneaker over his mouth. There is a faraway grinding sound, like pebbles knocking together inside a rag. "You," the captain says, pointing at Joseph. "You are the one whose mother has been killed?"

Joseph blinks. "She sold vegetables in the market at Mazien Town," he says. "I have not seen her for three months."

The captain takes the gun from the holster on his hip and holds it out to Joseph. "This parasite has killed probably one thousand people," the captain says. "Mothers and daughters. It makes me sick to look at him." The captain's hands are on Joseph's hips; he draws Joseph forward as if they are dancing. The light reflecting off the tennis court is dazzling. The boys in the chairs watch, whisper. The soldier who brought Joseph leans against the fence and lights a cigarette.

The captain's lips are in Joseph's ear. "You do your mother a favor," he murmurs. "You do the whole country a favor."

The gun is in Joseph's hand—its handle is warm and slick with sweat. The pain in his head quickens. Everything before him—the dusty and still rows of trees, the captain breathing in his ear, the man on the asphalt, crawling now, feebly, like a sick child—stretches and blurs; it is as though the lenses of his glasses have liquefied. He thinks of his mother making that final walk to the market, the sun and shadow of the long trail, the wind muscling through the leaves. He should have been with her; he should have gone in her stead. He should be the one who felt the ground open beneath him, the one who disappeared. They bombed her into vapor, Joseph thinks. They bombed her into smoke. Because she thought we needed the money.

"He is not worth the blood in his body," the captain whispers. "He is not worth the air in his lungs."

Joseph lifts the pistol and shoots the prisoner through the

head. The sound of the shot is quickly swallowed, dissipated by the thick air, the heavy trees. Joseph slumps to his knees; glittering rockets of light detonate behind his eyes. Everything reels in white. He collapses onto his chest, and faints.

⌣

He wakes on the floor inside the plantation house. The ceiling is bare and cracked and a fly buzzes against it. He stumbles from the room and finds himself in a hallway with no doors at either end and columns of rubber trees below stretching out nearly to the horizon. His clothes are damp; his money—even the bills beneath the soles of his boots—is gone.

At the doorway two boys loll in lounge chairs. Behind them, through the fence of the tennis court, Joseph can see the body of the man he has killed, unburied, slumped on the asphalt. He descends through the long rows of trees. None of the soldiers he sees pays him any mind. After an hour or so of walking he reaches a road; he waves to the first car that passes and they give him water to drink and a ride to the port city of Buchanan.

Buchanan is at peace—no tribes of gun-toting boys patrol the streets; no planes roar overhead. He sits by the sea and watches the dirty water wash back and forth along the pilings. There is a new kind of pain in his head, dull and trembling, no longer sharp; it is the pain of absence. He wants to cry; he wants to throw himself into the bay and drown himself. It would be impossible, he thinks, to get far enough away from Liberia.

He boards a chemical tanker and begs work washing pans in the galley. He scrubs the pans carefully enough, the hot spray washing over him as the tanker bucks its way across the Atlantic, into the Gulf of Mexico and through the Panama Canal. In the bunkroom he studies his shipmates and wonders if they can tell he is a murderer, if he wears it like a mark on his forehead. At night he leans over the bow rail and watches the hull as it cleaves the darkness. Everything feels empty and ragged; he feels as if he has left behind a thousand unfinished tasks, a thousand miscalculated ledgers. The waves continue on their anonymous journeys. The tanker churns north up the Pacific Coast.

⌣

He disembarks in Astoria, Oregon; the immigration police tell him he is a refugee of war and issue him a visa. Some days later, in the hostel where he stays, he is shown an ad in a newspaper: *Handy person needed for winter season to tend Ocean Meadows, a ninety-acre estate, orchard and home. We're desperate!*

Joseph washes his clothes in the bathroom sink and studies himself in a mirror—his beard is long and knotted; through the lenses of his glasses, his eyes look warped and yellow. He remembers the definition from his mother's dictionary: *Desperate: beyond hope of recovery, at one's last extreme.*

He takes a bus to Bandon, then thirty miles down 101, and walks the last two miles down an unmarked dirt road. Ocean Meadows: a bankrupted cranberry farm turned summer playground, the original house demolished to make way for a three-story mansion. He picks his way past the shrapnel of broken wine bottles on the porch.

"I am Joseph Saleeby, from Liberia," he tells the owner, a stout man in cowboy boots called Mr. Twyman. "I am thirty-six years old, my country is at war, I seek only peace. I can fix your shingles, your deck. Anything." His hands shake as he says this. Twyman and his wife retreat, shout at each other behind the kitchen doors. Their gaunt and taciturn daughter drags a bowl of cereal to the dining table, eats quietly, leaves. The clock on the wall chimes once, twice.

Eventually Twyman returns and hires him. They have advertised for two months, he says, and Joseph is the only applicant. "Your lucky day," he says, and eyes Joseph's boots warily.

They give him a pair of old coveralls and the apartment above the garage. During his first month the estate bulges with guests: children, babies, young men on the deck shouting into cell phones, a parade of smiling women. They are millionaires from something to do with computers; when they get out of their cars they inspect the doors for scratches; if they find one they lick their thumbs and try to buff it out. Half-finished vodka tonics on the railings, guitar music from loudspeakers dragged onto the porch, the whine of yellow jackets around half-cleaned plates, plump trash bags piling up in the shed: these are their leavings, these are Joseph's chores. He fixes a burner on the stove, sweeps sand out of the hallways, scrubs salmon off the walls after a food fight. When he isn't working he sits on the edge of the tub in his apartment and stares at his hands.

In September Twyman comes to him with a list of winter duties: install storm windows, aerate the lawns, clear ice from the roof and walkways, make sure no one comes to rob the house. "Can you handle that?" Twyman asks. He leaves keys to the caretaker's pickup and a phone number. The next morning everybody is gone. Silence floods the place. The trees swing in the wind as if shaking off a spell. Three white geese crawl out from under the shed and amble across the lawn. Joseph wanders the main house, the living room with its massive stone fireplace, the glass atrium, the huge closets. He lugs a television halfway down the stairs but cannot summon the will to steal it. Where would he take it? What would he do with it?

Each morning the day ranges before him, vast and empty. He walks the beach, fingering up stones and scanning them for uniqueness—an embedded fossil, the imprint of a shell, a glittering vein of mineral. It is rare that he doesn't pocket the stone; they are all unique, all beautiful. He brings them to his apartment and sets them on the sills—a room lined with rows of pebbles like small, unfinished battlements, fortifications against tiny invaders.

For two months he speaks to no one, sees no one. There is only the slow, steady tracking of headlights along 101, two miles away, or the contrails of a jet as its hurtles overhead, the sound of it lost somewhere in the space between sky and earth.

○

Rape, murder, an infant kicked against a wall, a boy with a clutch of dried ears suspended from his neck: in nightmares Joseph replays the worst things men do to each other. He sweats through his blankets and wakes throttling his pillow. His mother, his money, his neat, ordered life: all are gone—not finished, but vanished, as if some madman kidnapped each element of his life and dragged it to the bottom of a dungeon. He wants terribly to do something good with himself; he wants to do something right.

In November five sperm whales strand on the beach a half mile from the estate. The largest—slumped on the sand a few hundred yards north of the others—is over fifty feet long and is half the size of the garage where Joseph lives. Joseph is not the first to discover them: already a dozen Jeeps are parked in the dunes; men run back and forth between the animals, lugging buckets of seawater, brandishing needles.

Several women in neon anoraks have lashed a rope around the flukes of the smallest whale and are trying to tow it off the sand with a motorized skiff. The skiff churns and skates over the breaking waves; the rope tightens, slips and bites into the whale's fluke; the flesh parts and shows white. Blood wells up. The whale does not budge.

Joseph approaches a circle of onlookers: a man with a fishing pole, three girls with plastic baskets half full of clams. A woman in a blood-smeared lab coat is explaining that there is little hope of rescuing the whales: already they are overheating, hemorrhaging, organs pulping, vital tubes conceding to the weight. Even if the whales could be towed off the beach, she says, they would probably turn and swim back onto shore. She has seen this happen before. "But," she adds, "it is a great opportunity to learn. Everything must be handled carefully."

The whales are written over with scars; their backs are mottled with pocks and craters and plates of barnacles. Joseph presses his palm to the side of one and the skin around the scar trembles beneath his touch. Another whale slaps its flukes against the beach and emits clicks that seem to originate from the center of it. Its brown bloodshot eye rolls forward, then back.

For Joseph it is as if some portal from his nightmares has opened and the horrors crouched there, breathing at the door, have come galloping through. On the half-mile trail back to Ocean Meadows, he falters in his step and has to kneel, his body quaking, the ragged clouds coursing overhead. Tears pour from his eyes. His flight has been futile; everything remains unburied, floating just at the surface, a breeze away from being dredged back up. And why? Save yourself, the neighbors had told him. Save yourself. Joseph wonders if he is beyond saving, if the only kind of man who can be saved is the man who never needed saving in the first place.

He lies in the trail until it is dark. Pain rolls behind his forehead. He watches the stars blazing in their lightless tracts, their twisting and writhing, their relentless burning, and wonders what the woman meant, what he should be learning from this.

⌒

By morning four of the five whales have died. From the dunes they look like a flotilla of black submarines run aground. Yellow tape has been strung around them on stakes and the crowds have swelled further: there are new, more civilian spectators—a dozen Girl Scouts, a mail carrier, a man in wing tips posing for a photo.

The bodies of the whales have distended with gas; their sides sag like the skin of withered balloons. In death the white cross-hatchings of scars on their backs look like ghastly lightning strokes, nets the whales have snared themselves in. Already the first and largest of them—the cow that stranded several hundred yards north of the others—has been beheaded, its jaw turned up at the sky, bits of beach sand stuck to the fist-sized teeth. Using chainsaws and long-handled knives, men in lab coats strip blubber from its flanks. Joseph watches them haul out steaming purple sacs that must be organs. Onlookers mill around; some, he sees, have taken souvenirs, peeling off thin membranes of skin and rolling them up in their fists like gray parchment.

The researchers in lab coats labor between the ribs of the largest whale, finally manage to extract what must be the heart—a massive lump of striated muscle, bunched with valves at one end. It takes four of them to roll it onto the sand. Joseph cannot believe the size of it; maybe this whale had a large heart or maybe all whales have hearts this big, but the heart is the size of a riding mower. The tubes running into it are large enough to stick his head into. One of the researchers jabs it with a needle, draws some tissue and deposits it in a jar. His colleagues are already back in the whale; there is the sound of a saw starting up. The researcher with the needle joins the others. The heart steams lightly in the sand.

Joseph finds a forest service cop eating a sandwich in the dunes.

"Is that the heart?" he asks. "That they've left there?"

She nods. "They're after the lungs, I think. To see if they're diseased."

"What will they do with the hearts?"

"Burn them, I'd guess. They'll burn everything. Because of the smell."

☽

All day he digs. He chooses a plot on a hill, concealed by the forest, overlooking the western edge of the main house and a slice of lawn. Through the trunks behind him he can just see the ocean shimmer between the treetops. He digs until well after dusk, setting out a lantern and digging in its white circle of light. The earth is wet and sandy, rife with stones and roots, and the going is rough. His chest feels like it has cracks running through it. When he sets down the shovel, his fingers refuse to straighten. Soon the hole is deeper than Joseph is tall; he throws dirt over the rim.

Hours after midnight he has a tarp, a shovel, a tree saw and an alloy-cased hand winch in the bed of the estate's truck, the load rattling softly as he eases over the back lawn of the house and down the narrow lane to the beach. Tribes of white birch stand bunched and storm-broken in the headlights like bundles of shattered bones; their branches scrape the sides of the truck.

Twin campfires smolder by the four whales to the south but nobody is near the cow to the north, and he has no trouble driving past the hanks of kelp at tideline to the dark, beheaded hulk lying at the foot of the dunes like the caved-in hull of a wrecked ship.

Viscera and blubber is everywhere. Intestines lie unfurled across the beach like parade streamers. He holds a flashlight in his teeth and, through the giant slats of its ribs, studies the interior of the whale: everything is wet and shadowed and run-together. A few yards away the heart sits in the sand like a boulder. Crabs tear plugs from its sides; gulls squabble in the shadows.

He lays the tarp over the beach, anchors the hand winch to a crossbar at the head of the bed of the truck and hooks the bow-shackle through the grommets on the corners of the tarp. With great difficulty he rolls the heart onto the plastic; then it is merely a matter of winching the entire gory bundle into the bed. He turns the crank, the gears ratcheting loudly; the winch tackle growls; the corners of the tarp come up. The heart inches toward him, plowing through the sand, and soon the truck takes its weight.

The first pale streaks of light show in the sky as he parks the pickup beside the hole he has made above the property. He lowers the tailgate and lays the tarp flat. The heart, stuck all over with sand, lies in the bed like a slain beast. Joseph wedges his body between it and the cab, and pushes. It rolls out easily enough, sliding heavily over the slick tarp, and bounces into the hole with a wet, heavy thump.

He kicks out the extra pieces of flesh and muscle and gore still in the flatbed and drives slowly, in a daze, down the hill and back onto the beach where the other four whales lie in various stages of decomposition.

Three men stand over the dregs of a campfire, soaked in gore, drinking coffee from Styrofoam cups. The heads of two of the whales are missing; all the teeth from the remaining heads have been taken away. Sand fleas jump from the carcasses. There is a sixth whale lying in the sand, Joseph sees, a near-term fetus hauled from the body of its mother. He gets out, steps over the yellow tape and walks to them.

"I'll take the hearts," he says. "If you're done with them."

They stare. He takes the tree saw from the back of the truck bed and goes to the first whale, lifting the flap of skin and stepping inside the great tree of its ribs.

A man seizes Joseph's arm. "We're supposed to burn them. Save what we can and burn the rest."

"I'll bury the hearts." He does not look at the man but keeps his eyes away, on the horizon. "It will be less work for you."

"You can't . . ." But he has released Joseph, who is already back in the whale, sawing at tissue. With the tree saw as his flensing knife he hacks through three ribs, then a thick, dense tube that could be an artery. Blood spurts onto his hands: congealed and black and slightly warm. The cavern inside the whale smells, already, like rot, and twice Joseph has to step back and breathe deeply, the saw hanging from his fist, his forearms matted with blood, the front of his coveralls soaked from mucus and blubber and seawater.

He had told himself it would be like cleaning a fish, but it is completely different—it's more like eviscerating a giant. The plumbing of the whale is on a massive scale; housecats could gallop through its veins. He parts a final layer of blubber and lays a hand on what he decides must be the heart. It is still a bit damp, and warm, and very dark. He thinks: I did not make the hole large enough for five of these.

It takes ten minutes to saw through three remaining veins; when he does the heart comes loose easily enough, sliding toward him and settling muscularly against his ankles and knees. He has to tug his feet free. A man appears, thrusts a syringe into the heart and draws up some matter. "Okay," the man says. "Take it."

Joseph tows it into the truck. He does this all morning and all afternoon, hacking out the hearts and depositing them in the hole on the hill. None of the hearts were as big as the first whale's but they are huge, the size of the range in Twyman's kitchen or the engine in the truck. Even the fetus's heart is extraordinary; as big as a man's torso, and as heavy. He cannot hold it in his arms.

By the time Joseph is pushing the last heart into the hole on the hill, his body has begun to fail him. Purple halos spin at the fringes of his vision; his back and arms are rigid and he has to walk slightly bent over. He fills the hole, and as he leaves it, a mound of earth and muscle, stark amid a thicket of salmonberry with the trunks of spruce falling back all around it, high above the property in the late evening, he feels removed from himself, as though his body were a clumsy tool needed only a little longer. He parks in the yard and falls into bed, gore-soaked and unwashed, the door to the apartment open, the hearts of all six whales wrapped in earth, slowly cooling. He thinks: I have never been so tired. He thinks: at least I have buried something.

◡

During the following days he does not have the energy or will to climb out of bed. He tortures himself with questions: Why doesn't he feel any better, any more healed? What is revenge? Redemption? The hearts are still there, sitting just beneath the earth, waiting. What good does burying something really do? In nightmares it always manages to dig itself out. Here was a word from his mother's dictionary: *Inconsolable: not to be consoled, spiritless, hopeless, brokenhearted.*

An ocean between himself and Liberia and still he will not be saved. The wind brings curtains of yellow-black smoke over the trees and past his windows. It smells of oil, like bad meat frying. He buries his face in the pillow to avoid inhaling it.

☽

Winter. Sleet sings through the branches. The ground freezes, thaws, freezes again into something like sludge, immovably thick. Joseph has never seen snow; he turns his face to the sky and lets it fall on his glasses. He watches the flakes melt, their spiked struts and delicate vaulting, the crystals softening to water like a thousand microscopic lights blinking out.

He forgets his job. From the window he notices he has left the mower in the yard but the will to return it to the garage does not come. He knows he ought to flush the pipes in the main house, sweep the deck, install storm windows, switch on the cables to melt ice from the shingles. But he does not do any of it. He tells himself he is exhausted from burying the whale hearts and not from a greater fatigue, from the weight of memory all around him.

Some mornings, when the air feels warmer, he determines to go out; he throws off the covers and pulls on his trousers. Walking the muddy lane down from the main house, cresting the dunes, the sea laid out under the sky like molten silver, the low forested islands and gulls wheeling above them, a cold rain slashing through the trees, the sight of the world—the utter terror of being out in it—is too much for him, and he feels something splitting apart, a wedge falling through the center of him. He clenches his temples and turns, and has to go sit in the toolshed, among the axes and shovels, in the dark, trying to find his breath, waiting for the fear to pass.

○

Twyman had said the coast didn't get much snow but now the snow comes heavily. It falls for ten days straight and because Joseph does not switch on the de-icing cables, the weight of it collapses a section of the roof. In the master bedroom warped sheets of plywood and insulation sag onto the bed like ramps to the heavens. Joseph splays on the floor and watches the big clusters of flakes fall through the gap and gather on his body. The snow melts, runs down his sides, freezes again on the floor in smooth, clear sheets.

He finds jars of preserves in the basement and eats them with his fingers at the huge dining room table. He cuts a hole in a wool blanket, pulls it over his head and wears it like a cloak. Fevers come and go like wildfires; they force him to his knees and he must wait, wrapped in the blanket, until the shivers pass.

In a sprawling marble bathroom he studies his reflection. His body has thinned considerably; tendons stand out along his forearms; the slats of his ribs make drastic arcs across his sides. A yellow like the color of chicken broth floats in his eyes. He runs his hand over his hair, feels the hard surface of skull just beneath the scalp. Somewhere, he thinks, there is a piece of ground waiting for me.

He sleeps, and sleeps, and dreams of whales inside the earth, swimming through soil like they would through water, the tremors of their passage quaking the leaves. They breach up through the grass, turning over in a spray of roots and pebbles, then fall back, disappearing through the ground which stitches itself over them, whole again.

○

Warblers in the fog, ladybugs traversing the windows, fiddleheads nosing their way up through the forest floor—spring. He crosses the yard with the blanket over his shoulders and examines the first pale sleeves of crocuses rising from the lawn. Swatches of dirty slush lie melting in the shade. A memory rises unbidden: every April in his home, in the hills outside Monrovia, a wind blew down from the Sahara and piled red dust inches deep against the walls of the house. Dust in his ears, dust on his tongue. His mother fought back with brooms and whisks, enlisted him in the defense. Why? he would ask. Why sweep the steps when tomorrow they'll be covered again? She would look at him, fierce and disappointed, and say nothing.

He thinks of the dust, blowing now through the gaps in the shutters, piling up against the walls. It hurts him to imagine it: their house, empty, soundless, dust on the chairs and tables, the garden plundered and grown over. Stolen goods still stacked in the cellar. He hopes someone has crammed the place with explosives and bombed it into splinters; he hopes the dust will close over the roof and bury the house forever.

‿

Soon—who is to say how many days had passed?—there is the sound of a truck grinding up the drive. It is Twyman; Joseph is discovered. He retreats to the apartment, crouches behind the windowsill and his neatly stacked rows of pebbles. He takes one, rolls it in his palm. There is shouting in the main house. He watches Twyman stride across the lawn.

Cowboy boots thud upon the stairs. Already Twyman is bellowing.

"The roof! The floors are flooded! The walls are buckling! The mower's rusted to hell!"

Joseph wipes his glasses with his fingers. "I know," he says. "It is not good."

"Not good?! Damn! Damn! Damn! Damn!" Twyman's throat is turning red; the words clog on their way out. "My God!" he manages to spit. "You fucker!"

"It is okay. I understand."

Twyman turns, studies the pebbles along the sills. "Fucker! Fucker!"

⌒

Twyman's wife drives him north in a sleek, silent truck, the wipers slipping smoothly over the windshield. She keeps one hand in her purse, clenched around what Joseph guesses to be Mace or perhaps a gun. She thinks I am an idiot, thinks Joseph. To her I am a barbarian from Africa who knows nothing about work, nothing about caretaking. I am disrespectful, I am a nigger.

They stop at a red light in Bandon and Joseph says, "I will get out here."

"Here?" Mrs. Twyman glances around as if seeing the town for the first time. Joseph climbs out. She keeps her hand in the purse. "*Duty,*" she says. "It's an issue of duty." Her voice tremors; inside, he can see, she is raging. "I told him not to hire you. I told him what good is it hiring someone who runs from his country at the first sign of trouble? He won't know duty, responsibility. He won't be able to understand it. And now look."

Joseph stands, his hand on the door. "I never want to see you again," she says. "Close the fucking door."

⌒

For three days he lies on a bench in a laundromat. He studies cracks in the ceiling tiles; he watches colors drift across the undersides of his eyelids. Clothes turn loops behind portholes in the dryers. *Duty: behavior required by moral obligation.* Twyman's wife was right; what does he understand about that? He thinks of the hearts lumped into the earth, ground bacteria chewing microscopic labyrinths through their centers. Hadn't burying those hearts been the right thing, the decent thing to do? Save yourself, they said. Save yourself. There were things he had been learning at Ocean Meadows, things yet unfinished.

Hungry but not conscious of his hunger, he walks south down the road, loping through the sogged, muddy grass on the shoulder. All around him the trees stir. When he hears a car or truck approaching, tires hissing over the wet pavement, he retreats into the woods, draws his blanket around him and waits for it to pass.

Before dawn he is back on Twyman's property, high above the main house, hiking through dense growth. The rain has stopped, and the sky has brightened, and Joseph's limbs feel light. He climbs to the small clearing between the trunks where he buried the whale hearts and lays down armfuls of dead spruce boughs for a bed and lies among them on top of the buried hearts, half buried himself, and watches the stars wheel overhead.

I will become invisible, he thinks. I will work only at night. I will be so careful they will never suspect me; I will be like the swallows on their gutter, the insects in their lawn, concealed, a scavenger, part of the scenery. When the trees shift in the wind, so I will shift, and when rain falls I will fall too. It will be a kind of disappearing.

This is my home now, he thinks, looking around him. This is what things have come to.

꩜

In the morning he parts the brambles and peers down at the house where two vans are on the lawn, ladders propped against the siding, the small figure of a man kneeling on the roof. Other men cart boxes or planking into the house. There is the industrious sound of banging.

On the shady hillside below his plot of ground Joseph finds mushrooms standing among the leaves. They taste like silt and make his stomach hurt but he swallows them all, forcing them down.

He waits until dusk, squatting, watching a slow fog collect in the trees. When it is finally night he goes down the hill to the tool-shed beside the garage and takes a hoe from the wall and fumbles in the shadows around the seed box. In a paper pouch he can feel seeds—this he tucks into the pocket of his trousers and retreats, back through the clubfoot and fern, onto the wet, needled floor of the forest, to the ring of trunks and his small plot. In the dim, silvery light he opens the packet. There are maybe two palmfuls of seeds, some thin and black like thistle, some wide and white, some fat and tan. He stows them in his pocket. Then he stands, lifts the hoe, and drives it into the earth. A smell comes up: sweet, wealthy.

All through the smallest hours he turns earth. There is no sign of whale hearts; the soil is black and airy. Earthworms come up flailing, shining in the night. By dawn he is asleep again. Mosquitoes whine around his neck. He does not dream.

◡

The next night he uses his index finger to make rows of tiny holes, and drops one seed like a tiny bomb into each hole. He is so weak from hunger that he must stop often to rest; if he stands quickly his vision floods away and the sky rushes into the horizon, and for a moment it feels like he will dissolve. He eats several of the seeds and imagines them sprouting in his gut, vines pushing up his throat, roots twisting from the soles of his shoes. Blood drips from one of his nostrils; it tastes like copper.

In the ruins of a cranberry press he finds a rusted five-gallon drum. There is a small, vigorous brook that threads between boulders by the beach and he fills the drum with the water and carts it, sloshing and spilling, up the hill to his garden.

He eats kelp, salmonberries, hazelnuts, ghost shrimp, a dead sculpin washed up by the tide. He tears mussels from rocks and boils them in the salvaged drum. One midnight he creeps down to the lawn and gathers dandelions. They taste bitter; his stomach cramps.

The workmen finish rebuilding the roof. The tide of people builds. Mrs. Twyman arrives one afternoon with a flourish of activity; she whirls across the deck in a business suit, a young man at her heels taking notes in a pad. Her daughter takes long, lonesome hikes across the dunes. The evening parties begin, paper lanterns hung from the eaves, a swing band blowing horns in the gazebo, laughter drifting on the wind.

With the hoe and several hours of persistence Joseph manages to knock a chickadee from a low bough and kill it. In the dead of night he roasts it over a tiny fire; he cannot believe how little meat there is on it; it is all bone and feather. It tastes of nothing. Now, he thinks, I really am a savage, killing tiny birds and tearing the tendons from their bones with my teeth. If Mrs. Twyman saw me she would not be surprised.

○

Besides daily carting water up the hill and splashing it over the rows of seeds, there is little to do but sit. The scents of the forest run like rivers between the trunks: growing, rotting. Questions come in bevies: Is the soil warm enough? Didn't his mother start plants in small pots before setting them in the ground? How much sun do seeds need? And how much water? What if these seeds were wrapped in paper because they were sterile, or old? He worries the rust from his watering drum will foul the garden; he scrapes it as clean as he can with a wedge of slate.

Memories, too, volunteer themselves up: three charred corpses in the smoking wreck of a Mercedes, a black beetle crossing the back of a broken hand. The head of a boy kicked open and lying in red dust, Joseph's own mother pushing a barrow of compost, the muscles in her legs straining as she crosses the yard. For thirty-five years Joseph had envisioned a quiet, safe thread running through his life—a thread made for him, incontrovertible, assured. Trips to the market, trips to work, rice with cayenne for lunch, trim columns of numbers in his ledger: these were life, as regular and probable as the sun's rising. But in the end that thread turned out to be illusion—there was no rope, no guide, no truth to bind Joseph's life. He was a criminal; his mother was a gardener. Both of them turned out to be as mortal as anything else, the roses in her garden, whales in the sea.

Now, finally, he is remaking an order, a structure to his hours. It feels good, tending the soil, hauling water. It feels healthy.

○

In June the first green noses of his seedlings begin to show above the soil. When he wakes in the evening and sees them in the paling light, he feels his heart might burst. Within days the entire plot of ground, an unbroken black a week ago, is populated with small dashes of green. It is the greatest of miracles. He becomes convinced that some of the shoots—a dozen or so proud thumbs pointed at the sky—are zucchini plants. On his hands and knees he examines them through the scratched lenses of his glasses: the stalks are already separating into distinct blades, tiny platters of leaves poised to unfold. Are there zucchinis in there? Big shining vegetables carried somehow in the shoots? It doesn't seem possible.

He agonizes over what to do next. Should he water more, or less? Should he prune, mulch, heel in, make cuttings? Should he limb the surrounding trees, clear some of the bramble away to provide more light? He tries to remember what his mother had done, the mechanics of her gardening, but can only recall the way she stood, a fistful of weeds trailing from her fist, looking down at her plants as if they were children, gathered at her feet.

He finds a nest of fishing tackle washed up on the rocks, untangles the monofilament and coils it around a block of driftwood. Around the dull and rusty hook he sheathes an earthworm; he weights the line and lowers it into the sea from a ledge. Some nights he manages to hook a salmon, grab it around the tail and knock its head against a rock. In the moonlight he lays it on a flat stone and eviscerates it with a piece of oyster shell. The meat he roasts over a tiny fire and eats thoughtlessly, chewing as he scuttles back up the rocks, into the woods. He does not think of taste; he goes about eating in the same manner he might go about digging a hole: it is a job, vaguely troubling, hardly satisfying.

The mansion, like the garden, swings into life. Every night there are the sounds of parties: music, the clink of silver against china, laughter. He can smell their cigarettes, their fried potatoes, the gasoline of landscapers' weedeaters and tractors. Cars rotate through the driveway. One afternoon Twyman appears on the deck and begins firing a shotgun into the trees. He is dressed in shorts and dark socks and stumbles across the planks of the deck. He reloads the gun, shoulders it, fires. Joseph crouches against a trunk. Does he know? Has Twyman seen him out there? The shot tears through the leaves.

By mid-June the stems of his plants are inches high. When he sticks his face close he can see that several of the buds have separated into delicate flowers; what looked like a solid green shoot was actually a tightly folded blossom. He feels like shouting with joy. Because of their pale, toothed leaflets, he decides some of the seedlings might be tomatoes, so he tries to construct small trellises with sticks and vine, as his mother used to do with wire and string, upon which the plants might climb. When he finishes he picks his way down the hillside to the sea and kicks a depression in the dunes and sleeps.

An hour later he wakes to see a sneaker shuffle past, hardly ten yards away. Adrenaline rockets to the tips of his fingers. His heart riots inside his chest. The sneaker is small, clean, white. Its mate moves past him, dragging through the sand, moving toward the sea.

He could run. Or he could ambush the person, claw him to death or drown him or fill his throat with sand. He could rise screaming and improvise from there. But there is no time for anything—on his stomach he flattens himself as much as possible and hopes his shape in the darkness resembles driftwood, or a tangled mess of kelp.

But the sneakers do not slow. Their owner labors down the front of the dunes, stooped and straining, lugging in the basket of its arms what looks to Joseph like a pair of cinder blocks. When it crosses the tideline Joseph raises his head and makes out features: curly, unbound hair, small shoulders, thin ankles. A girl. There is something wrong with the way she carries her head, the way it lolls on her neck, the way her shoulders ride so low—she looks defeated, overcome. She stops often to rest; her legs strain beneath her as she muscles her load forward. Joseph lowers his eyes, feels the cool sand against his chin, and tries to calm his heartbeat. Above him the clouds have blown away, and the spray of stars sends a frail light onto the sea.

When he looks again the girl is a hundred feet away. In the surf she squats with what looks like a bight of rope and runs it through the holes in a cinder block—she seems to be lashing her wrist to it. As he watches she fastens one wrist to one block, the other to the other. Then she struggles to her feet, dragging the blocks and staggering into the water. Waves clap against her chest. The blocks drop into the water with heavy splashes. She goes to her knees, then to her back, and floats, arms pulled behind and under her, still affixed to the cinder blocks. The flux of water bears her up, then closes over her chin and she is gone.

Joseph understands: the cinder blocks will hold her down and she will drown.

He lets his forehead back down against the sand. There is only the sound of waves collapsing against the shore and that starlight, faint and clean, reflecting off the mica in the sand. It is the same all over the world, Joseph thinks, in the smallest hours of the night. He wonders what would have happened if he had decided to sleep elsewhere, if he had spent one more hour framing trellises in the garden, if his seedlings had failed to shoot. If he had never seen an ad in a newspaper. If his mother had not gone to market that day. Order, chance, fate: it does not matter what brought him here. The stars burn in their constellations. Beneath the surface of the ocean countless lives are being lived out every minute.

He runs down the dunes and dives into the water. She floats just below the waves, her eyes closed; her hair washed out in a fan. Her shoelaces, untied, drift in the current. Her arms disappear beneath her into the murk.

She is, Joseph realizes, Twyman's daughter.

He dives under and lifts one of the cinder blocks from the sand and frees her wrist. With his arms beneath her body, dragging the other block, he hauls her onto the sand. "Everything is okay," he tries to say, but his voice is unused and it cracks and the words do not come. For a long moment nothing happens. Goose pimples stand up on her throat and arms. Then she coughs and her eyes fly open. She scrambles up, one arm still tied to its anchor, and flails her feet. "Wait," Joseph says. "Wait." He reaches down and lifts the block and frees her wrist. She pulls back, terrified. Her lips tremble; her arms shake. He can see how young she is—maybe fifteen years old, small pearls in her earlobes, big eyes above pink, unmarked cheeks. Water pours from her jeans. Her shoelaces trail in the sand.

"Please," he says. "Don't." But she is already gone, running hard and fast over the slope of the dunes, in the direction of the house.

Joseph shivers; the ragged blanket he still wears over his shoulders drips. If she tells someone, he considers, there will be searches. Twyman will comb the woods with his shotgun; his guests will make a game of capturing the trespasser in the woods. He must not let them find the garden. He must find a new place to sleep, acres away from the house, a damp depression in a thicket or—better still—a hole in the ground. And he will stop making fires; he will eat only those things he is willing to eat cold. He will visit the garden only every third night, only in the darkest, deepest hours, carrying water to his plants, being careful to cover his tracks. . . .

Out on the sea the reflected stars quiver and shake. The crest of each wave is limned with light, a thousand white rivers running together—it is beautiful. It is, he thinks, the most beautiful thing he has ever seen. He watches, shivering, until the sun begins to color the sky behind him, then trots down the beach, into the forest.

◡

Four nights later: jazz, a woman on the porch making slow turns in the twilight, her skirt flaring out. Softly he creeps into his garden to weed, to yank out intruders. The music washes through the trees, piano, a saxophone. He strains to see the shoots standing up from the dirt. Blight—tiny bull's-eyes of rot—stains many of the leaves. A slug is chewing another shoot and a few of the plants have been cropped off at the ground. Over half the seedlings are dead or dying. He knows he should fence off the garden, spray the plants with something to protect them. He ought to construct a blind and stake out whatever is grazing the garden, scare it off or bludgeon it with the hoe. But he cannot—he can hardly afford the luxury of weed pulling. Everything must be done softly, must be made to look untended.

No longer does he go down to the shore or cross the lawns of the estate—they make him feel exposed, naked. He prefers the cover of the woods, the towering firs, the patches of giant clover and groves of maples; here is just one of many, here he is small.

○

With a flashlight she begins searching the woods at night. He knows it is she because he has hidden in a hollowed nurse log and waited for her to pass; first the light swinging frantically through the ferns, then her pinched, scared face, eyes unblinking. She moves noisily, snapping twigs, breathing hard on the hills. But she is determined; her light prowls the woods, ranges over the dunes, hurries across the lawn. Every night for a week he watches the light drifting across the property like a displaced star.

Once, in a moment of courage, he calls hello, but she doesn't hear. She continues on, stepping down through the dark shapes of the trees, the noise of her passage and the beam of the light growing fainter until they finally disappear.

○

On a stump not a hundred yards from his garden she begins leaving food: a tuna sandwich, a bag of carrots, a napkin full of chips. He eats them but feels slightly guilty about it, as if he's cheating, as if it's unfair that she's making it easier for him.

After another week of midnights, watching her blunder through the forest, he cannot stand it anymore and places himself in the field of her light. She stops. Her eyes, already wide, widen. She switches off her flashlight and sets it in the leaves. A pale fog hovers in the branches. They have a sort of standoff. The girl does not seem threatened although she keeps her hands just off her hips like a gunfighter.

Then she begins to move her arms in a short, intricate dance, striking the palm of one hand with the edge of the other, circling her fingers through the air, touching her right ear, finally pointing both index fingers at Joseph.

He does not know what to make of it. Her fingers repeat the dance: her hands draw a circle; the palms turn up; the fingers lock. Her lips move but no sound comes out. There is a large silver watch on her wrist which rides up and down her forearm as she gesticulates.

"I don't understand." His voice cracks from disuse. He waves toward the house. "Go away. I'm sorry. You must not come through here anymore. Someone will come looking for you." But the girl is running through the routine a third time, rolling her hand, tapping her chest, moving her lips in silence.

And then Joseph sees; he places his hands over his ears. The girl nods.

"You cannot hear?" She shakes her head. "But you know what I say? You understand?" She nods again. She points to her lips, then opens her hands like a book: lip-reading.

She pulls a notebook from her shirt and opens it. With a pencil hung around her neck, she scribbles. She holds the page out. In the dimness he reads: *How do you live?*

"I eat what I can. I sleep in the leaves. I have all I need. Please go home, Miss. Go to bed."

I won't tell, she writes.

When she leaves he watches the light bob and sweep until it becomes just a spark, a firefly spiraling through the gloom. He is surprised when he realizes it makes him lonely, watching the light fade, as if, although he told her to go, he had hoped she would stay.

⌣

Two nights later, full moon, her light is back, wobbling through the forest. He knows he should leave; he should start walking north and not stop until he is a hundred miles into Canada. Instead he paces through the leaves, finally goes to her. She is wearing jeans, a hooded sweatshirt, a knapsack over her shoulders. She switches off the light as before. Moonlight spills over the boughs, sends a patchwork of shadows shifting over their shoulders. He leads her through the bramble, past the verbena, to a ledge overlooking the sea. At the horizon a lone freighter blinks its tiny light.

"I almost did it too," he says. "The thing you tried to do." She holds her hands before her like two thin and pale birds. "I was leaning over the bow of a tanker, looking down at the waves a hundred feet below. We were in the middle of the ocean. All I needed to do was push with my feet and I would have gone over."

She writes in her pad. *I thought you were an angel. I thought you had come to take me to heaven.*

"No," Joseph says. "No." She looks at him, looks away. *Why did you come back?* she writes. *After you got fired?*

The light of the ship begins to fade. "Because it's beautiful here," he says. "Because I had nowhere else to go."

⌣

A night later they again face each other in the dimness. Her hands flutter in front of her, rolling in loops, rising to her neck, her eyes. She touches an elbow, points at him.

"I'm going for water," he says. "You can come if you like."

She follows him down through the forest until they reach the stream. He leans over a lichened rock, finds his rusty drum, and fills it. They climb back through the ferns and moss and deadfall to the top of the hill. He pulls aside some cut boughs of spruce.

"This is my garden," he says, and steps in among the plants, tendrils clinging greenly to their trellises, creepers running out over the bare soil. In the air there is the fragrance of earth and leaf and sea. "This is why I came back. I needed to do this. It's why I stay."

☽

In the nights to come she visits the garden and they crouch among the plants. She brings him a blanket and a baguette he reluctantly chews. She brings him a book of sign language—several thousand cartoon drawings of hands, each with a word beneath. There are hands above *tree,* hands above *bicycle,* hands above *house.* He studies the pages, wonders how anyone could ever learn all the signs. Her name is Belle, he learns: he practices making it in the air with his long, clumsy fingers.

He teaches her to find pests—slugs, iridescent beetles, aphids, tiny red spider mites—and crush them between her fingers. Some of the vines have grown knee high; they range across the soil; rain pops against the leaves. "What is it like?" he asks her. "Is it very quiet? Is it silent?" She doesn't see him speak or else chooses not to answer. She sits and stares down at the house.

She brings a plant food that they mix with creek water and pour over the rows. Each time she leaves he finds himself watching her go, her body moving down through the trees, finally appearing down on the lawn, a dim silhouette slipping back into the house.

Some nights, sitting among ferns far from the garden, watching headlights creep down 101 in the distance, he clamps his palms over his ears and tries to imagine what it must be like. He shuts his eyes, tries to quiet himself. For a moment he thinks he has it; a kind of void, a nothingness, an oblivion. But it doesn't—it cannot—last; there is always noise, the flux and murmur of his body's machinery, a hum in his head. His heart beats and flexes in its cage. His body, in those moments, sounds to him like an orchestra, a rock band, an entire prison of inmates crowded into one cell. What must it be like to not hear that? To never know even the whisper of your own pulse?

⌣

The garden explodes into life; Joseph gets the impression it would grow even if the world was plunged into permanent darkness. Each night there are changes; clusters of green spheres materialize and swell on the tomato stems; yellow flowers emerge from the vines like burning lamps. He begins to wonder if the large, bushy creepers are zucchini after all—maybe they are squash, some kind of gourds.

But they are melons. Days later he and Belle find six pale spheres sitting in the soil under the broad leaves. Each night they seem to grow larger, drawing more mass from the earth. They nearly glow in the midnight. He cakes their flanks with mud, patting them down, hiding them. He coats the tomatoes, too—it seems to him that their pale yellows and reds must shine like beacons, easily visible from the lawns of the estate, too outrageous to miss.

⌣

She is in the garden, sitting and staring down at the house, and he leaves the cover of the forest to join her. He taps her shoulder and makes the sign for night, and the sign for how are you. Her face brightens; her fingers flash a response.

"Slow down, slow down," laughs Joseph. "Good night was as far as I got."

She smiles, stands, brushes off her knees. She's written something on her pad: *Something to show you.* From her knapsack she takes a map and unfolds it over the dirt. It is worn along its creases and very soft. When he takes the whole thing in, he can see that it is a map of the entire Pacific Coast of the Americas, beginning with Alaska and ending at Tierra del Fuego.

Belle points at herself, then the map. She draws her finger down a series of highways, all north-south, that she has highlighted in color. Then she places her hands on an imaginary steering wheel and mimes driving a car.

"You want to drive this? You are going to drive this far?"

Yes, she nods. Yes. She leans forward and with her pencil, writes, *When I turn sixteen I get a Volkswagen. From my father.*

"Can you even drive?"

She shakes her head, holds up ten fingers, then six. *When I'm sixteen.*

He studies the map awhile. "Why? I don't get it."

She looks away. She makes a series of signs he does not know. On the paper she writes, *I want to leave,* and underlines it furiously. The tip of the pencil breaks.

"Belle," Joseph says. "No one could drive that far. There probably aren't even roads the whole way." She is looking at him; her mouth hangs open.

"You are, what, fifteen years old? You cannot drive to South America. You would be kidnapped. You would run out of petrol." He laughs, then, and puts his hand over his mouth. After a moment he begins to work, his fingers prying a leaf miner from the underside of a melon. Belle studies her map in the paling light.

When he looks up she is gone, her light moving quickly down the hillside, disappearing. He watches the thin shape of her hurry across the lawn.

⌣

She stops coming into the woods. As far as he can tell, she stops going outside altogether. Maybe she uses the front door, he thinks. He wonders how long she'd harbored that strange dream—to drive from Oregon to Tierra del Fuego, alone, a deaf girl.

A week passes and Joseph finds himself crouching beside the trail to the beach, sleeping on the fringes of the dunes, waking several times in the afternoon and wandering in a circle, his heart quick-beating. After dawn he studies the sign language book, working his fingers into knots, his hands aching, admiring in his memory the precision of Belle's signing, the abrupt dips, the way her hands pour together like liquid, then stop, then worry and gnash like the teeth of gears grinding. He never imagined the body could be so eloquent.

But he is learning. It is as if he is learning all over again how to put the world into words. A tree is an open hand shaken twice by your right ear; whale is three fingers dipped through a sea made by the opposite forearm. The sky is two hands touched above the head, then swept apart, as though a rift has formed in the clouds and you are swimming through them, into heaven.

☽

Thunder over the ocean, ravens screaming in the high branches. A little longer, Joseph thinks. The tomatoes will be ready. It begins to rain—cold, earnest drops fly through the boughs. He has not seen Belle in two weeks when he finds her in the garden, wearing a blue raincoat, stooped among the rows of plants, yanking weeds from the ground and hurling them into the brambles. The drops pop off her shoulders. He watches for a moment. Lightning strobes the sky. Rain runs off the end of her nose.

He steps in among the plants, the tomatoes weighing dreamily on their stems, the melons a pale green against the gray mud on their flanks. He pulls a thin weed and shakes the mud from its roots. "Last year," he says, "whales died here. On the beach. Six of them. Whales have their own language, clicks and creaks and clinking like bottles being smashed together. On the beach they talked to each other as they died. Like old ladies."

She shakes her head. Her eyes are red. I'm sorry, he signs.

Please. He says, "I was stupid. Your idea is not any more strange than probably every idea I have ever had."

After a moment he adds, "I buried the hearts from the whales in the forest." He makes the sign for heart over his chest.

She looks at him, canting her head. Her face softens. What? she signs.

"I buried them here." He wants to say more, wants to tell her the whales' story. But does he even know it? Does he even know why they came ashore, what they do when they don't come ashore? What happens to the bodies of whales which do not strand—do they wash up, rolling in the surf one day, rotten and bloated? Do they sink? Are their bodies mulled over at the bottom of the oceans where some strange, deepwater garden can grow up through their bones?

She studies him, her hands spread in the dirt. It's her attention, he thinks. The way she fixes me with her eyes. The way I feel like she's listening all the time, enwombed in that impenetrable silence. Her pale fingers browse among the stems, a raindrop slips down the curve of a green tomato, he has a sudden need to tell her everything. All his petty crimes, the way his mother left for the market in the morning while he *slept*—a hundred confessions surge through him. He has been waiting too long; the words have been building behind a dyke and now the dyke is breached and the river is slipping its banks. He wants to tell her what he has learned about the miracles of light, the way a day's light fluxes in tides: pale and gleaming at dawn, the glare of noon, the gold of evening, the promise of twilight— every second of every day has its own magic. He wants to tell her that when things vanish they become something else, in death we rise again in the blades of grass, the splitting bodies of seeds. But his past is flooding out: the dictionary, the ledger, his mother, the horrors he has seen.

"I had a mother," he says. "She disappeared." He cannot tell if Belle is reading his lips; she is looking away, lifting a tomato and scraping some mud from its underside, letting it back down. Joseph squats in front of her. The storm stirs the trees.

"She had a garden. Like this but nicer. More . . . orderly."

He realizes he does not know how to talk about his mother; he has no words for it. "For years I stole money," he says. He is not sure she understands. Rain pours over his glasses. "And I killed a man." She looks over the top of his head and makes no sign.

"I did not even know who he was or if he was the man they said he was. But I killed him."

Now Belle looks at him with her forehead creased as if in fear and Joseph cannot bear the look but he cannot stop either. There are so many things to give words to: how beached whales smother themselves with the black cannons of their own bodies, the songs of the forest, starlight limning the crests of waves, the way his mother bent in furrows to scatter seeds. He wants to use hand signs that will remake them; he wants her to see his poor, sordid histories reassembled out of the darkness. Every corpse he passed and left unburied; the body of the man slumped on the tennis court; the stolen junk locked even now in the cellar of his mother's house.

Instead he speaks of the whales. "One of the whales," he says, "lived longer than the others. People were tearing skin and fat from the dead one beside it. It watched them do it with its big brown eye and in the end it beat the beach with its flippers, slapping the sand. I was as far away as the house is from us right now and I could feel the ground shaking."

Belle is looking at him, a dirty tomato in her palm. Joseph is on his knees. Tears are flooding his eyes.

☽

A ripening: one last warm day, a half dozen tanagers poised on a branch like golden flowers, a leaning of tomatoes to the sun. The silk of the melon flowers seem infused with light; any moment they could burst into flame. Joseph watches Belle fight on the lawn with her mother—they are returning from the beach. Belle slashes the air with her hands. Her mother flings down her beach chair, signs something back. Does the girl, Joseph wonders, carry her secrets deep within her? Or do they sit on the edges of her fingertips, ready to fly into language, ready to sign to her mother? *The African you fired lives in the woods. He embezzled money and killed a man.* Do secrets boil inside her like steam in a kettle? Or do they settle like seeds, waiting to open until the time is right? No, Joseph thinks, Belle understands. She has kept her secrets far better than I've kept mine.

He smells the sweet fruit of a tomato, pink now with a swatch of yellow on one side, and the aroma is almost too much to bear.

○

But in the morning he is discovered. It is just dawn and he is tearing mussels from the rocks and placing them in his rusted drum when a figure appears atop the dunes. Bars of light break through the trees and then—as if the sun conspired to give him away—a single ray fixes him against the water. Behind the figure appear several others; they tumble down the dunes, wading in the loose sand, laughing toward him.

They are carrying drinks and their voices sound drunken and he considers dumping his drum and turning and swimming out to sea to be swept away in some current and dashed forever against the rocks of a faraway place. When they get close to him they stop. Twyman's wife is with them and she walks right to him—her face flushed and twitching—and throws her drink against his chest and screams.

He does not think to get rid of the book of hand signs and when they see it tucked inside the waistband of his trousers things become more serious. Mrs. Twyman turns the book over in her hands and shakes her head and seems unable to speak. "Where did he get that?" the others say. Two men move to flank him, their faces quivering, their fists clenched.

They take him over the dunes, up the trail and across the lawn, past the garage where he lived, the shed he raided for his hoe and seeds. There is no sign of Belle. Mr. Twyman charges out of the house shirtless, hitching up his sweatpants. The words tangle inside him. "The nerve," he spits. "The *nerve.*"

There is the sound of sirens, far off. From the lawn Joseph tries to make out the spot atop the hill where the garden is, a small break in a bulwark of spruce, but there is only a smear of green, and soon they are pushing him forward into the house and there is nothing at all to see, only the massive dining table strewn with dishes and half-empty drinks and the faces all around him, spitting questions.

☽

They drive him, handcuffed, to Bandon and place him in an office with antique sirens and plastic softball trophies along the shelves. Two policemen sit on the edge of a desk and take turns repeating questions. They ask what he did with the girl, why, where they went. Twyman rages somewhere in the building: Joseph cannot hear the words but only the cracking of Twyman's voice as it reaches its limits. The policemen on the desk are blank-faced, leaning in.

"What did you eat? Did you eat anything? You don't look like you've eaten at all." "How much time did you spend with the girl? Where did you take her?" "Why don't you speak to us? We can make it easier for you." They ask for the fiftieth time how he got the book of sign language. I'm a gardener, he wants to tell them. Leave me be. But he says nothing.

They lock him in a cell where the texture has been painted off of everything—the cinder block walls, the floor, the frame of the cot, the bars in the window, all rounded over with coats of paint. Only the sink and toilet are unpainted, the curling design of a thousand scrubbings worked into the steel. The window looks onto a brick wall fifteen or so feet away. A naked bulb hangs from the ceiling, too high to reach. Even at night it burns, a tiny, unnatural sun.

He sits on the floor and imagines weeds overwhelming the garden, their blades hauling down the tomato plants, their interloping roots curling through whatever is left of the whales' hearts. He imagines the tomatoes blooming into full ripeness, drooping from the vines, black spots opening like burns on their sides, finally falling, eaten hollow by flies. The melons turning over and crumpling. Platoons of ants tunneling through rinds, bearing off shining chunks of fruit. In a year the garden will be nothing but salmonberry and nettle, no different than anywhere else, nothing to tell its story.

He wonders where Belle is. He hopes she is far away and tries to picture her behind the wheel of a Volkswagen, a forearm on the sill, some southern highway unrolling before her, the wide fields of the sea coming into view as she rounds a bend.

꙰

He does not eat the peanut butter sandwiches they slide under the bars. After two days the marshal stands at the bars and asks if he wants something else. Joseph shakes his head.

"A body has to eat," the marshal declares. He slides a pack of crackers through. "Eat these. You'll feel better."

Joseph does not. It is not protest or sickness, as the policemen seem to think. It is merely the idea of eating that makes him queasy, the idea of mashing food in his teeth and forcing lumps of it down his throat. He sets the crackers beside the sandwiches, on the rim of the sink.

The marshal watches him a full minute before turning to go. "You know," he says, "I'll put you in the hospital and you can die there."

A lawyer tries to coerce a story out of him. "What did you do in Liberia? These people think you're dangerous—they're saying you're retarded. Are you? Why won't you speak?" There is no fight in Joseph, no anger, no outrage at injustice. He is not guilty of their crimes but he is guilty of so many others. There has never been a man guilty of so much, he thinks, a man more deserving of penalty. "Guilty!" he wants to scream. "I have been guilty all my life." But he has no energy. He shifts and feels his bones settling against the floor. The lawyer, exasperated, departs.

There are no more gates within him, no more divisions. It is as if everything he has done in his life has pooled together inside him and slops dully against his edges. His mother, the man he has killed, the languishing garden—he will never be able to live it down, never live through it, never live enough to compensate for all the things he has stolen.

Two more days without food and he is taken to a hospital—they carry him like his skin is a bag inside which his bones knock together. He can remember only the dull pain of knuckles on his sternum. He wakes in a room, propped on a bed, with tubes plugged into his arms.

In half-dreams he sees terrible visions: the limbless bodies of men materialized on the bureau or the corner chair; the floor lined with corpses in the unnatural poses of death, flies on their eyes, dried blood in their ears. Sometimes when he wakes he sees the man he has killed kneeling on the foot of the bed, his blue beret in his lap, his arms still tied behind his back. The wound in his forehead is fresh, a drill hole rimmed in black, his eyes open. "I have never even *been* in an airplane," he says. Any minute now a nurse will come into the room and see the dead man kneeling on the foot of the bed and that will be it. Finally, Joseph thinks, I must pay for it.

There are other visitors: Mrs. Twyman in the corner chair, her thin arms crossed over her chest. Her eyes are on his; purple stains like bruises throb beneath her eye sockets. "What?" she screams. "What?" And Belle comes, or what might have been Belle—Joseph wakes and remembers her sliding open the window, pointing at gulls on the Dumpsters. But he does not know if he dreamed it, if she is on her way to Argentina, if she even thinks of him. His window is closed, the curtains drawn. When the nurse opens it he can see there are no Dumpsters, just lawn, a parking lot.

Another week or so and a lawyer comes, a clean-shaven pink man with acne around his collar. He reads to Joseph from a newspaper article that says Liberia has held democratic elections; Charles Taylor is the new president, the war is over, refugees are flooding back. "You are to be deported, Mr. Saleeby," he says. "It's very very good for you. The tools you stole and the trespassing—the court will drop these things. Negligence and the accusations of abuse are dropped too. You're absolved, Mr. Saleeby. Free."

Joseph leans back in his bed and realizes that he does not care.

⌣

A nurse announces a visitor. She has to help him from the bed and when he stands black spots fill his vision. She folds him into a wheelchair and carts him down the hall and out a side door into a small fenced courtyard.

It is so bright Joseph feels as if his head might crack open. She wheels him to a picnic table in the center of the lawn, fringed by a fence, with cars parked in a lot behind it, and returns the way she came. Joseph strains his eyes toward the sky; it is dazzling, a seething bowl of clouds. A bank of trees beyond the lot tosses in the wind—half the leaves are down and the branches swing together. It is autumn, he realizes. He imagines the blackened, withered roots of his garden, the shriveled tomatoes and wrinkled leaves, a frost paralyzing everything. He wonders if this is where they'll leave him, finally, to die. The nurse will return in a few days, empty him from the chair and bury what's left, the leather of his skin pulling back, the black seed of his heart giving way, the bones settling into the earth.

A door opens into the courtyard and from the doorway steps Belle. She has her knapsack over her shoulders and she walks toward Joseph with a shy smile and seats herself at the picnic table. Beneath the collar of her windbreaker he can see the strap of her shirt, a pale collarbone, a trio of freckles above it. The wind lifts strands of her hair and sets them back down.

He holds his head in his hands and studies her and she studies him. She makes the sign for how are you and Joseph tries to make it back. They smile and sit. Sun winks off the cars in the lot. "Is this real?" Joseph asks. Belle cocks her head. "Are you real? Am I awake?" She squints and nods as if to say, of course. She points over her shoulder, at the parking lot. I drove here, she signs. Joseph says nothing but smiles and props his head in his hands because his neck will not hold it up.

Then she seems to remember why she has come and takes the knapsack from her shoulder and produces two melons, which she sets on the table between them. Joseph looks at her with his eyes wide. "Are those . . . ?" he asks. She nods. He takes one of the melons in his hands. It is heavy and cool; he raps his knuckles against it.

Belle takes a penknife from the pocket of her windbreaker and stabs the other melon, cutting in an arc across its diameter, and when, with a tiny sound of yielding, the melon splits into two hemispheres, a sweet smell washes up. In the wet, stringy cup within are dozens of seeds.

Joseph scoops them out and spreads them over the wood of the table, each white and marbled with pulp and perfect. They shine in the sun. The girl saws a wedge from one of the halves. The flesh is wet and shining and Joseph cannot believe the color—it is as if the melon carried light within it. They each lift a chunk of it to their lips and eat. It seems to him that he can taste the forest, the trees, the storms of the winter and the size of the whales, the stars and the wind. A tiny gob of melon slides down Belle's chin. Her eyes are closed. When they open she sees him and her mouth splits into a smile.

They eat and eat and Joseph feels the wet pulp of the melon slipping down his throat. His hands and lips are sticky. Joy mounts in his chest; any moment his whole body could dissolve into light.

They eat the second melon too, again taking the seeds from the core and spreading them over the table to dry. When they are done they divide the seeds and the girl wraps each half in a piece of notebook paper and they put the damp packets of seeds in their pockets.

Joseph sits and feels the sun come down on his skin. His head feels weightless, as though it would float away if not for his neck. He thinks: If I had to do it over again, I'd bury the whole whales. I'd sow the ground with bucketfuls of seeds—not just tomatoes and melons, but pumpkins and beans and potatoes and broccoli and maize. I'd fill the beds of a hundred dumptrucks with seeds. Huge gardens would come up. I'd make a garden so huge and colorful everyone would see it; I'd let the weeds grow and the ivy, everything would grow, everything would get its chance.

Belle is crying. He takes her hands and holds her thin, articulate fingers against his own. He wonders if the dust has piled up against the walls of the house in the hills outside Monrovia. He wonders if hummingbirds still flit between the cups of the flowers, if by some miracle his mother could be there, kneeling in the soil, if they could work together cleaning away the dust, sweeping, brooming it up, carrying it out the door and pitching it into the yard, watching it unfurl in great rust-colored clouds, to be taken up by the wind and scattered somewhere else.

"Thank you," he says, but cannot be sure if he says it aloud. The clouds split and the sky brims over with light—it pours onto them, glazing the surface of the picnic table, the backs of their hands, the wet, carved bowls of the melon rinds. Everything feels very tenuous, just then, and terribly beautiful, as if he is straddling two worlds, the one he came from and the one he is going to. He wonders if this is what it was like for his mother, in the moments before she died, if she saw the same kind of light, if she felt like anything was possible.

Belle has reclaimed her hands and is pointing somewhere far off, somewhere over the horizon. Home, she signs. You are going home.

A Tangle by the Rapid River

Mulligan gathers his things: his fly rod, a coffee-browned thermos, Ziplocs plumped with potato sticks, deer jerky, ginger-snaps, extra socks in a knapsack. A fly box from the basement. Breakfast: sausage sizzled in oil, two slabs of pumpernickel slathered with margarine, coffee in a chipped mug. He chews in the worn door frame between the kitchen and bedroom and watches his wife sleep. Her bulk rounded under blankets. Her gray undergarments on the wooden chair. Ever since their first night she has slept like this, like an ox. Since that fine and giddy wedding night, when he held her long after she slept, and told her things and she did not wake up. He told her once that it was as if some huntsman with his hounds comes to drag her into the night and hold her until dawn. Some wraithy night huntsman with slaverous hounds on tethers. Mulligan says her name. She sleeps her hard vacant sleep. Before he leaves he stokes the fire.

In the lane, above the walnut trees, the moon floats halved and white, a cold-bleached fossil. Shreds of cloud scud out to sea. Overnight, it seems, autumn was ridden out of the trees, the branches stripped, the yard buried under leaves. Mulligan chews a stalk of brown grass, unlocks the frosty truck cab. This, he thinks, might as well be winter: stony skies, crows tearing apart old trees, the ravening questions of owls, the round faces of ponds filmed with ice. Soon the trout and salmon will retreat to deepest pools and hang over the pebbled bottoms, motionless, unblinking, while the river kinks in ice-bound channels and freezes above them. Mulligan will retreat too, putter in his basement, tie flies by lamplight.

The truck moves sluggishly, the fuel thick, the high beams yellow and feeble. The highway is wet and shadowed. The long slow splashing and headlight glare and the wet severed trunks on the bed of a lumber truck grinding up the highway are the only things about, and a family of starlings, wing to wing on a split rail. One of them on one leg. Their eyes calm in the sweep of headlights.

At Weatherbee's Convenience by four-thirty, Mulligan stands in the harlequin light amid stacked glossies, shelved candy, cigarette packs, lotto tickets in silver rolls, discount milk signs. Little bells ribboned to the door jingle. The slushee machine makes its slow pink churn. He fills his thermos with Weatherbee's stale coffee, sets a newspaper and coins on the counter where Weatherbee sleeps on his elbows.

Weatherbee blinks, dry-eyed, coming back from a long way off. You?

Mulligan nods.

Like a goddamn alarm clock.

When you get to be my age, Mulligan says, sleep is not so different from being awake. You just kind of shut your eyes and you're there.

Weatherbee grinds his palms into his eyes. Fishing the Rapid again?

Thought I'd try.

You go up there every day. With a newspaper and a coffee.

Mulligan shrugs, his eyes already out the door. I don't know. Most every day. I'm going today.

Weatherbee wipes the counter and yawns. I thought retirement was for sleeping, he says. The door levers shut behind Mulligan.

The post office is dark, the windows shut, one short light, a fragile filament cast across rows of brass mailboxes. A lumber truck splashes down the highway. Mulligan walks to a post box, unlocks it and peers inside. One letter. Thick paper, and smooth. He slips it into his shirt pocket. From a zippered pocket in his jacket he takes another letter, addressed with his own tiny printing. He sets this letter in the post box, closes it and goes out.

He points the truck into the hills, the flanks of naked tree slopes, the fallen leaves beginning their slow slide into the earth, a few stars fading behind ropes of cloud. The pocked and mudded logging roads—four unmarked turns, fording a stone-choked creek and the truck gurgling, warming, pressing over slick clay, beneath the clear-cut hillsides, stacks of limbless birch in bound rolls on the road flanks and hacked from the dim tangle of woods, savage mudferns and rust-stalked blackberry—end in a small clay clearing, where the noses of granite boulders peek from the earth, where fishermen park. His is the first truck.

He pulls on his waders, fits his rod and reel, and leans it against the truckcab. He stuffs his knapsack with the Ziplocked jerky, gingersnaps, potato sticks, extra socks, and the newspaper. He zips the fly box into his vest, pulls a wool cap over his head. Then he sits a moment, breathes, and his breath fogs the windshield. A cloud stretches over the moon.

His fingers find the letter in his shirt pocket, the thick paper, the smooth envelope. He puts on his reading glasses, opens the letter, finds a flattened flower. In the stale cablight, the ignition buzzing, he reads the round cursive:

Dearest Mulligan,

It could hardly be more confusing. You say you feel the same way as I, yet you glide along with your life, your fishing—and her—as if all was well and good and this were normal. But all is not well! This secrecy wears at me. These letters we trade in a post office box, the harried days when she thinks you are fishing, when half of you is at the river anyway, these are not enough, not nearly enough. I am addicted to you, I think. Maybe I am greedy, maybe wanting you all for myself is selfish. Isn't love real, Mully, or was that a lie, too?

Oh, I don't know, maybe I will wait forever, you do make me happy. You and your quiet shyness. Your thoughtfulness. I am feeling so poorly and there was only your letter that said you are really going to the river today and now I think I know what longing truly is. My body aches. It is time you made a choice.

P.S. If you married me and left to go fishing, would you really go fishing?

He folds the flower into the card and the card back into the envelope and slides the envelope into the newspaper inside his pack and locks the truck. He walks to the river then, plunging along the mazed and moss-bottomed trail through thickets, weeds, brambles, fungus-wrapped trunks, down a sodden ravine where the earth sucks at his boots and flings round drops of mud onto his wader legs. The carpet of the forest is clotted with leaves; more sail down as he steps. There is rhythm to it: the tip of his fly rod jouncing, his boots stepping, spent leaves drifting, the river's whisper from the depths of the woods.

Mulligan plunges through a last thicket. On the bank, beside the Rapid River pouring along, sleek and glazed and black, he feels an old feeling, the irresistible tug of moving water and his blood trundling with it and a kind of joy splits his lips. He stands on the bank, his breath tossing clouds, and by penlight reads the letter again, fingers its edges, slides it back inside the folded newspaper. The clouds have piled up in the west, and soon the last stars are gone. The blotted moon offers a film of light. He ties a Hairwing to his tippet, wades into the river and fishes.

Before long he sees the penlights of other fishers, upstream, over his right shoulder, but it is not so hard to pretend he is alone. With numb fingers he keeps his line tailored so that his fly does not skate or slide but simply drifts and he runs his fly where few fishermen can.

Daybreak comes silently and simply with no more than a thin hem of pink and he is a little disappointed in it, because there is none of the glory of an August sunrise and soon the light around him is gray and day is begun. The tea-colored river purls around his waders, thick and clingy, the way river water gets when it is cold. Upstream the other fishers work their stretches of river, roll-casting to the opposite bank, a bearded man with a cigarette on his lip and another farther up.

But there is plenty of water, Mulligan thinks, and plenty of fish. He works carefully downstream, takes his time, casts to each pool, runs his fly around every boulder, searches under branches and in eddies across the river. He knows where every golden and weeded stone is placed and how the river threads over it.

But he doesn't. There are places he doesn't know, new places, innumerable tiny changes: a clot of submerged timber, a place where the river has undercut the bank and caved it. Clumps of leaves in several spots where he thought the water ran faster. He has not been here in weeks and it hurts him to know the river has poured on without him.

Around eleven the clouds thin slightly, and the sun tracking in its blue and windy space angles in weakly and lights the hills and muddy clear-cut to the east. The wind heaves; the birches rattle. Mulligan steps numb-legged out of the river and kicks each foot to warm it. He opens his knapsack and pours himself some of Weatherbee's coffee. He chews a gingersnap awhile, but it is dry and the coffee is much better. He unfolds his newspaper and sits against the lichened trunk of a birch to read, but instead sits and feels the coffee warm his stomach and watches yellow leaves shuttle downriver and makes wagers with himself about which leaves will pass him first and which will be trapped in eddy or snag. It brings him pleasure when the river funnels a leaf well and quickly, delivering it downstream without complication. Everything runs into the river, he thinks. Not just the leaves, but beetle corpses and heron bones and expired worms. Everything that starts on the hills eventually slides into the river. And the river spills it into the sea. Only the fish do it backward and he loves them for it.

He shivers a bit. The air is thin, cold, hard to breathe. It smells like beaten tin, like snow. It is early for snow and it makes him uneasy. He sits against the tree and crosses his wrists in his lap. A swallowtail, born too late, alights frantically on a thistle and pauses, flexing its wings. Mulligan blows gently and it flies, wandering dangerously low over the river, and is gone.

There are the tiny splashes and sucks of the river and he drifts into a shallow kind of sleep. The river threads over the stones and the wind breathes through the moss-mantled branches and the clouds skate over the hills in heaps. In his sleep he does not dream but on the underside of his eyelids he sees his wife, fisting bread dough and planting it in a buttered bowl. His wife bends, and he sees her wide back, her rotten ankles, her floured wrists. She covers the dough with a towel so it can plump.

When Mulligan looks up two people are standing over him.

Hey, they say. How is it, Mully?

Nothing yet. I can see them. Mostly undercuts. They aren't eating a whole lot. Maybe it's too cold.

The others nod. One is the bearded man with the cigarette. He looks into the river, squints, scratches his cheek. The other is a woman, thick and with a hard look to her. She is the niece of Mulligan's wife. A woman who fishes, hunts and gambles.

No maybes about it, she says. Her voice is loud and it makes Mulligan wince, a voice like that echoing along the river. She squats beside him, pries open one of his Ziplocs and tears herself a sinewy strip of jerky. My damn feet are froze.

The bearded man nods. Frost this morning, he adds. Snow tonight.

The niece chews jerky, runs her big-pupiled eyes over his things.

Did you see the swallowtail? Mulligan asks.

Swallowtail?

The butterfly. I saw a swallowtail.

The bearded man gives the niece a look.

How's my aunt? the niece barks. There is jerky in her teeth.

Mulligan wants to be rid of them. Well, he says. Fine.

The niece grabs the bag of gingersnaps. And you, Mully? How's retirement?

Fine. Fine and good.

I thought I'd see you here every day. You fishing somewhere else? Or my aunt putting you to work?

I don't know.

You're a softie, Mully, she says. Always have been.

You can have the cookies. If you want.

Her eyes fix him. The bearded one lights a cigarette. You don't want them? she asks. Her hand roots in the bag.

Mulligan shakes his head, looks down at his vest, runs a zipper on a pouch up and down. He wishes hard that they would leave him. The niece takes up the newspaper, folds a page back and says, Just need to see about the races. Mulligan is cold. They didn't believe him about the butterfly but he saw it.

Take that too, he says.

I just need to look for one second.

Take it. I'm not gonna read it. Mulligan wishes they would leave. It was nice sitting against the birch trunk and he does not like the smell of cigarettes or the loudness of the niece's voice.

We'll probably try below Middle Dam, the bearded man says. Mulligan nods, will not meet their eyes. The niece stands, rubs her palms along the thighs of her waders, then folds the newspaper into a rough square and wedges it under her arm.

Through half-chewed gingersnaps she spits, We'll holler if we get something.

Okay.

Something worth hollering about.

All right.

The bearded fisherman exhales smoke and gives a wave as they leave, ducking along the trail downstream, their boots shaking the moss knitted over the undercut roots of trees. Riddance, Mulligan faintly mumbles. He sits against the tree and sips his coffee, which has gone cold. He feels a bit unsteady. He thinks he can maybe feel the entire planet making its slow turn, and the roots of trees scrabbling around bedrock, and the clouds curling over the hills. Finally he takes his rod and wades back in.

It is afternoon, three or four, and he has been casting awhile, alone except for a pair of ravens who sweep and shout over the trees, when he gets his first fish. It is a sluggish strike, on a beaded nymph Mulligan had run through the same gravel pool ten times or more. The fish fights for its life, makes one jump and then Mulligan nets it, wets his hand and holds it. A red-flecked salmon, male, with a mean blunted head, black-eyed. The lower jaw beginning to develop its breeding hook. Its body jackknifes in his hand.

Mulligan holds it in the river, strokes its flanks and releases it. The fish sinks, turns over, then bursts away. Mulligan checks his knot and feels the energy run out of him, that tightness that always comes when he has a fish. It is not until he begins to cast again that he remembers, with a jolt, the letter tucked into the newspaper that he no longer has.

He splashes onto the rocks and the river pours off his waders and with trembling hands he snatches his knapsack and begins to stumble-run along the tangled riverbank. The blood is all out of his face. His feet are numb and they betray him, lifting too slowly over roots, thudding into fallen and rotten logs. It is like running with weights lashed to his ankles. He scrambles into the ravine and falls; his fists disappear in black mud. He struggles to his feet but wells of peat clutch his boots. Brambles grab for his waders. Seed thistles explode across his shins. He runs up the trail and the deep wood grasps at him, turns on him, fattens his terror, the tiny and once-lovely kingdoms now black and terrible, thin needles slipped through his ribs.

The path unspools much too slowly. His fly rod snags on brambles, the fly line is suddenly, immediately, miserably tangled, how do such things happen, how do such horrific tangles suddenly emerge from thin straight lines? He stops and blood howls in his ears. He pulls at his reel, but the line only cinches down more tightly and it seems the line is wrapped around an entire snarl of blackberry; plump thorns like the teeth of sharks hold it fast.

His shoulders slump. He squints ahead into the inscrutable thicket. Then he sits in the cold mud of the narrow fishermen's trail and works at the line, easing it free of barbs one by one. The heaving of his rib cage slows. The line begins to come free, loop by loop. All around him orange and yellow leaves spiral to earth.

When the line is untangled he spools it back onto his reel. He looks up through the branches at the clouded sky a long time. There is the sounding of the river, behind him, clucking and murmuring, voicing old notes. The front of his throat is white and stretched; his whiskers are silver.

Finally he wheels and plods back to the river. The first snowflakes sink from the sky and aim for the bronze coils of the Rapid River.

◡

It is well after dark and snow sifts through the thickets and Mulligan stands half frozen in the river and fishes in the feathered darkness. His hands and feet are numb; his back stings from ceaseless casting. Delicate flakes expire on the sliding water. He fishes on.

It is near midnight and the boughs sag from the weight of snow, and flakes fall still when a fish takes his fly and charges downstream, hauling from the reel in singing bursts and making it very clear who is in charge. Soon it runs the line to the backing. The blood in Mulligan's chest waxes, heats. His reel screams. The fish leaps once, twice, five times, a dim bullet twisting a yard above the river, beautiful, terrible, and then it is around a shallow bend and Mulligan can only hear it thrashing, panicking, yanking out the backing by the yard, its splashing mingled with the splashing of the river and the wind in the trees and the luminous descent of snow. The tide of blood in Mulligan's chest mounts and mounts until it seems he must burst.

The fish runs all the backing from the reel. Mulligan fumbles for the line with his bloodless fingers; the fish races on. The backing comes free, it was not tied on—who would think a fish could run out sixty yards of backing?—and the line slips through the guides on Mulligan's rod and he lunges for it and catches it between his palms, the line free of the rod altogether and the fish swimming far downriver pulls at the line between Mulligan's hands and he can feel the fish yard down against its tether, rise up and leap and smack the water, and the line slips through his hands and the fish breaks free and Mulligan is left, hands outstretched, a penitent, an imploring gesture.

The fly line floats slack upon the water. He shivers. His fly rod and emptied reel rest nose down in the gravel. The mute indifference of the woods is all around him. There is only the ceaseless suck of flowing water where the river glides endlessly through the forest and the snow, makes its faintest sliding whispers.

Mkondo

◡

[*mkondo,* noun. Current, flow, rush, passage, run, e.g., of water in a river or poured on the ground; of air through a door or window, i.e., a draft; of the wake of a ship, a track, the run of an animal.]

In October of 1983, an American named Ward Beach was sent to Tanzania by the Ohio Museum of Natural History to obtain the fossil of a prehistoric bird. Teams of European paleontologists had found something like the Chinese caudipteryx—a small, feathered reptile—in the limestone hills west of Tanga and the museum was eager to get one for itself. Ward was not a paleontologist (halfway to his doctorate he had given up) but he was a competent fossil hunter and an ambitious man. He did not like the work itself—backbreaking hours with a chisel and sifting pan, blind alleys, dead ends, disappointments—but he liked the idea behind the work. To discover fossils, he told himself, was to reclaim answers to important questions.

He was driving the nameless ridge he'd driven to the dig site

184

every day for two months when he came upon a woman running in the road. She wore sandals and a khanga tied loosely above her knees and her hair bounced against her back in a thick braid. The road narrowed and kinked as it climbed under a blazing sun, with a flat density of growth on both sides. He made to pass her but she darted in front of his truck. He braked, skidded, went up on two wheels and nearly slid over the edge. She did not look back.

Ward leaned over the wheel. Had that really happened? Had that woman dashed out in front of his truck? Up ahead she was sprinting now, her sandals raising dust. He followed. She ran as if chasing something, like a predator, running expertly and without wasted motion. He had never seen anything like her; she did not glance back, not once. He eased the truck closer until her heels were just missing the bumper. Above the engine noise he could hear her breath storming in and out. They went like this for ten minutes: Ward over the wheel, hardly breathing, possessed with something—anger, curiosity, maybe, already, desire; and the woman charging uphill, braid bouncing, her legs churning like pistons beneath her. She did not slow. When they reached the road's summit, a puddled hilltop steaming in the sun, she spun and leapt onto the hood of the truck. He braked; the truck slid heavily in the mud. She turned onto her back, hooked her hands around the sides of the windshield and gasped for air.

Keep driving! she yelled in English. I want to feel the wind!

He sat a moment, watching the back of her neck through the glass. Could he say no, after chasing her up the hill? Could he drive with her on the hood?

But already, as if his foot was not his own, he had let up on the brake and the truck was coasting downhill, gradually picking up speed. There were tight, desperate bends in the road: he watched the muscles in her arms tighten as she clenched the frame of the truck. He passed the dig site and drove on, for a half hour or more, over sheer, badly rutted roads, the braid of her hair swinging over the windshield, the cords in her shoulders standing out. The truck bounced over potholes, lilted into curves. Still she clung to the hood. Finally the road ended: there was a dense tangle of vines and below a steep ravine at the bottom of which the rusting frame of a car lay mangled and bent. Ward opened his door; he was nearly hyperventilating.

Miss, he began, are you . . .

Listen to my heart, she said. And he did—as if watching from a distance he saw himself get out and place his ear against her sternum. What he heard was like an engine, like the engine of the truck thrumming beneath her. He could hear the great muscle of her heart washing blood into the corridors of her body, the wind of her breath howling in her lungs. Never had he imagined a sound so alive.

I've seen you in the forest, she said. Digging in the clay with shovels. What are you looking for?

A bird, he stammered. An important bird.

She laughed. You look for birds in the earth?

It's a dead bird. We're looking for its bones.

Why don't you look for living birds? There are so many.

I'm not getting paid to look for them.

No? She climbed off the hood and stepped through the bamboo at the end of the road.

◡

Two nights later he was outside her parents' house wondering if he should have come. Her name was Naima; her parents, shy and prosperous tea farmers, lived above the bean fields and banana plantations on a small holding—four acres of tea, a three-room cottage and a glass-walled tea nursery—high in the Usambara Mountains, a craggy and forested range south of Kilimanjaro and west of the Indian Ocean, a last pocket of rainforest that had once stretched all the way to Tanzania from the West African coast. Locusts screamed in a bank of eucalyptus behind the nursery; the first stars guttered overhead. Ward had filled the flatbed of the truck with basketed flowers: hibiscus, lantana, honeysuckle, others he could not guess the names of.

Her parents stood in the doorway. Naima walked around the truck several times. Finally she reached in, pinched a daisy from its stem, and tucked it behind her ear. Can you catch me? she asked.

What? said Ward.

But already she was running, galloping around the tea nursery and into the trees. Ward glanced at her parents in the doorway—their faces were blank—and jogged after her. It was twice as dark under the canopy of leaves; exposed roots laced the path; branches lashed his chest. He caught one glimpse of her: leaping deadfall, dodging saplings. Then she was gone. It was so dark. He fell once, twice. There was a fork in the trail, then another; like arteries the trails branched out from central trunks, subdividing a hundred times; he had no idea which way she might have gone. He listened for her but heard only insects, frogs, leaves shifting.

Eventually he turned back, picking his way carefully down to the house. He helped her mother haul water from the creek; he drank tea with her father beside a charcoal fire. Still Naima didn't return. Her father shrugged over the rim of his teacup. Sometimes she is gone half the night, he said. She will come back. She always comes back. If I prevented her from going she would be unhappy. Her mother said Naima was old enough to make her own decisions.

When he left she still hadn't returned. It was a long way down to his hotel, two hours bouncing over potholed roads, and Ward could not shake the memory of her clinging to the hood of his truck, the way the cords in her arms strained against her skin, the arch of her fingers, the drumming of her heart. Two nights later he returned to her house, and again two nights after that. Each time he brought her something: a fossilized trilobite hung from a gold chain, a tiny wooden box with an array of purple crystals nested inside. She'd smile, lift the gift to the light or press it against her cheek. Thank you, she'd say. Ward would look down at his boots and mumble that it was nothing.

During dinner he'd describe where he was from: Ohio, the gleaming skyscrapers, the rows of town houses, the collection of butterflies in his museum. She listened avidly, her palms flat on the table, leaning forward. She asked many questions: What is the soil like? What kind of animals live there? Have you seen a tornado? He invented half-accurate natural histories of Ohio: dinosaurs battling on the plains; vast flocks of prehistoric geese flowing over stunted trees. But he didn't have language for what he really wanted to say; he couldn't explain how her wildness that day, on the road, had thrilled him as much as it terrified him. He couldn't tell her that at night, sweating in the folds of his mosquito net, he had begun to recite her name over and over, as if it were a spell that might summon her into his room.

Invariably, after dark, she'd gallop into the labyrinth of trails behind her house, challenging him to catch her. Each time he managed to pursue her a bit deeper down a path before he stumbled over a rock and cut his palm or fell into thorns and shredded his shirt. He began staying later and later into the night, tinkering in the tea nursery with her father or sitting at the table with her mother in polite, awkward silence. Always he had to leave before she returned, driving south toward the hotel in Tanga, with the truck shaking over the road and the first shafts of light springing above the mountains.

◡

Months steamed forward: December, January, February. Ward got the museum a complete fossil of their prehistoric bird—its delicate needle-sized bones folded into a block of limestone—and they wanted him back in Ohio. His airplane ticket was for the first of March but he delayed it and begged two weeks of vacation time and a room in Korogwe, a small town beneath the mountains where Naima lived. Every day for those two weeks he crossed the river and drove north into the labyrinth of muddy switchbacks that dead-ended at her parents' home.

He brought her tennis shoes and T-shirts; packets of pumpkin seeds for her mother, paperback novels for her father. Naima would give him that same inscrutable smile. At dinner she asked more about the world he came from: What does winter *smell* like? How does it feel to lie down in snow? But every night, chasing her farther through the forest, he lost her. Tell me what to do! he'd shout into the darkening hills. Tell me which way you've gone! And when he lay on the cot in his room, gripped with exhaustion, her name spilled from his lips: Naima, Naima, Naima.

The date for his return ticket passed, his visa expired, his malaria medication ran out. He wrote the museum to beg a month of unpaid leave. The Long Rains came: violent showers followed by choking humidity, steam in the streets, rainbows on the mountains. Sometimes a deluge swept goats into the river by his hotel. From his balcony Ward would watch them drift past, speeding between the banks, paddling hard to keep their noses above the water, and he felt sometimes that he was like those goats, swept up in circumstances beyond his control, swimming hard against the current, churning with silent desperation. Maybe living was no more than getting swept over a riverbed and eventually out to sea, no choices to make, only the vast, formless ocean ahead, the frothing waves, the lightless tomb of its depths.

He began to long for home, the steady seasons, the mild air, the ordinariness of the land. As his truck wound down through the hills, alone and after midnight, he'd gaze westward where the hills sloped a bit lower and imagine that Ohio lay just over the next ridge. His house was there, his bookshelves and his Buick; he imagined the refrigerator stocked with cheese and eggs and cold milk, daffodils standing primly in their beds. He was tired of sleeping in mosquito nets, tired of brown shower-water, tired of eating boiled maize in silence with Naima's mother and father. Although he had been in Africa only five months he could feel himself becoming saturated with fatigue; his heart was moldering, crumbling. The sun broiling overhead and the fire inside his chest—it was too much; he was going to burn up.

⌣

Then April: the wettest days. The museum sent a telegram to the hotel. They had been unable to replace him and wanted him back. They offered a promotion to curator and a pay raise. To accept he would have to report by the first of June.

Two months. He began to run. The sky was a furnace, the sun was blazing and white, but he ran as much as his body could stand, staggering up hills, lunging back to the hotel. At first he made it only a few miles before the heat bowed him under. The people along the roads stared unabashedly, this curiosity, this big mzungu gasping through the streets. But as he strengthened they soon lost interest—a few even clapped him on. By the end of April he could run ten, then fifteen, then twenty kilometers. His skin grew darker, his muscles leaner.

Every day he sent a driver into the mountains with a gift: desiccated moths, fossilized corals, a blue jar with eight tiny medusae floating inside. Three swallowtail butterflies pinned to velvet in a small plastic case. Returning to his hotel, his heart sounding evenly in his chest, Ward began to feel the glimmers of something burgeoning inside, a strange and bottomless strength emerging from the pit of him. Flesh fell from his body. His appetite was endless. By the middle of May he could run and keep running and felt, suddenly one morning, moving out past the basket merchants and the clay pits south of town, the vast pan of the sea glittering before him and the blue smoke of charcoal fires hanging above the beaches, that he could run forever.

◡

It wasn't until late May that Ward drove north once more, across the Pangani, up the intricate, rutted roads, above the plantations, and into the rainforest. His legs crackled with a new energy—she would not get away this time. She met him at the door, breathless: he had brought his last gift. He stood trembling with his fists balled at his sides and watched her unwrap the silver ribbon from the box. Inside was a living monarch butterfly. It danced from between her hands and began to wander through the house.

It was sent here from the museum in a cocoon, Ward said, watching it bump against the ceiling. It must have just emerged. Naima was looking at him.

You look different, she said. You've changed.

All through dinner her attention passed over his face, his arms, the veins on the backs of hands. She lit a paraffin candle on the table and a twisting reflection of the flame stood twinned in her eyes.

I've come, he announced, to ask you to come home with me and be my wife.

Before he could stand she was past him and he charged after her, knocking over his chair, running beneath the eucalyptus, pounding up the trails. The night was dark and moonless, but he had become more agile and felt that new strength singing in his legs. He bounded past trunks, hurdled vines, spun down the path. Within twenty minutes he was deeper into the forest than he had ever been, climbing a steep trail after her. She was wearing a white dress and he kept his eye on it as he charged forward.

He chased her through the trees, into the bamboo above the trees, and eventually above the bamboo into an open woodland where sedge and tussock and heather grew in lumps among huge flat stones and bizarre tall plants like needled cabbages stood in the dimness swaying on stalks. Several times he came to a fork in the path and had to choose which way to go. Up ahead, every few minutes, he would glimpse her, springing forward. She was so fast—he had forgotten how fast.

He tracked her through a field of boulders, then a long swath of mud. He ran in her footprints, matching her strides. His lungs howled; blood thumped in his ears. Her tracks took him to a ridge, past a series of tall boulders and to the edge of a bluff. He stopped. Just below the horizon the ocean sprawled, reflecting back a dizzying smear of stars. He gazed all around him, hoping for a glimpse of white, the river of her body swinging in the night. But she was nowhere. He had lost her: it was a dead end—had he, despite all his confidence, taken the wrong trail? He pivoted, retreated, reapproached the cliff's edge. He was certain he'd seen her dress flit between the boulders on which his hands now rested. And there were her tracks in the mud. Behind was the way he had come. Ahead waited what looked like nothing, space, a spiral of constellations reflected and real, and the hiss and splash of water on rocks somewhere far below.

A star fell from the sky; then another. Blood ticked in his ears. He leaned over the precipice, and although he could see nothing but those distant pinholes in the darkness, he felt a confidence, a resolution, and closed his eyes and stepped forward.

Years later he would look back and wonder: the footprints, the white dress—were these ways she revealed herself to him, ways she allowed him to catch her? Was he chasing her as a predator chases prey, or was he baited forward—was he the prey? Did he drive her off the cliff or did she lure him from its edge?

His fall took forever, too long, but then there was the smack of water beneath his shoes and on the bottoms of his forearms, and he was underwater, and back up, alive, gasping. From the mild current that flowed around him he knew he was in a river. The walls of a gorge lifted up around him. The river floated him to a gravel bar. He sat, half in the water, arms stinging, and tried to recover his breath.

She was standing on the far bank. Her skin was as dark as the river, darker even, and as she came toward him it seemed that her lower body dissolved and became part of the river itself. When she reached him she held out a hand and he took it. Though her hand was hot he could feel it tremble. Swallows drew loops above them; a crane, hunting minnows along the far bank, paused, its beak poised, one foot held above the water.

What a risk she was taking—what a fabulous, miraculous risk. Even Ward could see that she was the one stepping off a cliff's edge, plunging through the darkness. She looked over his head, at the stars rioting in the sky. Yes, she said.

◡

The next Sunday they were married by a priest in Lushoto.

A week in her parents' home: he slept in her room; they hardly spoke; they filled their frames of vision with each other. Ward could not bear to have her out of his sight: he wanted to follow her to the outhouse, wanted to help her dress. Naima found herself trembling nearly all the time. She threw herself into him; she was hurtling down the path she had chosen as quickly as her body would carry her. On the airplane they held hands. He watched the green and furrowed hills sliding far below and felt vaguely triumphant.

◡

In her window seat Naima tried to imagine herself hurtling through the sky, not cramped into this tunnel with strangers but really flying, arms stretched out, rafts of clouds scrolling by. She clenched her eyes, balled her fists; the vision would not come.

When Naima was ten she invented a game and called it Mkondo. Mkondo was this: from the network of trails behind her parents' home, she'd choose a path she'd never traveled and follow it until it ended. When she reached the end she had to take one step farther. Sometimes this meant merely stepping over nettles or crawling through a net of vines. Other times paths edged their way into gorges and dropped to a river—the brown and quiet Pangani or some nameless creek slashing past—and she would hitch her khanga to her thighs and, trembling, wade in. Of if, in the final pinch of a ravine, a trail dead-ended in a grove of cedar trees, she'd clamber up twenty feet to a branch, then take her step forward.

Her favorites were the trails that climbed high into the mountains, winding through fields of giant heather and tussock to terminate at some crumbling pinnacle, and she would stand at the end of the trail and lift her foot. Far off, above the trees nodding their heads in the wind, above the flat and dusty plains, clumps of clouds would soar in from the horizon. She'd lean into the pulsing gulf of air, with her foot poised over nothing, and space would flood around her, a vertigo against which she held back in blissful panic, fighting an urge she had, always, to continue on, to throw herself forward.

She'd run until she couldn't feel her legs moving beneath her, until past and future seemed to dissolve and there was only Naima—all the attention of the seething, tossing forest on her— and she'd feel a reckless urgency to accelerate, to run beneath the clouds and feel her core blaze into life; some rare nights, as she neared the end of a trail, she felt the shed of her body slip away, and for one electrifying moment she became a ray of light, speeding upward. It wasn't dissatisfaction as much as curiosity; it wasn't a fear of stasis as much as a need for movement. But those things—fear and dissatisfaction—were there too. She could not sit still; she hated picking tea; she dreaded school.

As Naima grew older she watched friends marry friends; young men assumed their father's jobs; young women became versions of their mothers. No one, it seemed, left the places they lived, the roads they traveled. At nineteen, at twenty-two, she was still racing through the forests, crawling through brambles, scrambling up riverbanks. Children called her mwendawazimu;

the tea pickers treated her as an outsider. By then Mkondo had become more than a game; it was the one way she could be certain she was alive.

Then Ward had arrived. He was different, significant; he spoke of places she had only dreamed of, he carried himself with a delicacy she had not seen before. (Ward stepping out of his truck, staring shyly at his feet, scraping at a fleck of clay on his shirt with a fingernail.) The gifts, the attention, the promise of something different, something glamorous—all these things attracted her. But it was not until he had leapt after her into the river that she was convinced. It was dark; he easily might have turned back.

On the plane she opened her eyes. This, she thought, this marriage, this one-way ticket to another continent, was just another round of Mkondo; it was only a matter of steeling yourself and taking that extra, final step.

‿

Ohio: bleak weather impended over the city like a shroud. Curtains of haze washed out the light; helicopters shuttled endlessly overhead; buses groaned through the streets like dying beasts. In Ward's neighborhood the houses were built within a foot of each other—Naima could lift a screen and reach into the neighbors' kitchen.

For those first months she threw herself so ardently into Ward that she managed to outrun her disappointment. It was love, the most desperate kind. She spent her afternoons glancing at the clock once a minute, waiting for the moment his bus would let him off at the end of the block, the sound of his keys at the door. Evenings they ran through the streets, dodging lampposts, hurdling newspaper boxes. Sometimes they stayed up until dawn talking; when Monday morning came—too soon—Naima wanted to hammer the door shut, bury his keys, pin him against the hallway floor.

Although the museum was not what she expected—cracked granite staircases, mounted mammals and bones on display, dioramas where plastic-eyed cavemen bent over plaster cookfires—she could see why Ward had such ambition for it. It was a musty, wistful place; a vision of what that country must once have been. They sat on the roof at night and watched traffic slug through the streets; they picnicked inside the fossilized rib cage of a brontosaur. In a marble hall the walls were covered with almost fifty thousand pinned butterflies, species from every region on earth. The colors on their wings took her breath away: dazzling blue halos, tiger stripes, false eyes. Ward beamed, named them one by one. It was his favorite place. Even later, after he had been promoted several times, he would return to the hall of butterflies to dust them off, straighten their labels, inspect new additions.

But the more time she spent there the more the museum unnerved her. Nothing grew, nothing lived. Even the light seemed dead, falling from naked bulbs screwed into the ceilings. The people there obsessed over names and classifications of things, as if the first orange-winged butterfly had emerged from its cocoon named *Anthocharis cardamines,* as if the essence of ferns was explained by a dried specimen tacked to posterboard and labeled *Dennstaedtiaceae.* The curators had taken Ward's prehistoric bird, taped an index card to it, and locked it in a glass cube. What kind of natural history was that? She wanted to haul in barrows of earth and dump them on the floor. See this grub? she'd announce, shaking one at the old guard, at the visiting class of first-graders. See these slugs? *This* is natural history. This is what you come from.

Traffic, billboards, sirens, a stranger's unwillingness to look directly at her: these were not things she had expected, not things she could have prepared herself for. The leaves of trees—the few trees she could find—were stained with soot from the mills. The markets were lifeless and sterile: meat came packaged in plastic and she had to tear it open in the aisle to smell it. The neighbors pretended not to stare when she did laundry in the yard. You need something, she told herself, wringing Ward's shirts over the lawn. You need something or you are not going to make it here.

◡

Ward watched Naima drift through the house as if searching for something she'd lost; sometimes she complained of strange illnesses: invisible clamps around her throat, thick-headedness, rubbery insides. Once he brought her to dinner at an acquaintance's house, a Kenyan professor at the university. It will do you good, Ward told her. The professor's wife cooked chapatis, murmured hymns in Swahili. But Naima sat sullenly at the table and gazed outside. After dinner, when they took tea in the parlor, she stayed in the kitchen and sat on the floor, whispering to the housecat.

At night Ward tossed in self-loathing: how, he wondered, can you want something so badly, finally get it, and yet wind up discontented? And how can it happen so quickly? When he finally could sink into sleep his dreams boiled with faceless devils; he woke—gasping—with their talons on his windpipe.

Ward was changing too, or perhaps just reverting to something he had been before, easing back to a more familiar road. After only six months in Ohio, Naima could see the flush in his neck fade, the definition of his muscles wilt. She watched him tangle himself in the trappings of work: he'd return home at eight or nine, sheepish and apologetic. He brought paperwork home on weekends; he was placed in charge of museum publications, then membership management. I love you, Naima, he'd say, standing in the doorway to his study. But already he was not the same person who had arrived at her parents' door like a stag in rut, breathing hard, trembling with life.

They made love carefully, and in silence. Nothing ever came of it. Are you okay? he'd say afterward, panting, suddenly afraid to touch her, as if she were a flower he'd torn the petals from—an accident, too late. Are you okay?

‿

Her first February the weather stayed overcast every day all day. She felt the dead weight of snow on the roof; she rolled over each morning, lifted the curtain and groaned to see it gray again, never any sun, never any movement to the air. A mile away the flat and dismal towers of downtown stood against the sky like huge prisons. Buses roared through the slush.

She had come to Ohio; she had taken that final, extra step. Now what? she thought. Now what am I supposed to do? Turn back? By August—she had been there a year—she was sobbing at night. The Ohio sky had become a tangible weight, bending the stalk of her neck, loading down her shoulders. She slumped through the hours. Ward, anxious to try anything, drove her out of the city: barns on hills, threshers in fields. They sat on a friend's porch and ate fresh corn slathered in butter and pepper. She asked, What are those white boxes over there?

Bees. So all winter she hammered together frames in the basement and in April bought a queen and a three-pound package of workers from a farm supply store and set up a hive in Ward's backyard. Each evening, with a canvas veil over her head, lulling the bees with smoke from smoldering bunches of grass, she'd stand over the hive and watch it in all its industry, all its wildness. And she was happy. But the neighbors complained—they had kids, they said, and some of the kids were allergic. The bees were infesting their forsythia bushes, their potted geraniums. A woman had bees coming through her air conditioner. The neighbors began leaving notes under Ward's wiper blades, rude messages on the answering machine. Then: a threat of sabotage—*How would your bees take to some DDT?*—taped to a glass paperweight and hurled through the living room window. Two cops stood on the porch with their hats behind their backs. City ordinance, they said, no bees.

Ward offered to help her get rid of them but she refused. She had never driven a car. She stopped and started, nearly leveled two children on tricycles. Finally she stalled in a field off the interstate, opened the trunk and watched the bees spiral out, angry, confused, swarming. A dozen stung her: on the arms, a knee, an ear. She wept, hated herself for it.

⌣

She stuck bird feeders to the bedroom windows with suction cups, lured squirrels into the kitchen with tea biscuits. She studied ants as they navigated the front walk, watched them heave the desiccated bodies of beetles onto their shoulders and freight them through the forest of the lawn. But it was not enough—it was not wilderness, not exactly, not at all. Chickadees and pigeons, mice and chipmunks. Houseflies. Trips to the zoo to watch a pair of dirty zebras eat hay. This was a life, this was how people chose to live? Somewhere inside she could feel winds dying, the gales of her youth stifled. She was learning that in her life everything— health, happiness, even love—was subject to the landscape; the weathers of the world were inseparable from the weathers of her soul. There were doldrums in her arteries, gray skies in her lungs. She heard a pulse inside her ear, a swishing cadence of blood and it was time, the steady marking of every moment as it sailed past, unrecoverable, lost forever. She mourned each one.

⌣

Winter—her third in Ohio—she crossed to Pennsylvania in Ward's Buick and returned with a pair of immature red-tailed hawks, orphans bought from a chicken farmer who had shot their mother and advertised them in the paper. They were fully fledged, hot and bristling, with hooked beaks and sharp black talons and fire-colored eyes. She lashed leather rufters over their heads and tied them to a wooden block in the basement. Each morning she fed them cubes of raw chicken. As a kind of training she carried them around the house, hooded, perched on a heavily gloved wrist, stroking their wings with a feather and talking to them.

The hawks were full of hate. At night wild cries reverberated from the basement. Naima would wake and experience the strange sensation that the world had inverted—the sky arched beneath her, the hawks were circling in the basement, shouting up. She lay in bed and listened. Then, all too familiar, the phone would ring: the neighbors wondered why it sounded like children were shrieking in Ward's cellar.

She was learning: wildness was not something she could make or something she could bring to her, it had to be there on its own, a miracle she had to be lucky enough to happen across, traveling one day along a path and arriving at its end. She went to the birds each night. She carried them to opposite ends of the basement, stroked them with the feather and talked to them in Swahili, in Chagga. But still they squalled. Can't you just muzzle them? Ward would shout from his study. Until they outgrow this? But hatred was not something they would outgrow, it was in them; she could see it brimming behind their eyes.

After a week of this, the neighbors calling and the police summoned twice to the front step, Ward sat her down. Naima, he said, the police are going to take the hawks away. I'm sorry.

Let them come, she said. But that night she carried one of the birds to the backyard, removed its hood, and set it free. It flapped clumsily into the air, trying its wings, and settled onto the gable. There it began to screech, sharply and regularly, like a siren. It hammered at the roof with its beak, sending scraps of shingle into the air; it dropped to the front porch and threw itself at the front window. Then it perched on the mailbox and resumed screaming. Naima ran around to the front, thrilled, breathless.

Five minutes later the police were shining flashlights in the windows. Ward stood on the sidewalk in his sweatpants, shaking his head, gesturing at the screeching hawk, which was now perched on the gutter. Porch lights up and down the block switched on. Two men in coveralls pulled their truck onto the lawn and tried to snare the hawk with long-poled nets. It screamed at them, dive-bombed their heads. Finally, at the peak of the noise, sirens wailing, men shouting and the bird crying savagely at them all, there was a gunshot, an explosion of feathers, and afterward, a silence. A sheepish cop reholstered his handgun. What was left of the bird fell in a lump behind the hedges. Fragments of feather drifted up, spinning into the darkness.

She waited until the police were gone and the neighbors' lights had gone out. Then she went downstairs, took the other hawk and set it free in the backyard. It lifted drunkenly into the sky and vanished over the city. She stood in the yard, listening, watching the spot in the haze where she had last seen it, a black speck against a field of gray.

☾

It has to stop, Ward said. What will you haul in here next? A crocodile? An elephant? He shook his head, circled his wide arms around her. In just three years his body had become soft enough to repulse her. Why not go to college? he'd say. You could walk to campus. But when she imagined college she thought of her dreary days in the schoolhouse in Lushoto, the heat of classrooms, the impatience of mathematics, bland two-dimensional maps pinned to walls. Green for land, blue for water, stars for capital cities. Schoolmasters obsessed with naming things that had existed unnamed for a million years.

Every day she went to bed early and slept late. She yawned: huge, widemouthed yawns that seemed to Ward not so much yawns as noiseless screams. Once, after Ward left for work, she climbed onto the first city bus that stopped and rode it until the driver announced last stop; she found herself at the airport. She wandered the terminal, watched the names of cities shuffle up and down the monitors: Denver, Tucson, Boston. With Ward's credit card she bought a ticket to Miami, folded it into her pocket and listened for the boarding calls. Twice she walked to the jetway but balked, turned around. On the bus back she found herself crying. Had she forgotten how to take that extra step? How had it happened so quickly?

⌣

She complained about the humidity in the summer and the cold in the winter. She claimed illness when Ward offered to take her to dinner; he'd tell her something about the museum and she'd look away, not even pretending to listen. Without thinking about it she referred to the house—still, after four years—as his house. It's *our* house, Naima, he'd insist, thumping the wall with his fist, *our* kitchen. *Our* spice rack. He began to wonder if she'd leave; he became certain he'd wake one day and find her gone, a note on the mantel, a suitcase missing from the closet.

He'd come home late and meet her on the stairs. I had a lot of work, he'd say. And she'd go past him, out into the night, moving in the opposite direction.

In his office he took a notepad from a drawer and wrote: *I see now that I cannot give you what you need. You need movement and life and things I can't even guess at. I am an ordinary man with an ordinary life. If you have to leave me to find the things you need, I understand. No one who has ever seen you run beneath the trees or hang on to the hood of his truck could ever again be entirely happy without you, but I could try. I could live, anyway.*

He signed the page, folded it, and stowed it in his pocket.

⌣

The twining of their lives: born on different halves of the world; brought together by chance and curiosity; leveraged apart by the incompatibility of their respective landscapes. While Ward was sitting on the bus, heading home, his letter in his pocket, another letter, tucked into the guts of an airplane, shuttled from truck to truck, hand to hand, was waiting in their Ohio mailbox: a letter from Tanzania, from the brother of Naima's father. Naima brought it in, set it on the counter and stared at it. When Ward came home he found her in the basement, on the floor, cocooned in an afghan.

He waved a finger in front of her eyes, brought her tea that she did not drink. He pried the letter from her fist and read it. Her parents had died together, when a section of the road to Tanga gave way in a rush of mud, rolling the truck into a gorge. She had already missed the burial by a week but Ward offered to send her anyway: he knelt before her and asked if she'd like him to make arrangements. No answer. He laid his hands on her cheeks and raised her head; when he released it, it fell back onto her chest.

He slept beside her in his shirt and tie on the concrete floor. In the morning he took the letter he had written her and shredded it. Then he carried her to the car and drove her to the county hospital. A nurse wheeled her to a room and plugged a tube into her arm. She'd be okay, the nurse said, they would help her.

But this was not the kind of help she needed: white walls, fluorescent lights, the smells of sickness and disease slinking through the halls. Twice a day they pushed pills into her mouth. She drifted through the hours; her pulse ticked slowly through her head. How many days did she lie with the television burbling, her heart emptied, her senses dulled? She could see the white moons of faces rising and falling as people bent over her: a doctor, a nurse, Ward, always Ward. Her fingers found the metal railings of her bed; her nose brought the sterile smells of hospital food: instant potatoes, medicinal squash. The TV hummed incessantly. Her sleep was gray and dreamless. When she tried to remember her parents she could not. Soon Tanzania would be gone from her altogether—like her orphaned hawks she would know no home except where she was kept, hooded and tied, against her will. What next? Would they come in and shoot her?

Was it morning? Had she been there two weeks? She tore the tube from her arm, heaved her way out of bed and stumbled from the room. She could feel drugs in her body slowing her muscles, dumbing her reflexes. Her head felt like it was a glass globe resting precariously on her shoulders—one wrong movement and it would fall; it would take her the rest of her life to sweep up the pieces.

In the hall, amid rolling gurneys and hustling orderlies, she saw lines of tape on the floor fanning out like the paths of her youth. She picked one and tried to follow it. After some time— she could not say how long—a nurse was at her elbow, turning her, shepherding her back to her room.

⌣

They began locking her door. Peas for dinner; soup for lunch. She felt herself sliding away; the muscle of her heart had thinned and blood slopped around inside. Something deep and untrammeled within her had died, diseased somehow, trampled. How had it happened? Hadn't she guarded it carefully? Hadn't she secured it away in the center of her?

After the hospital—she could not say how many days she was locked in that room—Ward brought her home and installed her in a chair by the window. She watched buses, taxicabs, neighbors plodding back and forth with their heads down. An immense emptiness had settled inside her; her body was a desert, windless and dark. Africa could not have seemed farther away. Sometimes she wondered if it even existed, if her whole history was just some dream, some fable meant for children. Look where impulsiveness can get you, the storyteller would say, wagging his finger in the child's eyes. Look what happens when you stray.

◡

Spring passed, summer and fall. Naima did not get out of bed until noon or later. With the slow revolution of seasons only the tiniest memories—the squeaks of robin chicks begging worms from their mother, snow sifting through a streetlight—trickled back. They came to her as if through a thick wall of glass; their meanings were changed and they had lost their context, their edge, their wild savor. Even her dreams came back eventually, but these too were altered. She dreamed a train of camels sauntering through a woodland, orange clouds looming over the canopy of a forest, but in these scenes she was nowhere to be found—she gazed at places but could not enter them, witnessed beauty but could not experience it. It was as though she had been excised neatly out of each moment. The world had become like an exhibit at Ward's museum: pretty and nostalgic and watered down, something old and sealed off you weren't allowed to touch.

Some mornings, watching from the bed as Ward tied his tie, the tail of his shirt hanging over the plump backs of his thighs, she felt resentment foam up from some rotting place within her and she'd turn onto her stomach and hate him for hounding her through the rainforest, for leaping from the rim of that cliff. Everything had unraveled between them: Ward had given up trying to reach her and she had given up allowing herself to be reached. She had been in Ohio five years but it felt like fifty.

◡

Evening. She was squatting on the back steps, half asleep, when a line of geese skimmed over the gable of the house. They passed so low she could see the definition of their feathers, the smooth black curves of their bills, the simultaneous, coordinated blink of their eyes. She felt the sudden power of their wings as the air they displaced shifted over her. They moved steadily toward the horizon, bleating, alternating leaders. She watched until they were gone and then watched the spot they had disappeared into and wondered: What avenue did they follow? What strange and hidden switch in their heads was thrown each winter, what sent them shuttling down the same invisible pathways to the same southern waters? How glorious the sky was, she thought, and how unknowable. Long after they were gone she trained her eyes skyward, waiting, hoping.

It was 1989; she was thirty-one years old. Ward was eating a cupcake—a stalactite of frosting hung from his bottom lip. She went in and stood before him. Okay, she said. I want to go to college.

He stopped chewing. Well, he said. All right then.

‍‌ʘ

In a gymnasium students milled between stalls labeled Government, Anthropology, Chemistry. One booth—decorated with glossy photographs—caught her eye. A volcano ringed with snow. The cracked seat of a chair. A series of photos of a bullet exiting an apple. She studied the images, filled out paperwork: Photography 100, Introduction to the Camera. Ward had an old Nikon 630 in the basement and she dusted it off and brought it to the first class.

That will never do, her instructor said. It is all I have, she said. He fiddled with the loading door, explained how light would seep in and spoil her photos.

I can hold it shut, she said. Or I'll tape it. Please. Tears sprung to her eyes.

Well, the instructor said, we'll see what we can do.

Their second day he led the students onto the campus. We're snapping a *few* exposures here, he called. Don't burn your film. Focus on the structures, people.

The students fanned out, aiming their lenses at the cornerstones of buildings, the chiseled end of a handrail, the domed cap of a fire hydrant. Naima walked to a grizzled, bent oak leaning out of a triangle of lawn between sidewalks. Her camera was taped shut with electrical tape. It contained twenty-four exposures. She hardly understood what that meant, to have twenty-four exposures in her machine. F-stop, ASA, depth of field, all this meant nothing. But she leaned forward, pointed the lens up, where the leafless branches shifted against the sky, and waited. The cloud cover was thick but she could see a rift forming. She waited. In ten minutes the clouds parted gently, a thin ray of light nudged through, illuminating the oak, and she made her exposure.

◡

Two days later, in the darkroom, she watched the instructor unclip the black coil of her negatives from the line where they were drying. He nodded and handed the strip to her. She raised them as he had done, to the bulb, and suddenly, seeing the rendered image of what she had captured only days before—oak branches bloomed over with sun, a fracture in the haze beyond— she felt a darkness tear away from her eyes. Shivers ran down her arms; joy founted up. It was rapture, the oldest feeling, a sensation like rising from the thick canopy of forest and turning, looking out over the treetops, seeing the world again, for the first time.

That night she could not sleep. She burned. She was three hours early for the next class.

◡

They made contact sheets, then prints. In the darkroom she watched the developing bath intently, waiting for the grain of her photo to emerge on the paper—it floated in, first faint, then gray, then fully there, and it struck her as the most beautiful magic she'd ever seen. Developer, stop-bath, fixer. So simple. She thought: I was made and set here to give voice to this.

After class the instructor called her over. He leaned over the prints and pointed out how she'd trapped a telephone wire in this frame, how she could have extended that exposure a bit longer. Good, though, he said, a good first set. But it's a bit wrong, too. Your camera lets light in—can you see here how the fringe is washed out? And here the tree looks flat; there is no background, no point of reference. He took his glasses off and leaned back, pontificating now. How to render three dimensions in two, the world in planar spaces. It's the central challenge for every artist, Naima.

Naima stepped back, reexamined her photo. Artist? she thought. An artist?

○

Every day she went out and snapped pictures of clouds: altonimbus, cirrocumulus, the cross-hatching of contrails, a child's balloon drifting over train tracks. She caught the skyline of the city reflected in the bottom of a cloud, two puff-ball cumulus drifting across the face of a puddle. A cerulean rhombus of sky mirrored in the eye of a dog, killed minutes earlier by a bus. She began to see the world in terms of angles of light; windows, bulbs, the sun, the stars. Ward would leave money for groceries on the counter but she'd spend it on film; she wandered into neighborhoods she'd never seen before; she squatted in someone's front yard, motionless, for an hour, waiting for a thick raft of stratus clouds to rupture, to see if the light might saturate the thin spar of a spider's web trussed between two blades of grass.

Again there were phone calls: we saw your wife squatting by a dead dog, Ward, taking *pictures* of it. She took pictures of our trash cans. She stood on the hood of your car for an hour, Ward, staring at the sky.

He tried talking to her. So Naima, he'd try, how's class? Or: Are you being careful out there? He had been promoted again and spent nearly all of his time at benefits, on the phone, walking the museum with donors in tow. By then he and Naima were miles apart—their trails had diverged and were unrolling through different continents. She'd show Ward the exposures and he'd nod. You're doing so great, he'd say and touch her on the back. I like this one, and he'd hold up a print she disliked, a patch of iridescence in a cirrus cloud drifting past the moon. She didn't mind; the kindling of her soul had caught fire. Nothing could slow her. Let Ward and his neighbors turn their eyes down, she would turn her eyes to the skies. She alone would witness these orange and purple and blue and white world-travelers, these bossed and gilded shape-shifters that came scudding overhead. Each morning, stepping out the front door, she felt the hard, dark center of her flare up.

⌣

Photography 100 ended. She earned an A. In the fall she took two more photography courses: Contemporary Photography and Techniques of the Darkroom. One professor lavished praise and offered to direct an independent study, saying, I think it's best if we let you continue down this path you're on. And Naima *was* on a path, she could sense it stretching out in front of her. She clicked and clicked. By the end of the semester she had won a student prize for her photo of the dead dog; people she had never seen before passed her in the halls and wished her well. In January a coffee shop called to offer a hundred dollars for a print of her first photo, the oak branches washed in light. By summer her work was made part of a group exhibition at a small gallery. It's her patience, a woman murmured. These photos remind you that each moment is here, then gone forever, that no two skies are ever the same. Another edged in to declare that Naima's work was perfectly ethereal, a sublime expression of the intangible.

She left early, escaping past a tuxedoed waiter with a tray of spring rolls, and marched into the dying light to take photographs: a wedge of sunset through a bridge buttress; the spinning rosette of light left by the moon as it eased behind a building.

◡

Late at night—it was April 1992—she felt that old feeling, the exhilaration of approaching a trail's end at a sprint. She stood on the marble steps of the Natural History Museum and studied the sky. It had rained during the afternoon and now the starlight fell cleanly through the air. The light of galaxies bathed her neck and shoulders, lifted the tide of blood in her heart—the sky was only yards deep. She could reach through it and seize the frigid center, set suns swaying like tiny droplets of mercury. Deep and shallow: the sky could be so many things.

Ward was in the hall of butterflies, unpacking a box filled with dead specimens. It had been packed poorly and many of the wings were torn, their powdery designs smeared. He was lifting them out and piecing them together on the floor. She shook him by his shoulder and said, I'm leaving. I'm going home. To Africa.

He leaned back but did not meet her eyes. When?

Now.

Wait until tomorrow.

She shook her head.

How will you get there?

I'll fly. Already she was turning, moving out of the hall, the soft sounds of her footfalls fading into silence. Although he knew she meant by airplane, later that night, alone in their bed, Ward couldn't help but imagine her spreading her arms, opening her hands, and gracefully, easily, lifting her body over the plains and hills, toward the ocean.

ᴐ

A photograph—impossible towers of cumulonimbus banked against the horizon, livid with lightning—came to Ward in the mail. He shook the envelope but she'd sent only the photo. The next week another arrived: a lone rhinoceros silhouetted on the horizon, the trails of two falling stars intersecting above it. She didn't write a word, didn't sign her name. But the photos kept coming, two a month, sometimes more, sometimes less. Between them yawned Ward's life.

He sold his house, sold the furniture and bought a condo in the center of the city. He spent his weekends buying things: a gigantic television, two tile murals for the bathroom walls. He redecorated his office: rare seashells on the windowsill, Spanish leather stretched over the desktop. He became especially good at his job. Over paella, over maguro and gyoza, he could get nearly anyone to donate to the museum. He learned how to make himself invisible, a listener who spoke only when the person he was courting needed reassurance or time to compose what to say next. He tweaked their consciences by describing children pouring into the museum, thrilled them by showing animated footage of digitized dinosaurs on the museum's movie screen. His finale always involved a line like: We offer children the world. And they would clap him on the shoulder and say, Why not, Mr. Beach. Why not.

He did his best to see that the museum evolved. People wanted interactive exhibits, complicated robotics, miniature reproductions of Brazilian forests. He got to work before everybody else and stayed until everything had closed. He arranged to have a simulated ice age occur every forty-five minutes in a room off the lobby. He had a miniature savannah built, complete with sunning hippopotami, swaying acacias, a three-inch zebra being feasted on by a pride of tiny, meticulously savage lionesses. But still he was mourning, and something in his face gave it away.

How Ward Beach suffers so quietly, his neighbors said, the museum volunteers said. He should find someone new, they said. Someone a little more *grounded*. Someone with his taste.

He grew corn, tomatoes, snap peas. He sat by the window in a café and read the paper, smiled at the waitress as she set down his change. And every few weeks the envelopes came: nimbus clouds reflected in the wet pawprint of a lion; squall lines warping over the summit of Kilimanjaro.

☽

Another year passed. He dreamed of her. He dreamed she'd sprouted huge and glorious butterfly wings and circled the globe with them, photographing volcanic clouds rising from a Hawaiian caldera, tufts of smoke from bombs dropped over Iraq, the warped, diaphanous sheets of auroras unfurling over Greenland. He dreamed of catching her as she flew through a forest; his arms were great butterfly nets; just as he held them above her, about to close the mouths of the nets over her, he woke, his throat closing, and had to lean gasping over the bed.

Sometimes, on his way home, walking through the empty museum, the heels of his shoes clicking over the floors, Ward would pass the fossilized bird he had sent back from Tanzania almost twenty years before. Its bones, caught as they were in the limestone—the curves and needles of its winglike arms, the jacket of its ribs—were crumpled; its neck was miserably bent; it had died broken in pain. What a thing, half bird, half lizard, part one thing, part another, trapped forever between more perfect states.

☽

In his mail an envelope with a Tanzanian postmark arrived, the first in months. Happy Birthday, it said, scribbled in her lilting, girlish cursive. It was his birthday, a few days away. Inside was a photograph of dark, rich grass, deep in a gorge, bisected by a river, the flat panel of water shimmering with stars. He held it under his desk lamp. The grass, the curve of the riverbank—it seemed familiar.

He saw: it was their place, the stretch of river he had plunged into from a cliffside, where she had come to him, almost dissolving into the water. He withdrew the print from the light and set it facedown, and wept.

⏾

What did he regret most? Their chance meeting on the road, her decision to leap onto the hood of his truck? His decision to bring her to Ohio? Letting her go? Letting himself go?

He didn't have her address, a phone number, anything. Twice on the plane he got up and walked to the lavatory to look at himself in the mirror. Do you know what you're doing? he asked aloud. Are you crazy? In his seat he drank vodka like water. Far below his window the clouds revealed nothing.

He was forty-seven years old and he had walked into the chief curator's office and given his two weeks'. He'd bought his ticket, carefully packed his clothes. These were all cliff edges off which he'd had to step.

In the wet air of Dar es Salaam he felt old memories come springing back: the familiar pattern on a woman's khanga, the smell of drying cloves, the lopsided face of an amputee holding out her palm for coins. His first morning the sight of his shadow standing sharp and black against the hotel wall caused déjà vu.

The sensation stayed with him on the drive up the coast toward Tanga. The green and brown pan of the Maasai Steppe, punctuated here and there with thin spires of smoke; the sight of two dhows sailing out to Zanzibar: he felt he had seen all these things before, as if here he was, twenty years younger, driving up this road for the first time with a Land Rover full of shovels and sifting pans and chisels.

◡

Some things had changed: there was a hotel in Lushoto now with a menu in English, and hawkers out front who offered glamorous safaris at ridiculous prices. The Usambaras had changed too: hundreds more terraced plantations had been cut into the hillsides; antennas stood blinking on ridgelines. But these changes—cellular phones and taxi-vans and cheeseburgers on a menu—didn't matter. After all, he considered, wasn't this the land where the first thick-browed humans walked, under these same brooding mountains, with these same winds bringing them smells of rain, of drought? He read in a guidebook that humans hadn't witnessed the great migration of wildebeest and zebra up the Serengeti until 1900. A hundred years—in Ward's field, a century was a finger-snap. What change could a hundred years bring? What small fraction of time was that for the animals who had been charging up and down that plain, teaching their young how to live, forever?

◡

He slept deeply and peacefully and for the first time in years did not wake from a dream with something clenched around his throat. He drank coffee on the porch of his hotel and chewed a scone before setting off. He thought he would find her parents' house easily—how many times had he made that drive: fifty?—but the roads were changed, wider and graded; he would round a bend and think he knew where he was but the road would suddenly descend when it was supposed to climb; he'd be at plantation gates when he should have been at an intersection. Dead ends, turn-offs, U-turns.

After days of winding through the hills he began to ask anyone he saw about her parents, about her, if anyone knew of a place where a photographer might develop film. He asked tea pickers, tour guides, duka owners. A boy at the hotel desk said he mailed tourists' film to an address in Dar to have it developed but that only white people dropped off rolls of film. An old woman told Ward in broken sentences that she remembered Naima's parents but no one had lived in their home since they died many years ago. He bought the woman lunch and plied her with questions. Do you remember where they lived? Can you tell me how to drive there? She shrugged and waved vaguely at the mountains. The only way to find something, she said, is to lose it first.

☽

He had not expected this, the waiting and wandering, the hot hours in a rented car. He began to park at road ends and follow footpaths into the fields. Blisters ballooned on his heels; he sweated through his shirts. But he knew this was the way to find her: he would have to walk the tracks that wound over the mountains. He would have to find a way to get his path to cross hers— she would not leave footprints this time, or wear a white dress, or give herself away.

Each morning he set forth and tried to get himself lost. He fashioned a walking stick, bought a machete, tried to ignore trail-side signs in Swahili that might have warned of buffalo gorings or the prosecution of trespassers. Welts appeared on his calves, insect bites studded his forearms. His clothes shredded and tore; he hacked the sleeves off a coat and wore it through the woods like a postapocalyptic vest.

☽

After three weeks of day hikes he found himself on a thin track beneath cedars. It was nearly dark and he was completely lost. The track had taken him through so many turns he could not say which way was north or south; uphill might lead him out of the mountains or farther into them; he had no compass, no map. Impossible clusters of vines hung in nets from the trees. Unseen birds screamed at him from the canopy. He hiked on, laboring over the tight, overgrown trail.

Soon it was dark and the sounds of night rose up around him. He took his headlamp from his pack and strapped it over his hat. Rain was misting over the leaves—large drops fell into the sub-story and dampened his shoulders. Before long he realized he'd lost the trail. He aimed his light in every direction—it revealed rotting logs, a shooting vine threaded around a trunk, great beards of moss hanging from the branches. A giant colony of ants was on the move, coursing along a column, overtaking a log.

He was almost fifty years old, unemployed, separated from his wife, lost in the mountains of Tanzania. In the thin beam of his light he watched a water droplet slide into the body of a red flower. He thought about how in a few days its petals would fall to the forest floor and crumple, and wither, and eventually be incorporated into something else, tree bark, a berry, energy rifling through the limbs of a salamander. He plucked the flower from its stem, wrapped it carefully in a bandanna and stowed it in the top of his pack.

He walked all that night, feeling his way, falling and staggering to his feet. When dawn came he could have been in the same place he'd been during the night—he had no way to know. Rain washed through the gaps in the canopy. He was drenched. Nearly everything he'd learned during his life was suddenly and perfectly useless. To walk, to find water, to look for a trail—these were the only ambitions that mattered. Part of him knew he should have been afraid. Part of him said, You do not belong in this place, you will die here.

What had he been doing these past years? His memory burrowed backward: the feel of his leather desktop, the clink of silver on china, wine lists at balconied restaurants—this gave way to his youth, clay breaking thickly in his hands, triumph at finding a rare crinoid embedded in stone, fish vertebrae fossilized in a fragment of slate. He remembered seeing goats swept up in a deluge, bawling at the riverbanks. Hadn't he learned anything, then? Why hadn't that raw energy, that terrific confidence he felt leaping from the edge of a cliff, stayed with him? What if he died here, in this forest, alone? What would become of his bones? Would they crumple and fold into the earth, preserved as a riddle for some other species, hacking one day through stone, to solve? He hadn't done enough with his life. He hadn't seen that what he had in common with the world—with the trunks of trees and the marching columns of ants and green shoots corkscrewing up from the mud—was *life*: the first light that sent every living thing paddling forth into the world every day.

He wouldn't die—he couldn't. He was, only now, remembering how to live. Something in him wanted to sing out, wanted to shout: I'm lost completely, lost utterly. The shingling, coarse bark of a tree, raindrops plunking on the leaves, the sound of a toad moaning a love song somewhere nearby: all of it seemed terribly beautiful to him.

A single white moth, huge, the size of his hand, wandered by, veering between the vines. Ward moved forward.

☽

A path, the faintest trace of a trail, encroached on all sides, a narrow passage into the light. He found her parents' house that night, stumbling through a long field of nettles. The house stood low and small, faintly illuminated and with smoke issuing from the chimney, a cottage out of a fairy tale. The walls were overgrown with vine and the tea fields had become wild, dark things, grown over with bougainvillea and thistle. But the place was tended to: there was a vegetable garden out back, fat pumpkins lolling in the soil and corn standing tall and tasseled on its stalks. The flames of two candles burned in a window. Behind the screen he saw a large oak table, wooden cabinets, a cluster of tomatoes on a countertop. He called her name but there was no reply.

In the dying light of his headlamp he saw that the tea nursery had been slathered over with mud, from top to bottom, like a giant anthill. There was a sign nailed to the door. Darkroom, it said, in Naima's hand.

He dropped his pack and sat. He thought of her inside, lifting her negatives from one chemical bath to the next, raising them up and pinning them to a line to dry. All those moments, captured and doubled onto film, frozen, her own museum of natural history unfolding in front of her.

Before long the first hem of light lifted over the trees and he looked out over the knitted vine and thistle, across the dark plantations stretched out in neat, arcing rows, to where the first rays of light fell across the hills. He heard the sounds of her moving inside—the scrape of a shoe over the floor, the muffled splash of poured liquid. The huge, warped crown of the sun showed above the horizon. Maybe, he thought, the words will come to me. Maybe when she walks out that door I'll know precisely what to say. Maybe I'll say I'm sorry, or I understand, or Thank you for sending the photos. Maybe we'll watch the light wash the hills together.

He reached into his pack and removed the flower, the delicate crumpled bell shape of its body, and held it carefully in his lap, waiting.

ACKNOWLEDGMENTS

I am deeply grateful to Wendy Weil for her immediate and enduring enthusiasm; to Gillian Blake for making each of these stories stronger; to my parents and brothers, for everything; to Wendell Mayo and June Spence for lighting the way; to everybody who made time to read early versions of these stories, especially Lysley Tenorio, Al Heathcock, Melissa Fraterrigo, and Amy Quan Barry; to Neil Giordano for his invaluable help with the first story and to C. Michael Curtis for his with the second; to George Plimpton for his help with "The Caretaker"; to Hal and Jacque Eastman for their energy and example; to Mike Gawtry and Tyler Lund for being my field experts; to the Ohioana Library Association for its support, and finally to the Wisconsin Institute of Creative Writing, without which many of these stories could not have been written. If you have extra money, give it to them.

This book is dedicated to my wife, Shauna, for her unswerving faith, her intelligence, and her love.

Please turn the page for an excerpt from
Anthony Doerr's

MEMORY WALL

"Beautiful . . . Doerr writes about the big questions, the imponderables, the major metaphysical dreads, and he does it fearlessly. The stories in *Memory Wall* shouldn't work at all, and yet they do, spectacularly."

—*The New York Times Book Review*

"Doerr has returned with a second collection, one that signals his arrival as an important American voice. *Memory Wall* not only captivates from start to finish, it is the kind of book likely to restore your faith in the pleasures of storytelling."

—*The Boston Globe*

"It's fair to say that Anthony Doerr is doing things with the short story that have rarely been attempted and seldom achieved. The stories in *Memory Wall* have such scope and depth that they hit as hard as novels three times their length. Doerr has set a new standard, I think, for what a story can do."

—Dave Eggers, author of *Zeitoun* and *What Is the What*

Available everywhere in hardcover and ebook from Scribner.

MEMORY WALL

TALL MAN IN THE YARD

Seventy-four-year-old Alma Konachek lives in Vredehoek, a suburb above Cape Town: a place of warm rains, big-windowed lofts, and silent, predatory automobiles. Behind her garden, Table Mountain rises huge, green, and corrugated; beyond her kitchen balcony, a thousand city lights wink and gutter behind sheets of fog like candleflames.

One night in November, at three in the morning, Alma wakes to hear the rape gate across her front door rattle open and someone enter her house. Her arms jerk; she spills a glass of water across the nightstand. A floorboard in the living room shrieks. She hears what might be breathing. Water drips onto the floor.

Alma manages a whisper. "Hello?"

A shadow flows across the hall. She hears the scrape of a shoe on the staircase, then nothing. Night air blows into the room—it smells of frangipani and charcoal. Alma presses a fist over her heart.

Beyond the balcony windows, moonlit pieces of clouds drift over the city. Spilled water creeps toward her bedroom door.

"Who's there? Is someone there?"

The grandfather clock in the living room pounds through the seconds. Alma's pulse booms in her ears. Her bedroom seems to be rotating very slowly.

"Harold?" Alma remembers that Harold is dead but she cannot help herself. "Harold?"

Another footstep from the second floor, another protest from a floorboard. What might be a minute passes. Maybe she hears someone descend the staircase. It takes her another full minute to summon the courage to shuffle into the living room.

Her front door is wide open. The traffic light at the top of the street flashes yellow, yellow, yellow. The leaves are hushed, the houses dark. She heaves the rape gate shut, slams the door, sets the bolt, and peers out the window lattice. Within twenty seconds she is at the hall table, fumbling with a pen.

A man, she writes. *Tall man in the yard.*

MEMORY WALL

Alma stands barefoot and wigless in the upstairs bedroom with a flashlight. The clock down in the living room ticks and ticks, winding up the night. A moment ago Alma was, she is certain, doing something very important. Something life-and-death. But now she cannot remember what it was.

The one window is ajar. The guest bed is neatly made, the coverlet smooth. On the nightstand sits a machine the size of a microwave oven, marked *Property of Cape Town Memory Research Center.* Three cables spiraling off it connect to something that looks vaguely like a bicycle helmet.

The wall in front of Alma is smothered with scraps of paper. Diagrams, maps, ragged sheets swarming with scribbles. Shining among the papers are hundreds of plastic cartridges, each the size of a matchbook, engraved with a four-digit number and pinned to the wall through a single hole.

The beam of Alma's flashlight settles on a color photograph of a man walking out of the sea. She fingers its edges. The man's pants are rolled to the knees; his expression is part grimace, part grin. Cold water. Across the photo, in handwriting she knows to be hers, is the name *Harold*. She knows this man. She can close her eyes and recall the pink flesh of his gums, the folds in his throat, his big-knuckled hands. He was her husband.

Around the photo, the scraps of paper and plastic cartridges build outward in crowded, overlapping layers, anchored with pushpins and chewing gum and penny nails. She sees to-do lists, jottings, drawings of what might be prehistoric beasts or monsters. She reads: *You can trust Pheko.* And *Taking Polly's Coca-Cola.* A flyer says: *Porter Properties.* There are stranger phrases: *dinocephalians, late Permian, massive vertebrate graveyard.* Some sheets of paper are blank; others reveal a flurry of cross-outs and erasures. On a half-page ripped from a brochure, one phrase is shakily and repeatedly underlined: *Memories are located not inside the cells but in the extracellular space.*

Some of the cartridges have her handwriting on them, too, printed below the numbers. *Museum. Funeral. Party at Hattie's.*

Alma blinks. She has no memory of writing on little cartridges or tearing out pages of books and tacking things to the wall.

She sits on the floor in her nightgown, legs straight out. A gust rushes through the window and the scraps of paper come alive, dancing, tugging at their pins. Loose pages eddy across the carpet. The cartridges rattle lightly.

Near the center of the wall, her flashlight beam again finds the photograph of a man walking out of the sea. Part grimace, part grin. That's Harold, she thinks. He was my husband. He died. Years ago. Of course.

Out the window, beyond the crowns of the palms, beyond the city lights, the ocean is washed in moonlight, then shadow. Moonlight, then shadow. A helicopter ticks past. The palms flutter.

Alma looks down. There is a slip of paper in her hand. *A man,* it says. *Tall man in the yard.*

DR. AMNESTY

Pheko is driving the Mercedes. Apartment towers reflect the morning sun. Sedans purr at stoplights. Six different times Alma squints out at the signs whisking past and asks him where they are going.

"We're driving to see the doctor, Mrs. Alma."

The doctor? Alma rubs her eyes, unsure. She tries to fill her lungs. She fidgets with her wig. The tires squeal as the Mercedes climbs the ramps of a parking garage.

Dr. Amnesty's staircase is stainless steel and bordered with ferns. Here's the bulletproof door, the street address stenciled in the corner. It's familiar to Alma in the way a house from childhood would be familiar. As if she has doubled in size in the meantime.

They are buzzed into a waiting room. Pheko drums his fingertips on his knee. Four chairs down, two well-dressed women sit beside a fish tank, one a few decades younger than the other. Both have fat pearls studded through each earlobe. Alma thinks: Pheko is the only black person in the building. For a moment she cannot remember what she is doing here. But this leather on the chair, the blue gravel in the saltwater aquarium—it is the memory clinic. Of course. Dr. Amnesty. In Green Point.

After a few minutes Alma is escorted to a padded chair overlaid with crinkly paper. It's all familiar now: the cardboard pouch of rubber gloves, the plastic plate for her earrings, two electrodes beneath her blouse. They lift off her wig, rub a cold gel onto her scalp. The television panel shows sand dunes, then dandelions, then bamboo.

Amnesty. A ridiculous surname. What does it mean? A pardon? A reprieve? But more permanent than a reprieve, isn't it? Amnesty is for wrongdoings. For someone who has done something wrong. She will ask Pheko to look it up when they get home. Or maybe she will remember to look it up herself.

The nurse is talking.

"And the remote stimulator is working well? Do you feel any improvements?"

"Improvements?" She thinks so. Things do seem to be improving. "Things are sharper," Alma says. She believes this is the sort of thing she is supposed to say. New pathways are being forged. She is remembering how to remember. This is what they want to hear.

The nurse murmurs. Feet whisper across the floor. Invisible machinery hums. Alma can feel, numbly, the rubber caps being twisted out of the ports in her skull and four screws being threaded simultaneously into place. There is a note in her hand: *Pheko is in the waiting room. Pheko will drive Mrs. Alma home after her session.* Of course.

A door with a small, circular window in it opens. A pale man in green scrubs sweeps past, smelling of chewing gum. Alma thinks: There are other padded chairs in this place, other rooms like this one, with other machines prying the lids off other addled brains. Ferreting inside them for memories, engraving those memories into little square cartridges. Attempting to fight off oblivion.

Her head is locked into place. Aluminum blinds clack against the window. In the lulls between breaths, she can hear traffic sighing past.

The helmet comes down.

THREE YEARS BEFORE, BRIEFLY

Memories aren't stored as changes to molecules inside brain cells," Dr. Amnesty told Alma during her first appointment, three years ago. She had been on his waiting list for ten months. Dr. Amnesty had straw-colored hair, nearly translucent skin, and invisible eyebrows. He spoke English as if each word were a tiny egg he had to deliver carefully through his teeth.

"This is what they thought forever but they were wrong. The truth is that the substrate of old memories is located not inside the cells but in the extracellular space. Here at the clinic we target those spaces, stain them, and inscribe them into electronic models. In the hopes of teaching damaged neurons to make proper replacements. Forging new pathways. Re-remembering.

"Do you understand?"

Alma didn't. Not really. For months, ever since Harold's death, she had been forgetting things: forgetting to pay Pheko, forgetting to eat breakfast, forgetting what the numbers in her checkbook meant. She'd go to the garden with the pruners and arrive there a minute later without them. She'd find her hairdryer in a kitchen cupboard, car keys in the tea tin. She'd rummage through her mind for a noun and come up empty-handed: Casserole? Carpet? Cashmere?

Two doctors had already diagnosed the dementia. Alma would have preferred amnesia: a quicker, less cruel erasure. This was a corrosion, a slow leak. Seven decades of stories, five decades of marriage, four decades of working for Porter Properties, too many houses and buyers and sellers to count—spatulas and salad forks, novels and recipes, nightmares and daydreams, hellos and goodbyes. Could it all really be wiped away?

"We don't offer a cure," Dr. Amnesty was saying, "but we might be able to slow it down. We might be able to give you some memories back."

He set the tips of his index fingers against his nose and formed a steeple. Alma sensed a pronouncement coming.

"It tends to unravel very quickly, without these treatments," he said. "Every day it will become harder for you to be in the world."

Water in a vase, chewing away at the stems of roses. Rust colonizing the tumblers in a lock. Sugar eating at the dentin of teeth, a river eroding its banks. Alma could think of a thousand metaphors, and all of them were inadequate.

She was a widow. No children, no pets. She had her Mercedes, a million and a half rand in savings, Harold's pension, and the house in Vredehoek. Dr. Amnesty's procedure offered a measure of hope. She signed up.

The operation was a fog. When she woke, she had a headache and her hair was gone. With her fingers she probed the four rubber caps secured into her skull.

A week later Pheko drove her back to the clinic. One of Dr. Amnesty's nurses escorted her to a leather chair that looked something like the ones in dental offices. The helmet was merely a vibration at the top of her scalp. They would be reclaiming memories, they said; they could not predict if the memories would be good ones or bad ones. It was painless. Alma felt as though spiders were stringing webs though her head.

Two hours later Dr. Amnesty sent her home from that first session with a remote memory stimulator and nine little cartridges in a paperboard box. Each cartridge was stamped from the same beige polymer, with a four-digit number engraved into the top. She eyed the remote player for two days before taking it up to the upstairs bedroom one windy noon when Pheko was out buying groceries.

She plugged it in and inserted a cartridge at random. A low shudder rose through the vertebrae of her neck, and then the room fell away in layers. The walls dissolved. Through rifts in the ceiling, the sky rippled like a flag. Then Alma's vision snuffed out, as if the fabric of her house had been yanked downward through a drain, and a prior world rematerialized.

She was in a museum: high ceiling, poor lighting, a smell like old magazines. The South African Museum. Harold was beside her, leaning over a glass-fronted display, excited, his eyes shining—look at him! So young! His khakis were too short, black socks showed above his shoes. How long had she known him? Maybe six months?

She had worn the wrong shoes: tight, too rigid. The weather

had been perfect that day and Alma would have preferred to sit in the Company Gardens under the trees with this tall new boyfriend. But the museum was what Harold wanted and she wanted to be with him. Soon they were in a fossil room, a couple dozen skeletons on podiums, some as big as rhinos, some with yardlong fangs, all with massive, eyeless skulls.

"One hundred and eighty million years older than the dinosaurs, hey?" Harold whispered.

Nearby, schoolgirls chewed gum. Alma watched the tallest of them spit slowly into a porcelain drinking fountain, then suck the spit back into her mouth. A sign labeled the fountain *For Use by White Persons* in careful calligraphy. Alma felt as if her feet were being crushed in vises.

"Just another minute," Harold said.

Seventy-one-year-old Alma watched everything through twenty-four-year-old Alma. She *was* twenty-four-year-old Alma! Her palms were damp and her feet were aching and she was on a date with a living Harold! A young, skinny Harold! He raved about the skeletons; they looked like animals mixed with animals, he said. Reptile heads on dog bodies. Eagle heads on hippo bodies. "I never get tired of seeing them," young Harold was telling young Alma, a boyish luster in his face. Two hundred and fifty million years ago, he said, these creatures died in the mud, their bones compressed slowly into stone. Now someone had hacked them out; now they were reassembled in the light.

"These were our ancestors, too," Harold whispered. Alma could hardly bear to look at them: They were eyeless, fleshless, murderous; they seemed engineered only to tear one another apart. She wanted to take this tall boy out to the gardens and sit hip-to-hip with him on a bench and take off her shoes. But Harold pulled her along. "Here's the gorgonopsian. A gorgon. Big as a tiger. Two, three hundred kilograms. From the Permian. That's only the second complete skeleton ever found. Not so far from where I grew up, you know." He squeezed Alma's hand.

Alma felt dizzy. The monster had short, powerful legs, fist-size eyeholes, and a mouth full of fangs. "Says they hunted in packs," whispered Harold. "Imagine running into six of those in the bush?" In the memory twenty-four-year-old Alma shuddered.

"We think we're supposed to be here," he continued, "but it's all just dumb luck, isn't it?" He turned to her, about to explain, and as he did shadows rushed in from the edges like ink, flowering over the entire scene, blotting the vaulted ceiling, and the school-girl who'd been spitting into the fountain, and finally young Harold himself in his too small khakis. The remote device whined; the cartridge ejected; the memory crumpled in on itself.

Alma blinked and found herself clutching the footboard of her guest bed, out of breath, three miles and five decades away. She unscrewed the headgear. Out the window a thrush sang *chee-chweeeoo.* Pain swung through the roots of Alma's teeth. "My god," she said.

Continued . . .

Turn the page for a preview of Anthony Doerr's

All the Light
We Cannot See

A Novel

Available from Scribner May 2014

Zero

---

7 August 1944

Leaflets

At dusk they pour from the sky. They blow across the ramparts, turn cartwheels over rooftops, flutter into the ravines between houses. Entire streets swirl with them, flashing white against the cobbles. *Urgent message to the inhabitants of this town,* they say. *Depart immediately to open country.*

The tide climbs. The moon hangs small and yellow and gibbous. On the rooftops of beachfront hotels to the east, and in the gardens behind them, a half-dozen American artillery units drop incendiary rounds into the mouths of mortars.

Bombers

They cross the Channel at midnight. There are twelve and they are named for songs: *Stardust* and *Stormy Weather* and *In the Mood* and *Pistol-Packin' Mama*. The sea glides along far below, spattered with the countless chevrons of whitecaps. Soon enough, the navigators can discern the low moonlit lumps of islands ranged along the horizon.

France.

Intercoms crackle. Deliberately, almost lazily, the bombers shed altitude. Threads of red light ascend from anti-air emplacements up and down the coast. Dark, ruined ships appear, scuttled or destroyed, one with its bow shorn away, a second flickering as it burns. On an outermost island, panicked sheep run zigzagging between rocks.

Inside each airplane, a bombardier peers through an aiming window and counts to twenty. Four five six seven. To the bombardiers, the walled city on its granite headland, drawing ever closer, looks like an unholy tooth, something black and dangerous, a final abscess to be lanced away.

The Girl

In a corner of the city, inside a tall, narrow house at Number 4 rue Vauborel, on the sixth and highest floor, a sightless sixteen-year-old named Marie-Laure LeBlanc kneels over a low table covered entirely with a model. The model is a miniature of the city she kneels within, and contains scale replicas of the hundreds of houses and shops and hotels within its walls. There's the cathedral with its perforated spire, and the bulky old Château de Saint-Malo, and row after row of seaside mansions studded with chimneys. A slender wooden jetty arcs out from a beach called the Plage du Môle; a delicate, reticulated atrium vaults over the seafood market; minute benches, the smallest no larger than apple seeds, dot the tiny public squares.

Marie-Laure runs her fingertips along the centimeter-wide parapet crowning the ramparts, drawing an uneven star shape around the entire model. She finds the opening atop the walls where four ceremonial cannons point to sea. "Bastion de la Hollande," she whispers, and her fingers walk down a little staircase. "Rue des Cordiers. Rue Jacques Cartier."

In a corner of the room stand two galvanized buckets filled to the rim with water. Fill them up, her great-uncle has taught her, whenever you can. The bathtub on the third floor too. Who knows when the water will go out again.

Her fingers travel back to the cathedral spire. South to the Gate of Dinan. All evening she has been marching her fingers around the model, waiting for her great-uncle Etienne, who owns this house, who went out the previous night while she slept, and who has not returned. And now it is night again, another revolution of the clock, and the whole block is quiet, and she cannot sleep.

She can hear the bombers when they are three miles away. A mounting static. The hum inside a seashell.

When she opens the bedroom window, the noise of the airplanes becomes louder. Otherwise, the night is dreadfully silent: no engines, no voices, no clatter. No sirens. No footfalls on the cobbles. Not even gulls. Just a high tide, one block away and six stories below, lapping at the base of the city walls.

And something else.

Something rattling softly, very close. She eases open the left-hand shutter and runs her fingers up the slats of the right. A sheet of paper has lodged there.

She holds it to her nose. It smells of fresh ink. Gasoline, maybe. The paper is crisp; it has not been outside long.

Marie-Laure hesitates at the window in her stocking feet, her bedroom behind her, seashells arranged along the top of the armoire, pebbles along the baseboards. Her cane stands in the corner; her big Braille novel waits facedown on the bed. The drone of the airplanes grows.

The Boy

Five streets to the north, a white-haired eighteen-year-old German private named Werner Pfennig wakes to a faint staccato hum. Little more than a purr. Flies tapping at a far-off windowpane.

Where is he? The sweet, slightly chemical scent of gun oil; the raw wood of newly constructed shell crates; the mothballed odor of old bedspreads—he's in the hotel. Of course. L'hôtel des Abeilles, the Hotel of Bees.

Still night. Still early.

From the direction of the sea come whistles and booms; flak is going up.

An anti-air corporal hurries down the corridor, heading for the stairwell. "Get to the cellar," he calls over his shoulder, and Werner switches on his field light, rolls his blanket into his duffel, and starts down the hall.

Not so long ago, the Hotel of Bees was a cheerful address, with bright blue shutters on its facade and oysters on ice in its café and Breton waiters in bow ties polishing glasses behind its bar. It offered twenty-one guest rooms, commanding sea views, and a lobby fireplace as big as a truck. Parisians on weekend holidays would drink aperitifs here, and before them the occasional emissary from the republic—ministers and vice ministers and abbots and admirals—and in the centuries before them, windburned corsairs: killers, plunderers, raiders, seamen.

Before that, before it was ever a hotel at all, five full centuries ago, it was the home of a wealthy privateer who gave up raiding ships to study bees in the pastures outside Saint-Malo, scribbling in notebooks and eating honey straight from combs. The crests above the door lintels still have bumblebees carved into the oak; the ivy-covered fountain in the courtyard is shaped like a hive. Werner's favorites are five faded frescoes on the ceilings of the grandest upper rooms, where bees as big as children float against blue backdrops, big lazy drones and workers with diaphanous wings—where, above a hexagonal bathtub, a single nine-foot-long queen, with multiple eyes and a golden-furred abdomen, curls across the ceiling.

Over the past four weeks, the hotel has become something else: a fortress. A detachment of Austrian anti-airmen has boarded up every window, overturned every bed. They've reinforced the entrance, packed the stairwells with crates of artillery shells. The hotel's fourth floor, where garden rooms with French balconies open directly onto the ramparts, has become home to an aging high-velocity anti-air gun called an 88 that can fire twenty-one-and-a-half-pound shells nine miles.

Her Majesty, the Austrians call their cannon, and for the past week these men have tended to it the way worker bees might tend to a queen. They've fed her oils, repainted her barrels, lubricated her wheels; they've arranged sandbags at her feet like offerings.

The royal *acht acht,* a deathly monarch meant to protect them all.

Werner is in the stairwell, halfway to the ground floor, when the 88 fires twice in quick succession. It's the first time he's heard the gun at such close range, and it sounds as if the top half of the hotel has torn off. He stumbles and throws his arms over his ears. The walls reverberate all the way down into the foundation, then back up.

Werner can hear the Austrians two floors up scrambling, reloading, and the receding screams of both shells as they hurtle above the ocean, already two or three miles away. One of the soldiers, he realizes, is singing. Or maybe it is more than one. Maybe they are all singing. Eight Luftwaffe men, none of whom will survive the hour, singing a love song to their queen.

Werner chases the beam of his field light through the lobby. The big gun detonates a third time, and glass shatters somewhere close by, and torrents of soot rattle down the chimney, and the walls of the hotel toll like a struck bell. Werner worries that the sound will knock the teeth from his gums.

He drags open the cellar door and pauses a moment, vision swimming. "This is it?" he asks. "They're really coming?"

But who is there to answer?

Saint-Malo

Up and down the lanes, the last unevacuated townspeople wake, groan, sigh. Spinsters, prostitutes, men over sixty. Procrastinators, collaborators, disbelievers, drunks. Nuns of every order. The poor. The stubborn. The blind.

Some hurry to bomb shelters. Some tell themselves it is merely a drill. Some linger to grab a blanket or a prayer book or a deck of playing cards.

D-day was two months ago. Cherbourg has been liberated, Caen liberated, Rennes too. Half of western France is free. In the east, the Soviets have retaken Minsk; the Polish Home Army is revolting in Warsaw; a few newspapers have become bold enough to suggest that the tide has turned.

But not here. Not this last citadel at the edge of the continent, this final German strongpoint on the Breton coast.

Here, people whisper, the Germans have renovated two kilometers of subterranean corridors under the medieval walls; they have built new defenses, new conduits, new escape routes, underground complexes of bewildering intricacy. Beneath the peninsular fort of La Cité, across the river from the old city, there are rooms of bandages, rooms of ammunition, even an underground hospital, or so it is believed. There is air-conditioning, a two-hundred-thousand-liter water tank, a direct line to Berlin. There are flame-throwing booby traps, a net of pillboxes with periscopic sights; they have stockpiled enough ordnance to spray shells into the sea all day, every day, for a year.

Here, they whisper, are a thousand Germans ready to die. Or five thousand. Maybe more.

Saint-Malo: Water surrounds the city on four sides. Its link to the rest of France is tenuous: a causeway, a bridge, a spit of sand. We are Malouins first, say the people of Saint-Malo. Bretons next. French if there's anything left over.

In stormy light, its granite glows blue. At the highest tides, the sea creeps into basements at the very center of town. At the lowest tides, the barnacled ribs of a thousand shipwrecks stick out above the sea.

For three thousand years, this little promontory has known sieges.

But never like this.

A grandmother lifts a fussy toddler to her chest. A drunk, urinating in an alley outside Saint-Servan, a mile away, plucks a sheet of paper from a hedge. *Urgent message to the inhabitants of this town,* it says. *Depart immediately to open country.*

Anti-air batteries flash on the outer islands, and the big German guns inside the old city send another round of shells howling over the sea, and three hundred and eighty Frenchmen imprisoned on an island fortress called National, a quarter mile off the beach, huddle in a moonlit courtyard peering up.

Four years of occupation, and the roar of oncoming bombers is the roar of what? Deliverance? Extirpation?

The clack-clack of small-arms fire. The gravelly snare drums of flak. A dozen pigeons roosting on the cathedral spire cataract down its length and wheel out over the sea.

Number 4 rue Vauborel

Marie-Laure LeBlanc stands alone in her bedroom smelling a leaflet she cannot read. Sirens wail. She closes the shutters and relatches the window. Every second the airplanes draw closer; every second is a second lost. She should be rushing downstairs. She should be making for the corner of the kitchen where a little trapdoor opens into a cellar full of dust and mouse-chewed rugs and ancient trunks long unopened.

Instead she returns to the table at the foot of the bed and kneels beside the model of the city.

Again her fingers find the outer ramparts, the Bastion de la Hollande, the little staircase leading down. In this window, right here, in the real city, a woman beats her rugs every Sunday. From this window here, a boy once yelled, *Watch where you're going, are you blind?*

The windowpanes rattle in their housings. The anti-air guns unleash another volley. The earth rotates just a bit farther.

Beneath her fingertips, the miniature rue d'Estrées intersects the miniature rue Vauborel. Her fingers turn right; they skim doorways. One two three. Four. How many times has she done this?

Number 4: the tall, derelict bird's nest of a house owned by her great-uncle Etienne. Where she has lived for four years. Where she kneels on the sixth floor alone, as a dozen American bombers roar toward her.

She presses inward on the tiny front door, and a hidden catch releases, and the little house lifts up and out of the model. In her hands, it's about the size of one of her father's cigarette boxes.

Now the bombers are so close that the floor starts to throb under her knees. Out in the hall, the crystal pendants of the chandelier suspended above the stairwell chime. Marie-Laure twists the chimney of the miniature house ninety degrees. Then she slides off three wooden panels that make up its roof, and turns it over.

A stone drops into her palm.

It's cold. The size of a pigeon's egg. The shape of a teardrop.

Marie-Laure clutches the tiny house in one hand and the stone in the other. The room feels flimsy, tenuous. Giant fingertips seem about to punch through its walls.

"Papa?" she whispers.

Cellar

Beneath the lobby of the Hotel of Bees, a corsair's cellar has been hacked out of the bedrock. Behind crates and cabinets and pegboards of tools, the walls are bare granite. Three massive hand-hewn beams, hauled here from some ancient Breton forest and craned into place centuries ago by teams of horses, hold up the ceiling.

A single lightbulb casts everything in a wavering shadow.

Werner Pfennig sits on a folding chair in front of a workbench, checks his battery level, and puts on headphones. The radio is a steel-cased two-way transceiver with a 1.6-meter band antenna. It enables him to communicate with a matching transceiver upstairs, with two other anti-air batteries inside the walls of the city, and with the underground garrison command across the river mouth.

The transceiver hums as it warms. A spotter reads coordinates into the headpiece, and an artilleryman repeats them back. Werner rubs his eyes. Behind him, confiscated treasures are crammed to the ceiling: rolled tapestries, grandfather clocks, armoires, and giant landscape paintings crazed with cracks. On a shelf opposite Werner sit eight or nine plaster heads, the purpose of which he cannot guess.

The massive staff sergeant Frank Volkheimer comes down the narrow wooden stairs and ducks his head beneath the beams. He smiles gently at Werner and sits in a tall-backed armchair upholstered in golden silk with his rifle across his huge thighs, where it looks like little more than a baton.

Werner says, "It's starting?"

Volkheimer nods. He switches off his field light and blinks his strangely delicate eyelashes in the dimness.

"How long will it last?"

"Not long. We'll be safe down here."

The engineer, Bernd, comes last. He is a little man with mousy hair and misaligned pupils. He closes the cellar door behind him and bars it and sits halfway down the wooden staircase with a damp look on his face, fear or grit, it's hard to say.

With the door shut, the sound of the sirens softens. Above them, the ceiling bulb flickers.

Water, thinks Werner. I forgot water.

A second anti-air battery fires from a distant corner of the city, and then the 88 upstairs goes again, stentorian, deadly, and Werner listens to the shell scream into the sky. Cascades of dust hiss out of the ceiling. Through his headphones, Werner can hear the Austrians upstairs still singing.

. . . auf d'Wulda, auf d'Wulda, da scheint d'Sunn a so gulda . . .

Volkheimer picks sleepily at a stain on his trousers. Bernd blows into his cupped hands. The transceiver crackles with wind speeds, air pressure, trajectories. Werner thinks of home: Frau Elena bent over his little shoes, double-knotting each lace. Stars wheeling past a dormer window. His little sister, Jutta, with a quilt around her shoulders and a radio earpiece trailing from her left ear.

Four stories up, the Austrians clap another shell into the smoking breech of the 88 and double-check the traverse and clamp their ears as the gun discharges, but down here Werner hears only the radio voices of his childhood. *The Goddess of History looked down to earth. Only through the hottest fires can purification be achieved.* He sees a forest of dying sunflowers. He sees a flock of blackbirds explode out of a tree.